ALL THE DAYS OF MY LIFE

ALL THE DAYS OF MY LIFE

Poems to Console and Inspire

Edited by

PHILIP DAVIS
University of Liverpool

J. M. Dent London

First published in Great Britain in 1999
by J. M. Dent

A CIP catalogue record for this book is available
from the British Library.

ISBN 0 460 87967 7

Typeset by Deltatype Ltd, Birkenhead, Merseyside
Set in Monotype Sabon

Printed in Great Britain by
Butler & Tanner Ltd, Frome and London

J. M. Dent

Weidenfeld & Nicolson
The Orion Publishing Group Ltd
Orion House
5 Upper Saint Martin's Lane
London, WC2H 9EA

CONTENTS

INTRODUCTION

D. H. Lawrence thought it might be better if we stopped using the word 'love' for a hundred years or so. At the end of that time, we just might be able to use it as a real word again. But there are also other words that have become so well known as to obscure the fact that we don't really know what we mean by them – worn-out verbal talismans such as 'religious' or 'spiritual'. 'I hear and behold God in every object,' sings Walt Whitman rapturously, but then he immediately adds, more soberly, 'yet understand not God in the least.' It may well be good not to presume to understand too much. But there is also a lack of understanding which is connected with freely using the word 'God' too often and too indiscriminately, to stand for whatever you want it to. As the thirteenth-century mystic, Meister Eckhardt, more austerely puts it: '*Whatever* you say about God is untrue.'

But on the whole ours is not, I think, a time of strong formal belief but one of often hidden or unadmitted religious needs. Many would say nothing about God simply because they do not believe in any such existence. And that is right: you ought not to say you believe if you don't. Still, there are varieties of unbelief, and there must be many people who can't believe and yet cannot quite disbelieve either, but carry on with life somewhere vaguely in between the two. Can there be an anthology of religious verse in what often seems an unreligious age? This anthology is not a textbook or a prayerbook; it is a book, most of all perhaps, for people in that in-between situation, that working norm between conviction and scepticism wherein you find yourself thinking, 'But there must be *something*'. Or must there? This collection is,

vii

implicitly and not dogmatically, a guide to the perplexed, a holding-ground for the troubled, in an attempt to meet the religious needs of those who do not necessarily have formal religious beliefs. It takes its title from the religious poem, so deep in the memory of our language, that it is most likely that almost everyone will have heard or read it in time of trouble – Psalm 23 in the Authorized King James Version:

> The Lord is my shepherd; I shall not want.
> He maketh me to lie down in green pastures: he leadeth me beside the still waters.
> He restoreth my soul: he leadeth me in the paths of righteousness for his name's sake.
> Yea, though I walk through the valley of the shadow of death, I will fear no evil; for thou art with me; thy rod and thy staff they comfort me.
> Thou preparest a table before me in the presence of mine enemies: thou anointest my head with oil; my cup runneth over.
> Surely goodness and mercy shall follow me all the days of my life: and I will dwell in the house of the Lord for ever.

'Surely goodness and mercy shall follow me all the days of my life': my title omits that surety, although this book struggles often enough to find it again. *All the Days of My Life* does not offer God, but human voices in conditions of 'want', in times of need – a modern version of the ancient Psalms, where the great cry is like Doris Lessing's in her *Canopus in Argos* sequence of novels: what are we *for*?

And what is this book for? Imagine, in partial answer, an aged man reading the following from Eckhardt:

> Blessed are the poor in spirit... . See to it that you are stripped of all creatures, of all consolation from creatures. For certainly as long as creatures comfort and are able to comfort you, you will

certainly never find true comfort. But if nothing can comfort you save God, truly God will console you.

'Comfort' is another of our soft, soulfully degenerated words. We talk nowadays of wanting to feel not only comforted but comfortable ('It must be *such* a consolation to have a religion' – tell that to pained strugglers like C. H. Sisson or R. S. Thomas.) It is not what the word 'comfort' originally meant: it comes from the Latin, meaning 'with strength'. Even so, is our imagined old man, reading this, one of the old-fashioned Pious from a bygone age? Not entirely: 'Mr Sammler could not say that he literally believed what he was reading. He could, however, say that he cared to read nothing but this.'

The protagonist of Saul Bellow's novel, *Mr Sammler's Planet*, is a Jew not a Christian, a survivor of the Holocaust reading the great German mystic, a man left in the modern world without formal or literal beliefs, reading nonetheless not for aesthetic entertainment, not for fantasy, but for something that still somehow goes on for him within old religious writings. What is it that holds him? Thus says T. S. Eliot in *Four Quartets*:

There is only the fight to recover what has been lost
And found and lost again and again: and now, under conditions
That seem unpropitious.

In a poem entitled 'Happiness' Peter Porter speaks of being moved by the power of the language of George Herbert, fuelled by religious faith: 'His more can only make ours less'. Under conditions that seem faithless we too may seem diminished and lessened: in our modern secular days, when it comes to mourning, divorce may replace death and may even make one feel less able, or less entitled, to mourn freely. But we cannot be sure that the ancient human feelings do not go on in some way within modern forms or in people far younger than old Sammler. And, plausibly, even in the old propitious ages of belief it was never as straightforward and easy as we may now nostalgically imagine. In any comparison with past ages it is perhaps not for us to know of gain or loss. As T. S. Eliot says: 'For us there is only the trying. The rest is not our business'. Perhaps we do not know where we really are, or what we are really feeling or doing. Before his unspeakable experience in the 1930s and 1940s, Sammler was an intellectual sceptic who would not have gone near mystic literature. How could an historical disaster, sufficient to destroy belief in God and humanity alike, play a part if not in restoring belief at least in leaving some continued opening for it? How come these baffling contradictions?

This anthology does not confine itself, as Sammler did, to avowedly religious reading. On the contrary, each part begins with common experiences that are not necessarily to be called religious: the death of a child, spouse or friend, the feeling of loneliness, the fear of mortality in old age, a sudden sense of awe at the natural world. These times of trouble, loss, perplexity, gratitude, revelation or love reveal how so-called 'religious' needs are not remote, esoteric or narrowly sectarian, but part of recognizable human experience even in a nominally secular age. On occasions I have included poems as much for their recognition of a subject-matter as for their verbal treatment of it – however much the two cannot be entirely separated. But sometimes it is the lesser writers who are most valuable for taking you into a vulnerable area of being and simply staying there, whereas greater poets will move on, leaving the basics behind. So in this anthology there is a mixture of greater and lesser, for different times and different ways. But what this book is after are those founding emotional experiences, the basic human stuff, that leads people into those areas of seriousness from which deep mortal thinking proceeds. They may be places in which we cannot remain steadily for long, because we don't seem built for that (as George Eliot puts it in *Middlemarch*, 'It would be like hearing the grass grow and the squirrel's heart beat, and we should die of that roar which lies on the other side of silence'). But, equally, we cannot simply go away, whilst what is there keeps coming and going in us. So, that is what poetry is in this collection: a place of holdfast for our deepest thoughts as they emerge from anterior feelings and needs.

But poetry is not just the words on the page: poetry in its deepest sense exists in real life. There are, said Wordsworth, many silent and unknown poets in the world – existent every time we see or feel something which we don't or can't write down. In an essay in *The Paperback Tree*, on the experience of editing his own anthology of Australian religious verse, Les Murray says that our consciences, our ideologies, our dreams, our sense of ourselves are all of them poems, *our* poems – albeit ones that are usually too narrow or too small. And then there's Freud's poem, Marx's poem, or Jesus's poem, and those rich inexhaustible poems called religions. All these visions of the world have at their heart something of what Murray calls 'the poetic experience' – 'the thing poets and their readers share, and the thing we all seek from poetry'. That re-enlivening experience of life's depth is but a temporary clearing and opening, a renewal of serious feeling and mattering that suddenly takes over from the usual prosaic routine – and then goes again. For most, and perhaps for all people, that experience, even if repeatable, is inherently intermittent, like faith given in the midst of doubt, like a sense of religion found amidst secularism. That is because, says Murray, 'we are as it were not yet permitted to *live* there'. *All the Days of My Life* seeks to enable you to regain access to 'there' – to something mentally equivalent to what Larkin in 'Church Going' once called 'a serious house on serious earth' – and stay there, with memory, at least a little longer.

Therefore, this anthology is not simply for lovers of poetry, and not necessarily for those who are expert in reading verse or entirely 'comfortable' with it. Religion is difficult for us and, in a connected but also different way, poetry is difficult for us too.

The purpose of *All the Days of My Life* is to provide a guiding context in which poetry may be read slowly and meditatively as part of a life's ordinary struggle, day by day. If much here has to do with human trouble, the intention is not to depress, any more than it is vainly to cheer up, but is closer to what Wordsworth describes in *The Prelude*:

> thence may I select
> Sorrow that is not sorrow, but delight,
> And miserable love that is not pain
> To hear of, for the glory that redounds
> Therefrom to human kind and what we are.
>
> (1805–6 version) xii 244–8

Of course a sceptic (or that sceptical part of ourselves) will wonder if such art, like religion, isn't a mere compensation for our cares. What we create out of our needs may be fictional, for those needs themselves may have no other force of necessity beside our own in the universe. *All the Days of My Life* is agnostic on that question. We may have to set our sights lower these days, or we may need to create what we depend upon; or, again, we may find within the lowered sights or created values something which is not solely our invention. For the purposes of this anthology it does not matter, to begin with, if you think that religion is no more than an expression of human need or whether, alternatively, you believe that human need is a way to God even when the human beings involved do not yet explicitly realize it. I grant that, finally, this distinction – essentially the difference between believing in God or not – is more crucial than any other in existence. But people must start from wherever they find they are, and at the start at any rate the sources of the seriousness are less important than its felt presence.

In his book *And Our Faces, My Heart, Brief as Photos*, John Berger finely says that poems are like prayers – but, he goes on to say, 'in poetry there is no one behind the language being prayed to. It is the language itself which has to hear and acknowledge. For the religious poet, the Word is the first attribute of God. In all poetry words are a presence before they are a means of communication.' That helps to explain why this is an anthology of meditative as well as strictly religious verse, of concerns on that hinterland between the secular and the religious where much of the poetry selected here does its work. Indeed, it is poetry that makes thinking – even unfinished, unfulfilled thinking – meditative and not merely anxious. And yet it is also true that for George Herbert, for instance, there *was* a divine presence behind the language being prayed to. And in the case of other poets, who knows if their praying in their language and even to their own language isn't another of God's mysterious ways, acting through human work, without us knowing it? Similarly I do not in the first instance mind whether you think the modern poems in this selection are there to give 'relevance' and translated 'access' to the older, more religious, more potentially out-dated ones; or whether, contrariwise, the modern poems of ordinary experiences are there as a human ground from which you may see the older ones taking off and going further. In any case, it isn't simply one or the other, there are always complex ambivalences and impurities and individualities and varieties – and above all it doesn't quite matter what explicitly you *think* you think: it matters only what is happening to you, whatever you suppose you are doing.

I have divided this book into five sections, each of which has two or three sub-sections within it. This is not because I believe it is either right or possible to sectionalize human existence. But I want to offer the reader a manageable meditative framework, such that a section or sub-section, without dominating the poems within it, offers a sort of pathway or journey through common phases of experience as it if were the equivalent of a chapter in life's novel. I have taken the advice of the fourteenth-century mystical work *The Cloud of Unknowing* and tried, as far as possible, to stick to raw monosyllables, simple lump terms for life's basics. Thus the five major sections and their subsections are: *Common Sacraments* (Born, Marriage, Generations), *Here and Now* (Day/Night, Being, In Midst of All) *Out of the Depths* (Trouble, Lost), *Of Good* (Joy, Right) and *End* (Time, Death). Of course, as befits an anthology, readers should still feel free to read around as they wish. There are implicit cross-currents and overlaps *between* sections, whilst *within* them there are tacit contrasts between one predicament or temperament and another, as well as between ways ancient and modern. Thus, for instance, the juxtaposition between Thomas Hardy and his lesser known Wessex neighbour William Barnes offers, within the terms of 'Marriage', a contrast between Barnes's sheer goodness as a family man and Hardy's more equivocal regrets – a contrast painful not least, one suspects, to Hardy himself, the editor of a selection of the older man's verse. The reader should expect sudden, even violently moody movements from calm to fear, from love to lust, from celebration to stoicism, from I to Not I, and above all shifts from the ostensibly 'secular' to the so-called 'religious' and back again – as in the very nature of experience itself. This is a book for differing 'days of a life', for different times, stages, seasons, and ways of being:

> To every thing there is a season, and a time to every purpose under the heaven:
> A time to be born, and a time to die, a time to plant and a time to pluck up that which is planted;
> A time to kill, and a time to heal; a time to break down, and a time to build up;
> A time to weep, and a time to laugh; a time to mourn and a time to dance;
> A time to cast away stones, and a time to gather stones together; a time to embrace, and a time to refrain from embracing;
> A time to get, and a time to lose; a time to keep, and a time to cast away;

A time to rend, and a time to sew; a time to keep silence, and a
time to speak;
A time to love, and a time to hate; a time of war, and a time of
peace.

Ecclesiastes 3.1–8

It is not for me, I hope, to have imposed upon time's variety
some prescriptive model of straightforward linear progress: to
put it at its simplest, the sub-section 'Day/Night' ends with a
return to day again. Different sections offer different ending
points, of which some attempt resolutions, some are in lieu of
such, but all are open to the reader's meditative attention.

Inevitably, an anthology such as this is a personal and
individual selection, based on beliefs, loves, fears and prejudices,
as well as the need for exploratory checks and challenges. My
remit has been poetry originally in English: reluctantly, I have
come to the conclusion that generally for me, religious poetry,
outside the Authorized Version of the Bible, has not sufficient
reality in translation, despite the quite proper current concern
for pluralism of faiths. At any rate, though it lost me Dante,
Rilke, Celan, Mandelstam (a painful list), this decision alleviated
some pressure on space. Brief notes should suffice to help the
reader with the poetry of Robert Burns and William Barnes,
where dialect is a valuable defence of inherent vulnerability. I
am generally unhappy about using excerpts from epics such as
Milton's *Paradise Lost* or Wordsworth's *The Prelude*, which
require reading at length, and I have only allowed myself to
succumb to need on rare occasions where the alternative was to
lose almost all of Spenser or Milton or T. S. Eliot.

But this is also a personal anthology in a deeper sense. It is not
directly about great social themes or historical events. Rather it
seeks a 'something' that is personal and moving in its readers,
making them feel like individuals in their own being. That is to
say: the something that, both in the midst of all others and
beneath the consciousness of self, comes into and goes out of

this world with you. It may be the turn of a line, a sudden feeling or a transient memory, the small hold upon or total loss of one's self in crisis, or a very quiet voice inside. But emphatically it is 'all the days of *my* life', where the poet's 'my' makes you feel and think of yours too.

In short, what is offered here are my good things, which for me at least, even where they are painful, 'remain vividly in the memory, playing a protective or guiding role: moral refuges, perpetual starting points'. The words are Iris Murdoch's in *Metaphysics as a Guide to Morals*:

> Such points or places of spiritual power may be indicated by a tradition, suggested by work or subjects of study, emerge from personal crises or relationships, be gradually established or come suddenly: through familiarity with a good person or a sacred text, a sense of renewal in a particular place, a sudden vision in art or nature, joy experienced as pure, witnessing a virtuous action, a patient suffering, an absence of resentment, innumerable things in family life. We are turning here to an inexhaustible and familiar field of human resources. Every individual has a collection of such things.

Some influences to which I am indebted have been quoted in this introduction. I am also more directly grateful to some good people for counsel in discussing and preparing this volume: Brian Nellist, Douglas Oliver, Stanley Middleton, Les Murray, Sid Davis, Shelley Bridson, Tony Barley, Hilary Laurie, Anthony Rudolf and Jo Burns. In particular, Ian Pindar at Dent has been a most encouraging and sympathetic editor. But above all, there's my wife, Jane Davis, whose idea it was to compile such an anthology because she wanted one for her own needs: to her this book is dedicated.

PHILIP DAVIS

For Jane Davis

'Love's not Time's Fool'

ALL THE DAYS OF MY LIFE

SOMETHING?

But silent musings urge the mind to seek
Something, too high for syllables to speak.

Anne Finch, Countess of Winchilsea

There is No God

ARTHUR HUGH CLOUGH

'There is no God,' the wicked saith,
　'And truly it's a blessing,
For what he might have done with us
　It's better only guessing.'

'There is no God,' a youngster thinks,
　'Or really, if there may be,
He surely didn't mean a man
　Always to be a baby.'

'There is no God, or if there is,'
　The tradesman thinks, ' 'twere funny
If he should take it ill in me
　To make a little money.'

'Whether there be,' the rich man says,
　'It matters very little,
For I and mine, thank somebody,
　Are not in want of victual.'

Some others, also, to themselves
　Who scarce so much as doubt it,
Think there is none, when they are well,
　And do not think about it.

But country folks who live beneath
　The shadow of the steeple;

The parson and the parson's wife,
  And mostly married people;

Youths green and happy in first love,
  So thankful for illusion;
And men caught out in what the world
  Calls guilt, in first confusion;

And almost everyone when age,
  Disease, or sorrows strike him,
Inclines to think there is a God,
  Or something very like him.

The Evasion

C. H. SISSON

The life I lived was sombre and obscure
Or so it seemed, or so life always is;
The outward symptoms were ordinary,
Those of a commonplace which fails to please.

Whom? Me? Or was it I failed to please others?
As certainly I did, yet I have had
Friends and enough at all times of my life.
To say the only true friend is God.

As loving, perhaps. But I have never loved
Him, or found him at the end of time:
In the world, maybe, as a remote voice
Almost heard, never quite, like a half rhyme.

Or half seen like smoke on distant fields,
It might be mist, it might be rain falling.
The splendour of the sun was not my *métier*.
There might have been those who had a calling.

I am the wanderer of old stories
Or that one now making across the moor:
Old time is my time now, I am at home
With my incertitude for evermore.

'Come home to bounty' is a plausible
Request to make to those who are in need.

I look for nothing but what I find
And find nothing unless I seek indeed

As I do, can, will not. I go my way
Against expectation or surprise.
The moment that I turn is when I turn
Into the landscape and the landscape dies.

The Buried Life

MATTHEW ARNOLD

Light flows our war of mocking words, and yet,
Behold, with tears mine eyes are wet!
I feel a nameless sadness o'er me roll.
Yes, yes, we know that we can jest,
We know, we know that we can smile!
But there's a something in this breast,
To which thy light words bring no rest,
And thy gay smiles no anodyne.
Give me thy hand, and hush awhile,
And turn those limpid eyes on mine,
And let me read there, love! thy inmost soul.

Alas! is even love too weak
To unlock the heart, and let it speak?
Are even lovers powerless to reveal
To one another what indeed they feel?
I knew the mass of men conceal'd
Their thoughts, for fear that if reveal'd
They would by other men be met
With blank indifference, or with blame reproved;
I knew they lived and moved
Trick'd in disguises, alien to the rest
Of men and alien to themselves – and yet
The same heart beats in every human breast!
But we, my love! – doth a like spell benumb
Our hearts, our voices? – must we too be dumb?
Ah! well for us, if even we,
Even for a moment, can get free

9

Our heart, and have our lips unchain'd;
For that which seals them hath been deep-ordain'd!
Fate, which foresaw
How frivolous a baby man would be –
By what distractions he would be possess'd,
How he would pour himself in every strife,
And well-nigh change his own identity –
That it might keep from his capricious play
His genuine self, and force him to obey
Even in his own despite his being's law,
Bade through the deep recesses of our breast
The unregarded river of our life
Pursue with indiscernible flow its way;
And that we should not see
The buried stream, and seem to be
Eddying at large in blind uncertainty,
Though driving on with it eternally.

But often, in the world's most crowded streets,
But often, in the din of strife,
There rises an unspeakable desire
After the knowledge of our buried life;
A thirst to spend our fire and restless force
In tracking out our true, original course;
A longing to inquire
Into the mystery of this heart which beats
So wild, so deep in us – to know
Whence our lives come and where they go.
And many a man in his own breast then delves,
But deep enough, alas! none ever mines.
And we have been on many thousand lines,
And we have shown, on each, spirit and power;
But hardly have we, for one little hour,
Been on our own line, have we been ourselves –
Hardly had skill to utter one of all

The nameless feelings that course through our breast,
But they course on for ever unexpress'd.
And long we try in vain to speak and act
Our hidden self, and what we say and do
Is eloquent, is well – but 'tis not true!
And then we will no more be rack'd
With inward striving, and demand
Of all the thousand nothings of the hour
Their stupefying power;
Ah yes, and they benumb us at our call!
Yet still, from time to time, vague and forlorn
From the soul's subterranean depth upborne
As from an infinitely distant land,
Come airs, and floating echoes, and convey
A melancholy into all our day.

Only – but this is rare –
When a belovéd hand is laid in ours,
When, jaded with the rush and glare
Of the interminable hours,
Our eyes can in another's eyes read clear,
When our world-deafen'd ear
Is by the tones of a loved voice caress'd –
A bolt is shot back somewhere in our breast,
An air of coolness plays upon his face
And a lost pulse of feeling stirs again.
The eye sinks inward, and the heart lies plain,
And what we mean, we say, and what we would, we know.
A man becomes aware of his life's flow,
And hears its winding murmur; and he sees
The meadows where it glides, the sun, the breeze.

And there arrives a lull in the hot race
Wherein he doth for ever chase
That flying and elusive shadow, rest.

An air of coolness plays upon his face
And an unwonted calm pervades his breast.
And then he thinks he knows
The hills where his life rose,
And the sea where it goes.

The Darkling Thrush[1]

THOMAS HARDY

I leant upon a coppice gate
  When Frost was spectre-gray,
And Winter's dregs made desolate
  The weakening eye of day.
The tangled bine-stems scored the sky
  Like strings of broken lyres,
And all mankind that haunted nigh
  Had sought their household fires.

The land's sharp features seemed to be
  The Century's corpse outleant,
His crypt the cloudy canopy,
  The wind his death-lament.

[1] As if written in contrast to John Keble's 'To a Thrush Singing in the Middle of a Village, Jan. 1833' which contains the following stanzas:

Perhaps within thy carol's sound
  Some wakeful mourner lies,
Dim roaming days and years around,
  That ne'er again may rise.

He thanks thee with a tearful eye,
  For thou hast wing'd his spright
Back to some hour when hopes were nigh
  And dearest friends in sight;

That simple, fearless note of thine
  Has pierced the cloud of care,
And lit awhile the gleam divine
  That bless'd his infant prayer;

Ere he had known, his faith to blight,
  The scorner's withering smile;
While hearts, he deem'd, beat true and right,
  Here in our Christian Isle.

The ancient pulse of germ and birth
   Was shrunken hard and dry,
And every spirit upon earth
   Seemed fervourless as I.

At once a voice arose among
   The bleak twigs overhead
In a full-hearted evensong
   Of joy illimited;
An aged thrush, frail, gaunt, and small,
   In blast-beruffled plume,
Had chosen thus to fling his soul
   Upon the growing gloom.

So little cause for carolings
   Of such ecstatic sound
Was written on terrestrial things
   Afar or nigh around,
That I could think there trembled through
   His happy good-night air
Some blessed Hope, whereof he knew
   And I was unaware.

31 December 1900

A Letter from Brooklyn

DEREK WALCOTT

An old lady writes me in a spidery style,
Each character trembling, and I see a veined hand
Pellucid as paper, travelling on a skein
Of such frail thoughts its thread is often broken;
Or else the filament from which a phrase is hung
Dims to my sense, but caught, it shines like steel,
As touch a line, and the whole web will feel.
She describes my father, yet I forget her face
More easily than my father's yearly dying;
Of her I remember small, buttoned boots and the place
She kept in our wooden church on those Sundays
Whenever her strength allowed;
Grey haired, thin voiced, perpetually bowed.

'I am Mable Rawlins,' she writes, 'and know both your
    parents;'
He is dead, Miss Rawlins, but God bless your tense:
'Your father was a dutiful, honest,
Faithful and useful person.'
For such plain praise what fame is recompense?
'A horn-painter, he painted delicately on horn,
He used to sit around the table and paint pictures.'
The peace of God needs nothing to adorn
It, nor glory nor ambition.
'He is twenty-eight years buried,' she writes, 'he was called
    home,
And is, I am sure, doing greater work.'

The strength of one frail hand in a dim room
Somewhere in Brooklyn, patient and assured,
Restores my sacred duty to the Word.
'Home, home,' she can write, with such short time to live,
Alone as she spins the blessings of her years;
Not withered of beauty if she can bring such tears,
Nor withdrawn from the world that breaks its lovers so;
Heaven is to her the place where painters go,
All who bring beauty on frail shell or horn,

There was all made, thence their lux-mundi[1] drawn,
Drawn, drawn, till the thread is resilient steel,
Lost though it seems in darkening periods,
And there they return to do work that is God's.

So this old lady writes, and again I believe,
I believe it all, and for no man's death I grieve.

[1] Latin: light of the earth.

The Shadow on the Stone

THOMAS HARDY

I went by the Druid stone
That broods in the garden white and lone,
And I stopped and looked at the shifting shadows
    That at some moments fall thereon
    From the tree hard by with a rhythmic swing,
    And they shaped in my imagining
To the shade that a well-known head and shoulders[1]
    Threw there when she was gardening.

I thought her behind my back,
Yea, her I long had learned to lack,
And I said: 'I am sure you are standing behind me,
    Though how do you get into this old track?'
    And there was no sound but the fall of a leaf
    As a sad response; and to keep down grief
I would not turn my head to discover
    That there was nothing in my belief.

Yet I wanted to look and see
That nobody stood at the back of me;
But I thought once more: 'Nay, I'll not unvision
    A shape which, somehow, there may be.'
    So I went on softly from the glade,
    And left her behind me throwing her shade,
As she were indeed an apparition –
    My head unturned lest my dream should fade.

[1] Hardy's late wife, Emma. One day he had found her burning his
old love letters to her, behind that stone, so unhappy had their marriage
become.

from *Notes Toward a Supreme Fiction:*
It Must Give Pleasure

WALLACE STEVENS

He[1] imposes orders as he thinks of them,
As the fox and snake do. It is a brave affair.
Next he builds capitols and in their corridors,

Whiter than wax, sonorous, fame as it is,
He establishes statues of reasonable men,
Who surpassed the most literate owl, the most erudite

Of elephants. But to impose is not
To discover. To discover an order as of
A season, to discover summer and know it,

To discover winter and know it well, to find,
Not to impose, not to have reasoned at all,
Out of nothing to have come on major weather,

It is possible, possible, possible. It must
Be possible. It must be that in time
The real will from its crude compoundings come,

Seeming, at first, a beast disgorged, unlike,
Warmed by a desperate milk. To find the real,
To be stripped of every fiction except one,

---

[1] Canon Aspirin, the poet's alter ego.

The fiction of an absolute – Angel,
Be silent in your luminous cloud and hear
The luminous melody of proper sound.

Poetry and Religion

LES MURRAY

Religions are poems. They concert
our daylight and dreaming mind, our
emotions, instinct, breath and native gesture

into the only whole thinking: poetry.
Nothing's said till it's dreamed out in words
and nothing's true that figures in words only.

A poem, compared with an arrayed religion,
may be like a soldier's one short marriage night
to die and live by. But that is a small religion.

Full religion is the large poem in loving repetition;
like any poem, it must be inexhaustible and complete
with turns where we ask Now why did the poet do that?

You can't pray a lie, said Huckleberry Finn;
you can't poe one either. It is the same mirror:
mobile, glancing, we call it poetry,

fixed centrally, we call it religion,
and God is the poetry caught in any religion,
caught, not imprisoned. Caught as in a mirror

that he attracted, being in the world as poetry
is in the poem, a law against its closure.
There'll always be religion around while there is poetry

or a lack of it. Both are given, and intermittent,
as the action of those birds – crested pigeon, rosella parrot –
who fly with wings shut, then beating, and again shut.

Prayer

CAROL ANN DUFFY

Some days, although we cannot pray, a prayer
utters itself. So, a woman will lift
her head from the sieve of her hands and stare
at the minims sung by a tree, a sudden gift.

Some nights, although we are faithless, the truth
enters our hearts, that small familiar pain;
then a man will stand stock-still, hearing his youth
in the distant Latin chanting of a train.

Pray for us now. Grade I piano scales
console the lodger looking out across
a Midlands town. Then dusk, and someone calls
a child's name as though they named their loss.

Darkness outside. Inside, the radio's prayer –
Rockall. Malin. Dogger. Finisterre.[1]

---

[1] The shipping forecast, often the last thing people hear on the radio
at night.

Crossing the Bar[1]

ALFRED, LORD TENNYSON

Sunset and evening star,
   And one clear call for me!
And may there be no moaning of the bar,
   When I put out to sea,

But such a tide as moving seems asleep,
   Too full for sound and foam,
When that which drew from out the boundless deep
   Turns again home.

Twilight and evening bell,
   And after that the dark!
And may there be no sadness of farewell,
   When I embark;

For though from out our bourne of Time and Place
   The flood may bear me far,
I hope to see my Pilot face to face
   When I have crost the bar.

[1] Bar: bank, shoal or wall at the mouth of a harbour.

One Clear Call

DENNIS HASKELL

Holidays, the bush, dusty Coonabarabran
and out of the blue your friend has rung
you, caught on the hop; an engineer
who never looks at a book, whose father's died;

the service is soon; and he wants to read
something – not scriptural – literature perhaps:
the skilled academic that you are,
you suggest – a good choice – 'Crossing the Bar'.

'Where can I buy it?' he asks, 'and quickly?'
'I know it,' you say, down the glistening, impersonal wires,
'I'll repeat it, slowly.' He waits, still, fingers
at the ready, for the first poem he's heard since school.

So you start, inexpressively, enunciating each syllable,
' "Sunset and evening star, / And one clear call for me" ',
into a vast tide of silence at the end of the line,
the unmoving pen you cannot see, foaming at the words

until his wife picks up the mouthpiece, and the pen,
and you are Tennyson's mouthpiece, shaken a little
and wondering now, as you begin again
before a face you cannot see: ' "Sunset and evening star ..." '

until she is choking too, and her wrist falters
across the lines, registering the scatter of words

as they lift from Tennyson's death mouth and your own
   voice
where they have lain like subject matter of no one's choice,

that past sensation of syllables sweeping you and your friends
across the bar of technique, of grieving, of consolation.

The Empty Church

R. S. THOMAS

They laid this stone trap
for him, enticing him with candles,
as though he would come like some huge moth
out of the darkness to beat there.
Ah, he had burned himself
before in the human flame
and escaped, leaving the reason
torn. He will not come any more

to our lure. Why, then, do I kneel still
striking my prayers on a stone
heart? Is it in hope one
of them will ignite yet and throw
on its illumined walls the shadow
of someone greater than I can understand?

The Temple

C. H. SISSON

Who are they talking to in the big temple?
If there was a reply it would be a conversation:
It is because there is none that they are fascinated.
What does not reply is the answer to prayer.

Part One

COMMON SACRAMENTS

I

Born

The Lord bless thee, and keep thee:
The Lord make His face shine upon thee,
and be gracious unto thee.

The Bible, Authorized Version,
Numbers 6:24–5

Shadows in the Water

THOMAS TRAHERNE

In unexperienced infancy
Many a sweet mistake doth lie –
Mistake, though false, intending true,
A seeming somewhat more than view –
   That doth instruct the mind
   In things that lie behind
And many secrets to us show
Which afterwards we come to know.

Thus did I by the water's brink
Another world beneath me think;
And while the lofty spacious skies
Reversèd there abused mine eyes,
   I fancied other feet
   Came mine to touch and meet;
As by some puddle I did play
Another world within it lay.

Beneath the water people drowned;
Yet with another heaven crowned,
In spacious regions seemed to go,
Freely moving to and fro.
   In bright and open space
   I saw their very face;
Eyes, hands, and feet they had like mine;
Another sun did with them shine.

'Twas strange that people there should walk,
And yet I could not hear them talk;
That through a little watery chink,
Which one dry ox or horse might drink,
　　We other worlds should see,
　　Yet not admitted be;
And other confines there behold
Of light and darkness, heat and cold.

I called them oft, but called in vain;
No speeches we could entertain;
Yet did I there expect to find
Some other world, so please my mind.
　　I plainly saw by these
　　A new Antipodes,
Whom, though they were so plainly seen,
A film kept off that stood between.

By walking men's reversèd feet
I chanced another world to meet;
Though it did not to view exceed
A phantasm, 'tis a world indeed,
　　Where skies beneath us shine,
And earth by art divine
Another face presents below,
Where people's feet against ours go.

Within the regions of the air,
Compassed about with heaven's fair,
Great tracts of land there may be found
Enriched with fields and fertile ground;
　　Where many numerous hosts
　　In those far distant coasts,
For other great and glorious ends,
Inhabit, my yet unknown Friends.

Oh ye that stand upon the brink,
Whom I so near me, through the chink,
With wonder see, what faces there,
Whose feet, whose bodies, do ye wear?
    I my companions see
    In you, another me.
They seemed others, but are we;
Our second selves those shadows be.

Look, how far off those lower skies
Extend themselves! Scarce with mine eyes
I can them reach. Oh ye my friends,
What Secret borders on those ends?
    Are loftly heavens hurled
    'Bout your inferior world?
Are ye the representatives
Of other people's distant lives?

Of all the playmates which I knew
That here I do the image view
In other selves, what can it mean?
But that below the purling stream
    Some unknown Joys there be
    Laid up in store for me;
To which I shall, when that thin skin
Is broken, be admitted in.

The Retreat

HENRY VAUGHAN

Happy those early days, when I
Shin'd in my angel-infancy!
Before I understood this place
Appointed for my second race,
Or taught my soul to fancy aught
But a white, celestial thought;
When yet I had not walked above
A mile, or two, from my first love,
And looking back (at that short space)
Could see a glimpse of his bright face;
When on some gilded cloud or flower
My gazing soul would dwell an hour,
And in those weaker glories spy
Some shadows of eternity;
Before I taught my tongue to wound
My conscience with a sinful sound,
Or had the black art to dispense
A several sin to every sense,
But felt through all this fleshly dress
Bright *shoots* of everlastingness.
 O how I long to travel back
And tread again that ancient track!
That I might once more reach that plain
Where first I left my glorious train,
From whence th'Enlightened spirit sees
That shady city of palm-trees;
But (ah!) my soul with too much stay
Is drunk, and staggers in the way.

Some men a forward motion love,
But I by backward steps would move,
And when this dust falls to the urn,
In that state I came, return.

Woman to Child

JUDITH WRIGHT

You who were darkness warmed my flesh
where out of darkness rose the seed.
Then all a world I made in me;
all the world you hear and see
hung upon my dreaming blood.

There moved the multitudinous stars,
and coloured birds and fishes moved.
There swam the sliding continents.
All time lay rolled in me, and sense,
and love that knew not its beloved.

O node and focus of the world;
I hold you deep within that well
you shall escape and not escape –
that mirrors still your sleeping shape;
that nurtures still your crescent cell.

I wither and you break from me;
yet though you dance in living light
I am the earth, I am the root,
I am the stem that fed the fruit,
the link that joins you to the night.

Morning Song

SYLVIA PLATH

Love set you going like a fat gold watch.
The midwife slapped your footsoles, and your bald cry
Took its place among the elements.

Our voices echo, magnifying your arrival. New statue.
In a drafty museum, your nakedness
Shadows our safety. We stand round blankly as walls.

I'm no more your mother
Than the cloud that distils a mirror to reflect its own slow
Effacement at the wind's hand.

All night your moth-breath
Flickers among the flat pink roses. I wake to listen:
A far sea moves in my ear.

One cry, and I stumble from bed, cow-heavy and floral
In my Victorian nightgown.
Your mouth opens clean as a cat's. The window square

Whitens and swallows its dull stars. And now you try
Your handful of notes;
The clear vowels rise like balloons.

A Prayer for My Daughter

W. B. YEATS

Once more the storm is howling, and half hid
Under this cradle-hood and coverlid
My child sleeps on. There is no obstacle
But Gregory's wood and one bare hill
Whereby the haystack- and roof-levelling wind,
Bred on the Atlantic, can be stayed;
And for an hour I have walked and prayed
Because of the great gloom that is in my mind.

I have walked and prayed for this young child an hour
And heard the sea-wind scream upon the tower,
And under the arches of the bridge, and scream
In the elms above the flooded stream;
Imagining in excited reverie
That the future years had come,
Dancing to a frenzied drum,
Out of the murderous innocence of the sea.

May she be granted beauty and yet not
Beauty to make a stranger's eye distraught,
Or hers before a looking-glass, for such,
Being made beautiful overmuch,
Consider beauty a sufficient end,
Lose natural kindness and maybe
The heart-revealing intimacy
That chooses right, and never find a friend.

Helen being chosen found life flat and dull
And later had much trouble from a fool,[1]
While that great Queen,[2] that rose out of the spray,
Being fatherless could have her way
Yet chose a bandy-leggèd smith for man.
It's certain that fine women eat
A crazy salad with their meat
Whereby the Horn of Plenty[3] is undone.

In courtesy I'd have her chiefly learned;
Hearts are not had as a gift but hearts are earned
By those that are not entirely beautiful;
Yet many, that have played the fool
For beauty's very self, has charm made wise,
And many a poor man that has roved,
Loved and thought himself beloved,
From a glad kindness cannot take his eyes.

May she become a flourishing hidden tree
That all her thoughts may like the linnet be,
And have no business but dispensing round
Their magnanimities of sound,
Nor but in merriment begin a chase,
Nor but in merriment a quarrel.
O may she live like some green laurel
Rooted in one dear perpetual place.

My mind, because the minds that I have loved,
The sort of beauty that I have approved,
Prosper but little, has dried up of late,
Yet knows that to be choked with hate

---

[1] Helen of Troy left her husband, Menelaus, for Paris, son of Priam of Troy.

[2] Aphrodite, born of the sea, married Hephaestus, the Lame God of Fire.

[3] Zeus was suckled by the goat Amalthie whose horn, flowing with nectar and honey, broke off.

May well be of all evil chances chief.
If there's no hatred in a mind
Assault and battery of the wind
Can never tear a linnet from the leaf.

An intellectual hatred is the worst,
So let her think opinions are accursed.
Have I not seen the loveliest woman born[1]
Out of the mouth of Plenty's horn,
Because of her opinionated mind
Barter that horn and every good
By quiet natures understood
For an old bellows full of angry wind?

Considering that, all hatred driven hence,
The soul recovers radical innocence
And learns at last that it is self-delighting,
Self-appeasing, self-affrighting,
And that its own sweet will is Heaven's will;
She can, though every face should scowl
And every windy quarter howl
Or every bellows burst, be happy still.

And may her bridegroom bring her to a house
Where all's accustomed, ceremonious;
For arrogance and hatred are the wares
Peddled in the thoroughfares.
How but in custom and in ceremony
Are innocence and beauty born?
Ceremony's a name for the rich horn,
And custom for the spreading laurel tree.

---

[1] Yeat's beloved Maud Gonne, his equivalent to Helen of Troy, who never returned his love.

Epitaph. On her Son H.P. at St Syth's Church where her body also lies Interred

KATHERINE PHILIPS

What on Earth deserves our trust?
Youth and Beauty both are dust.
Long we gathering are with pain,
What one moment calls again.
Seven years childless marriage past,
A Son, a son is born at last:
So exactly limb'd and fair,
Full of good Spirits, Mien, and Air,
As a long life promisèd,
Yet, in less than six weeks dead.
Too promising, too great a mind
In so small room to be confin'd:
Therefore as for in Heav'n to dwell,
He quickly broke the Prison shell.
So the subtle Alchemist,
Can't with Hermes seal[1] resist
The powerful spirit's subtler flight,
But 'twill bid him long good night.
And so the Sun if it arise
Half so glorious as his Eyes,
Like this Infant, takes a shroud,
Buried in a morning Cloud.

[1] Even an Hermetic seal cannot prevent the soul's flight.

For a Five-year-old

FLEUR ADCOCK

A snail is climbing up the window-sill
Into your room, after a night of rain.
You call me in to see, and I explain
That it would be unkind to leave it there:
It might crawl to the floor; we must take care
That no one squashes it. You understand,
And carry it outside, with careful hand,
To eat a daffodil.

I see, then, that a kind of faith prevails:
Your gentleness is moulded still by words
From me, who have trapped mice and shot wild birds,
From me, who drowned your kittens, who betrayed
Your closest relatives, and who purveyed
The harshest kind of truth to many another.
But that is how things are: I am your mother,
And we are kind to snails.

False Friends-Like

WILLIAM BARNES

When I wer still a bwoy[1], an' mother's pride,
A bigger bwoy spoke up to me so kind-like,
'If you do like, I'll treat ye wi' a ride
In theäse[2] wheel-barrow here.' Zoo[3] I wer blind-like
To what he had a-worken in his mind-like,
An' mounted vor[4] a passenger inside;
An' comen to a puddle, perty wide,
He tipp'd me in, a-grinnen back behind-like.
Zoo when a man do come to me so thick-like,
An' sheäke my hand, where woonce he pass'd me by,
An' tell me he would do me this or that,
I can't help thinken o' the big bwoy's trick-like.
An', then, vor all I can but wag my hat
An' thank en, I do veel[5] a little shy.

[1] bwoy: Dorset dialect for 'boy'.
[2] theäse: this.
[3] Zoo: so.
[4] vor: for.
[5] veel: feel.

Epitaphs
(i)
On My First Daughter

BEN JONSON

Here lies to each her parents' ruth
Mary, the daughter of their youth:
Yet, all Heaven's gifts being Heaven's due,
It makes the father less to rue.
At six months' end she parted hence
With safety of her innocence;
Whose soul Heaven's Queen (whose name she bears)
In comfort of her mother's tears,
Hath placed amongst her virgin-train;
Where, while that severed doth remain,
This grave partakes the fleshly birth,
Which cover lightly, gentle earth.

(ii)
On My Son

BEN JONSON

Farewell, thou child of my right hand, and joy;
  My sin was too much hope of thee, loved boy.
Seven years thou wert lent to me, and I thee pay,
  Exacted by thy fate, on the just day.
O, could I lose all father now! For why
  Will man lament the state he should envy?
To have so soon 'scaped world's and flesh's rage,
  And, if no other misery, yet age?
Rest in soft peace, and, asked, say here doth lie
  Ben Jonson, his best piece of poetry.
For whose sake, henceforth, all his vows be such
  As what he loves may never like too much.

Infancy – A Fragment

GEORGE CRABBE

Who on the new-born light can back return,
And the first efforts of the soul discern –
Waked by some sweet maternal smile, no more
To sleep so long or fondly as before?
No! Memory cannot reach, with all her power,
To that new birth, that life-awakening hour.
No! all the traces of her first employ
Are keen perceptions of the senses' joy,
And their distaste – what then could they impart? –
That figs were luscious, and that rods had smart.

But, though the Memory in that dubious way
Recalls the dawn and twilight of her day,
And thus encounters, in the doubtful view,
With imperfection and distortion too;
Can she not tell us, as she looks around,
Of good and evil, which the most abound?

Alas! and what is earthly good? 'tis lent
Evil to hide, to soften, to prevent,
By scenes and shows that cheat the wandering eye,
While the more pompous misery passes by;
Shifts and amusements that awhile succeed,
And heads are turn'd, that bosoms may not bleed:
For what is Pleasure, that we toil to gain?
'Tis but the slow or rapid flight of Pain.
Set Pleasure by, and there would yet remain,
For every nerve and sense the sting of Pain:
Set Pain aside, and fear no more the sting,
And whence your hopes and pleasures can ye bring?

No! there is not a joy beneath the skies,
That from no grief nor trouble shall arise.

Why does the Lover with such rapture fly
To his dear mistress? – He shall show us why: –
Because her absence is such cause of grief
That her sweet smile alone can yield relief.
Why, then, that smile is Pleasure: – True, yet still
'Tis but the absence of the former ill:
For, married, soon at will he comes and goes;
Then pleasures die, and pains become repose,
And he has none of these, and therefore none of those.

Yes! looking back as early as I can,
I see the griefs that seize their subject Man,
That in the weeping Child their early reign began:
Yes! though Pain softens, and is absent since,
He still controls me like my lawful prince.
Joys I remember, like phosphoric light
Or squibs and crackers on a gala night.
Joys are like oil; if thrown upon the tide
Of flowing life, they mix not, nor subside:
Griefs are like waters on the river thrown,
They mix entirely, and become its own.
Of all the good that grew of early date,
I can but parts and incidents relate:
A guest arriving, or a borrow'd day
From school, or schoolboy triumph at some play:
And these from Pain may be deduced; for these
Removed some ill, and hence their power to please.

But it was Misery stung me in the day
Death of an infant sister made a prey;
For then first met and moved my early fears,
A father's terrors, and a mother's tears.
Though greater anguish I have since endured, –
Some heal'd in part, some never to be cured;
Yet was there something in that first-born ill,

So new, so strange, that memory feels it still!
  That my first grief: but, oh! in after-years
Were other deaths, that call'd for other tears.
No! that I cannot, that I dare not, paint –
That patient sufferer, that enduring saint,
Holy and lovely – but all words are faint.
But here I dwell not – let me, while I can,
Go to the Child, and lose the suffering Man.

  Sweet was the morning's breath, the inland tide,
And our boat gliding, where alone could glide
Small craft – and they oft touch'd on either side.
It was my first-born joy. I heard them say,
'Let the child go; he will enjoy the day.'
For children ever feel delighted when
They take their portion, and enjoy with men.
Give him the pastime that the old partake,
And he will quickly top and taw forsake.

  The linnet chirp'd upon the furze as well,
To my young sense, as sings the nightingale.
Without was paradise – because within
Was a keen relish, without taint of sin.

  A town appear'd, – and where an infant went,
Could they determine, on themselves intent?
I lost my way, and my companions me,
And all, their comforts and tranquillity.
Midday it was, and, as the sun declined,
The good, found early, I no more could find:
The men drank much, to whet the appetite;
And, growing heavy, drank to make them light;
Then drank to relish joy, then further to excite.
Their cheerfulness did but a moment last;
Something fell short, or something overpast.
The lads play'd idly with the helm and oar,
And nervous women would be set on shore,
Till 'civil dudgeon' grew, and peace would smile no more.

Now on the colder water faintly shone
The sloping light – the cheerful day was gone;
Frown'd every cloud, and from the gather'd frown
The thunder burst, and rain came pattering down.
My torpid senses now my fears obey'd,
When the fierce lightning on the eye-balls play'd.
Now, all the freshness of the morning fled,
My spirits burden'd, and my heart was dead;
The female servants show'd a child their fear,
And men, full wearied, wanted strength to cheer;
And when, at length, the dreaded storm went past,
And there was peace and quietness at last,
'Twas not the morning's quiet – it was not
Pleasure revived, but Misery forgot:
It was not Joy that now commenced her reign,
But mere relief from wretchedness and Pain.

So many a day, in life's advance, I knew;
So they commenced, and so they ended too.
All Promise they – all Joy as they began!
But Joy grew less, and vanish'd as they ran!
Errors and evils came in many a form, –
The mind's delusion, and the passions' storm.

The promised joy, that like this morning rose,
Broke on my view, then clouded at its close;
E'en Love himself, that promiser of bliss,
Made his best days of pleasure end like this:
He mix'd his bitters in the cup of joy,
Nor gave a bliss uninjured by alloy.

Intimations of Immortality from Recollections of Early Childhood

WILLIAM WORDSWORTH

There was a time when meadow, grove and stream,
The earth, and every common sight,
    To me did seem
    Apparelled in celestial light,
The glory and the freshness of a dream.
It is not now as it hath been of yore; –
    Turn wheresoe'er I may,
      By night or day,
The things which I have seen I now can see no more.

    The Rainbow comes and goes,
    And lovely is the Rose,
    The Moon doth with delight
Look round her when the heavens are bare;
    Waters on a starry night
    Are beautiful and fair;
The sunshine is a glorious birth;
But yet I know, where'er I go,
That there hath past away a glory from the earth.

Now, while the birds thus sing a joyous song,
    And while the young lambs bound
      As to the tabor's sound,
To me alone there came a thought of grief:
A timely utterance gave that thought relief,
    And I again am strong:
The cataracts blow their trumpets from the steep;

No more shall grief of mine the season wrong;
I hear the Echoes through the mountains throng,
The winds come to me from the fields of sleep,
     And all the earth is gay;
      Land and sea
     Give themselves up to jollity,
     And with the heart of May
     Doth every beast keep holiday; –
     Thou Child of Joy,
Shout round me, let me hear thy shouts, thou happy
      Shepherd-boy!

Ye blessed Creatures, I have heard the call
   Yet to each other make; I see
The heavens laugh with you in your jubilee;
   My heart is at your festival,
    My head hath its coronal,
The fulness of your bliss, I feel – I feel it all.
    Oh evil day! if I were sullen
    While Earth herself is adorning,
    This sweet May morning,
    And the children are culling
     On every side,
    In a thousand valleys far and wide,
    Fresh flowers; while the sun shines warm,
And the Babe leaps up on his Mother's arm: –
    I hear, I hear, with joy I hear!
    – But there's a Tree, of many, one,
A single Field which I have looked upon,
Both of them speak of something that is gone:
    The Pansy at my feet
    Doth the same tale repeat:
Whither is fled the visionary gleam?
Where is it now, the glory and the dream?

Our birth is but a sleep and a forgetting:
The Soul that rises with us, our life's Star,
        Hath had elsewhere its setting,
            And cometh from afar:
        Not in entire forgetfulness,
        And not in utter nakedness,
But trailing clouds of glory do we come
        From God, who is our home:
Heaven lies about us in our infancy!
Shades of the prison-house begin to close
        Upon the growing Boy,
But He beholds the light, and whence it flows,
        He sees it in his joy;
The Youth, who daily farther from the east
        Must travel, still is Nature's Priest,
        And by the vision splendid
        Is on his way attended;
At length the Man perceives it die away.
And fade into the light of common day.

Earth fills her lap with pleasures of her own;
Yearnings she hath in her own natural kind,
And, even with something of a Mother's mind,
        And no unworthy aim,
        The homely Nurse doth all she can
To make her Foster-child, her Inmate Man,
        Forget the glories he hath known,
And that imperial palace whence he came.

Behold the Child among his new-born blisses,
A six years' Darling of a pigmy size!
See, where 'mid work of his own hand he lies,
Fretted by sallies of his mother's kisses,
With light upon him from his father's eyes!
See at his feet, some little plan or chart,

Some fragment from his dream of human life,
Shaped by himself with newly-learned art;
    A wedding or a festival,
    A mourning or a funeral;
    And this hath all his heart,
    And unto this he frames his song:
    Then will he fit his tongue
To dialogues of business, love or strife;
    But it will not be long
    Ere this be thrown aside,
    And with new joy and pride
The little Actor cons another part;
Filling from time to time his 'humorous stage'
With all the Persons, down to palsied Age,
That life brings with her in her equipage;
    As if his whole vocation
    Were endless imitation.

Thou, whose exterior semblance doth belie
    Thy Soul's immensity;
Thou best Philosopher, who yet dost keep
Thy heritage, thou Eye among the blind,
That, deaf and silent, read'st the eternal deep,
Haunted for ever by the eternal mind, –
    Mighty Prophet! Seer blest!
    On whom those truths do rest,
Which we are toiling all our lives to find,
In darkness lost, the darkness of the grave;
Thou, over whom thy Immortality
Broods like the Day, a Master o'er a Slave,
A Presence which is not to be put by;
    (To whom the grave
Is but a lonely bed without the sense or sight
    Of day or the warm light,
A place of thought where we in waiting lie;)

Thou little Child, yet glorious in the might
Of heaven-born freedom on thy being's height,
Why with such earnest pains dost thou provoke
The years to bring the inevitable yoke,
Thus blindly with thy blessedness at strife?
Full soon thy Soul shall have her earthly freight,
And custom lie upon thee with a weight,
Heavy as frost, and deep almost as life!

     O joy! that in our embers
     Is something that doth live,
     That nature yet remembers
     What was so fugitive!
The thought of our past years in me doth breed
Perpetual benediction: not indeed
For that which is most worthy to be blest;
Delight and liberty, the simple creed
Of Childhood, whether busy or at rest,
With new-fledged hope still fluttering in his breast: –
     Not for these I raise
     The song of thanks and praise;
    But for those obstinate questionings
    Of sense and outward things,
    Fallings from us, vanishings;
    Blank misgivings of a Creature
Moving about in worlds not realized,
High instincts before which our mortal Nature
Did tremble like a guilty Thing surprised:
     But for those first affections,
     Those shadowy recollections,
     Which, be they what they may,
Are yet the fountain-light of all our day,
Are yet a master-light of all our seeing;
Uphold us, cherish, and have power to make
Our noisy years seem moments in the being

Of the eternal Silence: truths that wake,
>   To perish never:
Which neither listlessness, nor mad endeavour,
>   Nor Man nor Boy,
Nor all that is at enmity with joy,
Can utterly abolish or destroy!
>   Hence in a season of calm weather
>   Though inland far we be,
Our Souls have sight of that immortal sea
>   Which brought us hither,
>   Can in a moment travel thither,
And see the Children sport upon the shore,
And hear the mighty waters rolling evermore.

Then sing, ye Birds, sing, sing a joyous song!
>   And let the young Lambs bound
>   As to the tabor's sound!
We in thought will join your throng,
>   Ye that pipe and ye that play,
>   Ye that through your hearts to-day
>   Feel the gladness of the May!
What though the radiance which was once so bright
Be now for ever taken from my sight,
>   Though nothing can bring back the hour
Of splendour in the grass, of glory in the flower;
>   We will grieve not, rather find
>   Strength in what remains behind,
>   In the primal sympathy
>   Which having been must ever be;
>   In the soothing thoughts that spring
>   Out of human suffering;
>   In the faith that looks through death,
In years that bring the philosophic mind.

And O, ye Fountains, Meadows, Hills and Groves,
Forebode not any severing of our loves!
Yet in my heart of hearts I feel your might;
I only have relinquished one delight
To live beneath your more habitual sway.
I love the Brooks which down their channels fret,
Even more than when I tripped lightly as they;
The innocent brightness of a new-born Day
   Is lovely yet;
The Clouds that gather round the setting sun
Do take a sober colouring from an eye
That hath kept watch o'er man's mortality;
Another race hath been, and other palms are won.
Thanks to the human heart by which we live,
Thanks to its tenderness, its joys and fears,
To me the meanest flower that blows can give
Thoughts that do often lie too deep for tears.

2

Marriage

To have and to hold from this day forward,
for better for worse, for richer for poorer, in
sickness and in health, to love and to cherish,
till death us do part ...

Book of Common Prayer

There was never nothing more me pained

SIR THOMAS WYATT

There was never nothing more me pained
  Nor nothing more me moved
As when my sweet heart her complained
  That ever she me loved,
    Alas the while!

With piteous look she said and sight:
  'Alas what aileth me
To love and set my wealth so light
  On him that loveth not me?
    Alas the while!

'Was I not well void of all pain
  When that nothing me grieved?
And now with sorrows I must complain
  And cannot be relieved.
    Alas the while!

'My restful nights and joyful days
  Since I began to love
Be take from me. All thing decays
  Yet can I not remove.
    Alas the while!'

She wept and wrung her hands withal.
  The tears fell in my neck.
She turned her face and let it fall,

Scarcely therewith could speak,
   Alas the while!

Her pains tormented me so sore
   That comfort had I none
But cursed my fortune more and more
   To see her sob and groan,
      Alas the while!

Easter

EDMUND SPENSER

Most glorious Lord of life, that on this day,
   Didst make thy triumph over death and sin:
And having harrowed hell, didst bring away
   Captivity thence captive us to win:
   This joyous day, dear Lord, with joy begin,
And grant that we, for whom thou diddest die,
   Being with thy dear blood clean washed from sin,
May live for ever in felicity.
And that thy love we weighing worthily,
   May likewise love thee for the same again:
And for thy sake that all like dear didst buy,
   With love may one another entertain.
     So let us love, dear love, like as we ought,
     Love is the lesson which the Lord us taught.

from *Epithalamion*

EDMUND SPENSER

Early before the world's light-giving lamp,
His golden beam upon the hills doth spread,
Having dispersed the night's uncheerful damp,
Do ye awake, and with fresh lusty head,
Go to the bower of my beloved love,
My truest turtle dove,
Bid her awake; for Hymen is awake,
And long since ready forth his mask to move,
With his bright Tead that flames with many a flake,
And many a bachelor to wait on him,
In their fresh garments trim.
Bid her awake therefore and soon her dight,
For lo the wished day is come at last,
That shall for all the pains and sorrows past,
Pay to her usury of long delight:
And whilst she doth her dight,
Do ye to her of joy and solace sing,
That all the woods may answer and your echo ring.

Wake now, my love, awake; for it is time.
The Rosy Morn long since left Tithones bed,
All ready to her silver coach to climb,
And Phoebus 'gins to show his glorious head.
Hark how the cheerful birds do chant their lays
And carol of love's praise.
The merry Lark her matins sings aloft,
The thrush replies, the Mavis descant plays,
The Ouzell shrills, the Ruddock warbles soft,

So goodly all agree with sweet consent,
To this day's merriment.
Ah my dear love, why do ye sleep thus long,
When meeter were that ye should now awake,
T'await the coming of your joyous make,
And hearken to the birds' lovelearned song,
The dewy leaves among.
For they of joy and pleasance to you sing,
That all the woods them answer and their echo ring.

Now is my love all ready forth to come;
Let all the virgins therefore well await,
And ye fresh boys that tend upon her groom
Prepare your selves; for he is coming straight.
Set all your things in seemly good array
Fit for so joyful day,
The joyfulst day that ever sun did see.
Fair Sun, show forth thy favourable ray,
And let thy lifeful heat not fervent be
For fear of burning her sunshiny face,
Her beauty to disgrace.
O fairest Phoebus, father of the Muse,
If ever I did honour thee aright,
Or sing the thing, that mote thy mind delight,
Do not thy servant's simple boon refuse,
But let this day, let this one day, be mine,
Let all the rest be thine.
Then I thy sovereign praises loud will sing,
That all the woods shall answer and their echo ring.

Lo where she comes along with portly pace
Like Phoebe from her chamber of the East,
Arising forth to run her mighty race,
Clad all in white, that seems a virgin best.
So well it her beseems that ye would ween

Some angel she had been.
Her long loose yellow locks like golden wire,
Sprinkled with pearl, and pearling flowers a-tween,
Do like a golden mantle her attire,
And being crowned with a garland green,
Seem like some maiden Queen.
Her modest eyes abashed to behold
So many gazers, as on her do stare,
Upon the lowly ground affixed are.
Ne dare lift up her countenance too bold,
But blush to hear her praises sung so loud,
So far from being proud.
Nathlesse do ye still loud her praises sing.
That all the woods may answer and your echo ring.

Tell me, ye merchants' daughters, did ye see
So fair a creature in your town before,
So sweet, so lovely, and so mild as she,
Adorn'd with beauty's grace and virtue's store,
Her goodly eyes like Sapphires shining bright,
Her forehead ivory white,
Her cheeks like apples which the sun hath rudded,
Her lips like cherries charming men to bite,
Her breast like to a bowl of cream uncrudded,
Her paps like lilies budded,
Her snowy neck like to a marble tower,
And all her body like a palace fair,
Ascending up with many a stately stair,
To honour's seat and chastity's sweet bower.
Why stand ye still, ye virgins, in amaze,
Upon her so to gaze,
Whiles ye forget your former lay to sing,
To which the woods did answer and your echo ring.

But if ye saw that which no eyes can see,
The inward beauty of her lively spright,
Garnish'd with heavenly gifts of high degree,
Much more then would ye wonder at that sight,
And stand astonish'd like to those which read
Medusa's mazeful[1] head.
There dwells sweet love and constant chastity,
Unspotted faith and comely womanhood,
Regard of honour and mild modesty,
There virtues reigns as Queen in royal throne,
And giveth laws alone,
The which the base affections do obey,
And yield their services unto her will,
Ne thought of thing uncomely ever may
Thereto approach to tempt her mind to ill.
Had ye once seen these her celestial treasures,
And unrevealed pleasures,
Then would ye wonder and her praises sing,
That all the woods should answer and your echo ring.

Now welcome night, thou night so long expected,
That long day's labour dost at last defray,
And all my cares, which cruel love collected,
Hast summed in one, and cancelled for aye:
Spread thy broad wing over my love and me,
That no man may us see,
And in thy sable mantle us enwrap,
From fear of peril and foul horror free.
Let no false treason seek us to entrap,
Nor any dread disquiet once annoy
The safety of our joy:
But let the night be calm and quietsome,
Without tempestuous storms or sad affray:

---

[1] mazeful: amazing.

Like as when Jove with fair Alcmena lay,
When he begot the great Tirynthian groom[1]:
Or like as when he with thy self did lie,
And begot Majesty.
And let the maids and youngmen cease to sing:
Ne let the woods them answer, nor their echo ring.

And thou, great Juno, which with awful might
The laws of wedlock still dost patronize,
And the religion of the faith first plight
With sacred rites hast taught to solemnize:
And eeke for comfort often called art
Of women in their smart,
Eternally bind thou this lovely band,
And all thy blessings unto us impart.
And thou, glad Genius, in whose gentle hand
The bridal bower and genial bed remain,
Without blemish or stain,
And the sweet pleasures of their love's delight
With secret aid dost succour and supply,
Till they bring forth the fruitful progeny,
Send us the timely fruit of this same night.
And thou, fair Hebe[2], and thou, Hymen free,
Grant that it may so be.
Til which we cease your further praise to sing,
Ne any woods shall answer, nor your Echo ring.

[1] Hercules.
[2] Hebe: daughter of Jove and Juno. Hebe married Hercules.

To My Dear and Loving Husband

ANNE BRADSTREET

If ever two were one, then surely we.
If ever man were lov'd by wife, then thee;
If ever wife was happy in a man,
Compare with me ye women if you can.
I prize thy love more than whole mines of gold,
Or all the riches that the East doth hold.
My love is such that rivers cannot quench,
Nor aught but love from thee, give recompense.
Thy love is such I can no way repay,
The heavens reward thee manifold, I pray.
Then while we live, in love let's so persevere
That, when we live no more, we may live ever.

from *Paradise Lost Book IX*

JOHN MILTON

Much pleasure we have lost, while we abstained
From this delightful fruit, nor known till now
True relish, tasting; if such pleasure be
In things to us forbidden, it might be wished,
For this one tree had been forbidden ten.
But come, so well refreshed, now let us play,
As meet is, after such delicious fare;
For never did thy beauty since the day
I saw thee first and wedded thee, adorned
With all perfections, so inflame my sense
With ardour to enjoy thee, fairer now
Than ever, bounty of this virtuous tree.
  So said he, and forbore not glance or toy
Of amorous intent, well understood
Of Eve, whose eye darted contagious fire.
Her hand he seized, and to a shady bank,
Thick overhead with verdant roof embowered
He led her nothing loth; flowers were the couch,
Pansies, and violets, and asphodel,
And hyacinth, earth's freshest softest lap.
There they their fill of love and love's disport
Took largely, of their mutual guilt the seal,
The solace of their sin, till dewy sleep
Oppressed them, wearied with their amorous play.
Soon as the force of that fallacious fruit,
That with exhilarating vapour bland
About their spirits had played, and inmost powers
Made err, was now exhaled, and grosser sleep

Bred of unkindly[1] fumes, with conscious dreams
Encumbered, now had left them, up they rose
As from unrest, and each the other viewing,
Soon found their eyes how opened, and their minds
How darkened; innocence, that as a veil
Had shadowed them from knowing ill, was gone,
Just confidence, and native righteousness
And honour from about them, naked left
To guilty shame he covered, but his robe
Uncovered more, so rose the Danite[2] strong
Herculean Samson from the harlot-lap
Of Philistean Dalilah, and waked
Shorn of his strength, they destitute and bare
Of all their virtue: silent, and in face
Confounded long they sat, as strucken mute,
Till Adam, though not less than Eve abashed,
At length gave utterance to these words constrained.

O Eve, in evil hour thou didst give ear
To that false worm, of whomsoever taught
To counterfeit man's voice, true in our fall,
False in our promised rising; since our eyes
Opened we find indeed, and find we know
Both good and evil, good lost, and evil got,
Bad fruit of knowledge, if this be to know,
Which leaves us naked thus, of honour void,
Of innocence, of faith, of purity,
Our wonted ornaments now soiled and stained,
And in our faces evident the signs
Of foul concupiscence; whence evil store;
Even shame, the last of evils; of the first
Be sure then. How shall I behold the face
Henceforth of God or angel, erst with joy
And rapture so oft beheld? Those heavenly shapes

[1] unkindly: unnatural.
[2] Samson, of the tribe of Dan, was betrayed by Delilah (Judges 16).

Will dazzle now this earthly, with their blaze
Insufferably bright. O might I here
In solitude live savage, in some glade
Obscured, where highest woods impenetrable
To star or sunlight, spread their umbrage broad
And brown as evening: cover me ye pines,
Ye cedars, with innumerable boughs
Hide me, where I may never see them more.
But let us now, as in bad plight, devise
What best may for the present serve to hide
The parts of each from other, that seem most
To shame obnoxious, and unseemliest seen,
Some tree whose broad smooth leaves together sewed,
And girded on our loins, may cover round
Those middle parts, that this new comer, shame,
There sit not, and reproach us as unclean.
  So counselled he, and both together went
Into the thickest wood, there soon they chose
The fig-tree, not that kind for fruit renowned,
But such as at this day to Indians known
In Malabar or Decan[1] spreads her arms
Branching so broad and long, that in the ground
The bended twigs take root, and daughters grow
Above the mother tree, a pillared shade
High overarched, and echoing walks between;
There oft the Indian herdsman shunning heat
Shelters in cool, and tends his pasturing herds
At loop-holes cut through thickest shade: those leaves
They gathered, broad as Amazonian targe,[2]
And with what skill they had, together sewed,
To gird their waist, vain covering if to hide
Their guilt and dreaded shame; O how unlike
To that first naked glory. Such of late

[1] banyan or Indian fig.
[2] targe: shield.

70

Columbus found the American so girt
With feathered cincture,[1] naked else and wild
Among the trees on isles and woody shores.
Thus fenced, and as they thought, their shame in part
Covered, but not at rest or ease of mind,
They sat them down to weep, nor only tears
Rained at their eyes, but high winds worse within
Began to rise, high passions, anger, hate,
Mistrust, suspicion, discord, and shook sore
Their inward state of mind, calm region once
And full of peace, now tossed and turbulent:
For understanding ruled not, and the will
Heard not her lore, both in subjection now
To sensual appetite, who from beneath
Usurping over sovereign reason claimed
Superior sway: from thus distempered breast,
Adam, estranged in look and altered style,
Speech intermitted thus to Eve renewed.
    Would thou hadst hearkened to my words, and stayed
With me, as I besought thee, when that strange
Desire of wandering this unhappy morn,
I know not whence possessed thee; we had then
Remained still happy, not as now, despoiled
Of all our good, shamed, naked, miserable.
Let none henceforth seek needless cause to approve
The faith they owe; when earnestly they seek
Such proof, conclude, they then begin to fail.
    To whom soon moved with touch of blame thus Eve.
What words have passed thy lips, Adam severe,
Imput'st thou that to my default, or will
Of wandering, as thou call'st it, which who knows
But might as ill have happened thou being by,
Or to thy self perhaps: hadst thou been there,

[1] cincture: belt.

Or here the attempt, thou couldst not have discerned
Fraud in the serpent, speaking as he spake;
No ground of enmity between us known,
Why he should mean me ill, or seek to harm.
Was I to have never parted from thy side?
As good have grown there still a lifeless rib.
Being as I am, why didst not thou the head
Command me absolutely not to go,
Going into such danger as thou saidst?
Too facile then thou didst not much gainsay.
Nay didst permit, approve, and fair dismiss.
Hadst thou been firm and fixed in thy dissent,
Neither had I transgressed, nor thou with me.
　　To whom then first incensed Adam replied,
Is this the love, is this the recompense
Of mine to thee, ingrateful Eve, expressed
Immutable when thou wert lost, not I,
Who might have lived and joyed immortal bliss,
Yet willingly chose rather death with thee:
And am I now upbraided, as the cause
Of thy transgressing? Not enough severe,
It seems, in thy restraint: what could I more?
I warned thee, I admonished thee, foretold
The danger, and the lurking enemy
That lay in wait; beyond this had been force,
And force upon free will hath here no place.
But confidence then bore thee on, secure
Either to meet no danger, or to find
Matter of glorious trial; and perhaps
I also erred in overmuch admiring
What seemed in thee so perfect, that I thought
No evil durst attempt thee, but I rue
That error now, which is become my crime,
And thou the accuser. Thus it shall befall
Him who to worth in women overtrusting

Lets her will rule; restraint she will not brook,
And left to her self, if evil thence ensue,
She first his weak indulgence will accuse.

Thus they in mutual accusation spent
The fruitless hours, but neither self-condemning,
And of their vain contest appeared no end.

Crow's First Lesson

TED HUGHES

God tried to teach Crow how to talk.
'Love,' said God. 'Say, Love.'
Crow gaped, and the white shark crashed into the sea
And went rolling downwards, discovering its own depth.

'No, no,' said God, 'Say Love. Now try it. LOVE.'
Crow gaped, and a bluefly, a tsetse, a mosquito
Zoomed out and down
To their sundry flesh-pots.

'A final try,' said God. 'Now, LOVE.'
Crow convulsed, gaped, retched and
Man's bodiless prodigious head
Bulbed out onto the earth, with swivelling eyes,
Jabbering protest—

And Crow retched again, before God could stop him.
And woman's vulva dropped over man's neck and tightened.
The two struggled together on the grass.
God struggled to part them, cursed, wept—

Crow flew guiltily off.

Modern Love (i)

GEORGE MEREDITH

By this he knew she wept with waking eyes:
That, at his hand's light quiver by her head,
The strange low sobs that shook their common bed,
Were called into her with a sharp surprise,
And strangled mute, like little gaping snakes,
Dreadfully venomous to him. She lay
Stone-still, and the long darkness flowed away
With muffled pulses. Then, as midnight makes
Her giant heart of Memory and Tears
Drink the pale drug of silence, and so beat
Sleep's heavy measure, they from head to feet
Were moveless, looking through their dead black years,
By vain regret scrawled over the blank wall.
Like sculptured effigies they might be seen
Upon their marriage-tomb, the sword between;
Each wishing for the sword that severs all.

Modern Love (xii)

GEORGE MEREDITH

Not solely that the Future she destroys,
And the fair life which in the distance lies
For all men, beckoning out from dim rich skies:
Nor that the passing hour's supporting joys
Have lost the keen-edged flavour, which begat
Distinction in old times, and still should breed
Sweet Memory, and Hope, – earth's modest seed,
And heaven's high-prompting: not that the world is flat
Since that soft-luring creature I embraced
Among the children of Illusion went:
Methinks with all this loss I were content,
If the mad Past, on which my foot is based,
Were firm, or might be blotted: but the whole
Of life is mixed: the mocking Past will stay:
And if I drink oblivion of a day,
So shorten I the stature of my soul.

Sonnet 116

WILLIAM SHAKESPEARE

Let me not to the marriage of true minds
Admit impediments; love is not love
Which alters when it alteration finds,
Or bends with the remover to remove.
O no, it is an ever-fixèd mark
That looks on tempests and is never shaken;
It is the star to every wandering bark,
Whose worth's unknown, although his height be taken.
Love's not Time's fool, though rosy lips and cheeks
Within his bending sickle's compass come;
Love alters not with his brief hours and weeks,
But bears it out even to the edge of doom.
  If this be error and upon me proved,
  I never writ, nor no man ever loved.

Sonnet 110

WILLIAM SHAKESPEARE

Alas, 'tis true, I have gone here and there,
And made myself a motley to the view,
Gored mine own thoughts, sold cheap what is most dear,
Made old offences of affections new.
Most true it is that I have looked on truth
Askance and strangely; but, by all above,
These blenches gave my heart another youth,
And worse essays proved thee my best of love.
Now all is done, have what shall have no end;
Mine appetite I never more will grind
On newer proof, to try an older friend,
A god in love, to whom I am confined.
   Then give me welcome, next my heaven the best,
   Even to thy pure and most most loving breast.

The Vierzide Chairs[1]

WILLIAM BARNES

Though days do gaïn upon the night,
An' birds do teäke[2] a leäter[3] flight,
'Tis cwold[4] enough to spread our hands
Oonce now an' then to glowen brands.
Zoo[5] now we two, a-left alwone,
Can meäke a quiet hour our own,
Let's teäke, a-zitten feäce[6] to feäce,
Our pleäces by the vier pleäce,
Where you shall have the window view
Outside, an' I can look on you.

When oonce I brought ye hwome my bride,
In yollow glow o' zummer tide,
I wanted you to teäke a chair
At that zide o' the vier, there,
And have the ground an' sky in zight
Wi' feäce toward the window light;
While I back here should have my brow
In sheäde, an' zit where I do now,
That you mid zee the land outside,
If I could look on you, my bride.

---

[1] Barnes was a Dorset man, a scholar in many languages
including Dorset dialect, and a clergyman and schoolmaster. He
lost his wife in 1852, and was left with five children. Vierzide:
'Fireside'.
[2] teäke: take.
[3] leäter: later.
[4] cwold: cold.
[5] Zoo: so.
[6] feäce: face.

An' there the water-pool do spread,
Wi' swaÿen elems[1] over head,
An' there's the knap[2] where we did rove
At dusk, along the high-tree'd grove,
The while the wind did whisper down
Our whisper'd words; an' there's the crown
Ov Duncliffe hill, wi' wid'nen sheädes
Ov wood a-cast on slopen gleädes:
Zoo you injoy the green an' blue
Without, an' I will look on you.

An' there's the copse, where we did all
Goo out a-nutten in the fall,
That now would meäke, a-quiv'ren black,
But little lewth[3] behind your back;
An' there's the tower, near the door,
That we at dusk did meet avore
As we did gather on the green,
An' you did zee, an' wer a-zeen:
All wold zights welcomer than new,
A-look'd on as I look'd on you.

---

[1] elems: elms.
[2] knap: hillock.
[3] lewth: lewness, to lew as shelter.

The Wife A-Lost

WILLIAM BARNES

Since I noo mwore do zee your feäce,[1]
   Up steärs or down below,
I'll zit me in the lwonesome pleäce,
   Where flat-bough'd beech do grow:
Below the beeches' bough, my love,
   Where you did never come,
An' I don't look to meet ye now,
   As I do look at hwome.

Since you noo mwore be at my zide,
   In walks in zummer het,[2]
I'll go alwone where mist do ride,
   Drough[3] trees a drippèn wet:
Below the raïn-wet bough, my love,
   Where you did never come,
An' I don't grieve to miss ye now,
   As I do grieve at home.

Since now bezide my dinner-bwoard
   Your vaïce do never sound,
I'll eat the bit I can avword,[4]
   A-vield[5] upon the ground;
Below the darksome bough, my love,
   Where you did never dine,

[1] Since I no more do see your face. Julia was forty-seven.
[2] het: heat.
[3] Drough: through.
[4] avword: afford.
[5] A-vield: concealed.

An' I don't grieve to miss ye now,
　As I at hwome do pine.

Since I do miss your vaïce an' feäce
　In praÿer at eventide,
I'll praÿ wi' woone said[1] vaïce vor greäce
　To goo where you do bide;
Above the tree an' bough, my love,
　Where you be gone avore,[2]
An' be a-waïtèn vor me now,
　To come vor evermwore.

[1] woone said: one sad.
[2] avore: before.

The Going[1]

THOMAS HARDY

Why did you give no hint that night
That quickly after the morrow's dawn,
And calmly, as if indifferent quite,
You would close your term here, up and be gone
     Where I could not follow
     With wing of swallow
To gain one glimpse of you ever anon!

     Never to bid good-bye,
     Or lip me the softest call,
Or utter a wish for a word, while I
Saw morning harden upon the wall,
     Unmoved, unknowing
     That your great going
Had place that moment, and altered all.

Why do you make me leave the house
And think for a breath it is you I see
At the end of the alley of bending boughs
Where so often at dusk you used to be;
     Till in darkening dankness
     The yawning blankness
Of the perspective sickens me!

[1] Hardy admired Barnes and edited a selection of his poetry. A younger Dorset neighbour, Hardy had no such happiness in his marriage as did William Barnes. This poem sees his own wife's death as her way of leaving him, separating, divorcing even. Yet reading Emma's diary after her death Hardy had seen how happy they had been in their early days together and how unhappy she too had been in their later days.

You were she who abode
          By those red-veined rocks far West,
You were the swan-necked one who rode
Along the beetling Beeny Crest,
          And, reining nigh me,
          Would muse and eye me,
While Life unrolled us its very best.

Why, then, latterly did we not speak,
Did we not think of those days long dead,
And ere your vanishing strive to seek
That time's renewal? We might have said,
          'In this bright spring weather
          We'll visit together
Those places that once we visited.'

          Well, well! All's past amend,
          Unchangeable. It must go.
I seem but a dead man held on end
To sink down soon.... O you could not know
          That such swift fleeing
          No soul foreseeing –
Not even I – would undo me so!

My dearest dust, could not thy hasty day

LADY CATHERINE DYER

*from a monument erected by her in 1641 to her
husband, Sir William Dyer*

My dearest dust, could not thy hasty day
Afford thy drowsy patience leave to stay
One hour longer: so that we might either
Sate up, or gone to bed together?
But since thy finish'd labour hath possess'd
Thy weary limbs with early rest,
Enjoy it sweetly: and thy widow bride
Shall soon repose her by thy slumb'ring side.
Whose business, now, is only to prepare
My nightly dress, and call to prayer:
Mine eyes wax heavy and the day grows old.
The dew falls thick, my belov'd grows cold.
Draw, draw ye closed curtains: and make room:
My dear, my dearest dust; I come, I come.

The Voice

THOMAS HARDY

Woman much missed, how you call to me, call to me,
Saying that now you are not as you were
When you had changed from the one who was all to me,
But as at first, when our day was fair.

Can it be you that I hear? Let me view you, then,
Standing as when I drew near to the town
Where you would wait for me: yes, as I knew you then,
Even to the original air-blue gown!

Or is it only the breeze, in its listlessness
Travelling across the wet mead to me here,
You being ever dissolved to wan wistlessness,
Heard no more again far or near?

    Thus I; faltering forward,
    Leaves around me falling,
Wind oozing thin through the thorn from norward,
    And the woman calling.

Wife to Husband

CHRISTINA ROSSETTI

Pardon the faults in me,
 For the love of years ago:
  Good-bye.
I must drift across the sea,
 I must sink into the snow,
  I must die.

You can bask in this sun,
 You can drink wine, and eat:
  Good-bye.
I must gird myself and run,
 Though with unready feet:
  I must die.

Blank sea to sail upon,
 Cold bed to sleep in:
  Good-bye.
While you clasp, I must be gone
 For all your weeping:
  I must die.

A kiss for one friend,
 And a word for two, –
  Good-bye: –
A lock that you must send,
 A kindness you must do:
  I must die.

Not a word for you,
  Not a lock or kiss,
    Good-bye.
We, one, must part in two,
  Verily death is this:
    I must die.

After a Journey

THOMAS HARDY

Hereto I come to view a voiceless ghost;
  Whither, O whither will its whim now draw me?
Up the cliff, down, till I'm lonely, lost,
  And the unseen waters' ejaculations awe me.
Where you will next be there's no knowing,
  Facing round about me everywhere,
    With your nut-coloured hair,
And gray eyes, and rose-flush coming and going.

Yes: I have re-entered your olden haunts at last;
  Through the years, through the dead scenes I have tracked
    you;
What have you now found to say of our past –
  Scanned across the dark space wherein I have lacked you?
Summer gave us sweets, but autumn wrought division?
  Things were not lastly as firstly well
    With us twain, you tell?
But all's closed now, despite Time's derision.

I see what you are doing: you are leading me on
  To the spots we knew when we haunted here together,
The waterfall, above which the mist-bow shone
  At the then fair hour in the then fair weather,
And the cave just under, with a voice still so hollow
  That it seems to call out to me from forty years ago,
    When you were all aglow,
And not the thin ghost that I now fraily follow!

Ignorant of what there is flitting here to see,
  The waked birds preen and the seals flop lazily;
Soon you will have, Dear, to vanish from me,
  For the stars close their shutters and the dawn whitens
    hazily.
Trust me, I mind not, though Life lours,
  The bringing me here; nay, bring me here again!
      I am just the same as when
Our days were a joy, and our paths through flowers.

An Exequy

PETER PORTER

In wet May, in the months of change,
In a country you wouldn't visit, strange
Dreams pursue me in my sleep,
Black creatures of the upper deep –
Though you are five months dead, I see
You in guilt's iconography,
Dear Wife, lost beast, beleaguered child,
The stranded monster with the mild
Appearance, whom small waves tease,
(Andromeda upon her knees
In orthodox deliverance)
And you alone of pure substance,
The unformed form of life, the earth
Which Piero's brushes brought to birth
For all to greet as myth, a thing
Out of the box of imagining.

This introduction serves to sing
Your mortal death as Bishop King
Once hymned in tetrametric rhyme
His young wife, lost before her time;
Though he lived on for many years
His poem each day fed new tears
To that unreaching spot, her grave,
His lines a baroque architrave
The Sunday poor with bottled flowers
Would by-pass in their mourning hours,
Esteeming ragged natural life

('Most dearly loved, most gentle wife'),
Yet, looking back when at the gate
And seeing grief in formal state
Upon a sculpted angel group,
Were glad that men of god could stoop
To give the dead a public stance
And freeze them in their mortal dance.

The words and faces proper to
My misery are private – you
Would never share your heart with those
Whose only talent's to suppose,
Nor from your final childish bed
Raise a remote confessing head –
The channels of our lives are blocked,
The hand is stopped upon the clock,
No one can say why hearts will break
And marriages are all opaque:
A map of loss, some posted cards,
The living house reduced to shards,
The abstract hell of memory,
The pointlessness of poetry –
These are the instances which tell
Of something which I know full well,
I owe a death to you – one day
The time will come for me to pay
When your slim shape from photographs
Stands at my door and gently asks
If I have any work to do
Or will I come to bed with you.
O *scala enigmatica*,
I'll climb up to that attic where
The curtain of your life was drawn
Some time between despair and dawn –
I'll never know with what halt steps

You mounted to this plain eclipse
But each stair now will station me
A black responsibility
And point me to that shut-down room,
'This be your due appointed tomb.'

I think of us in Italy:
Gin-and-chianti-fuelled, we
Move in a trance through Paradise,
Feeding at last our starving eyes,
Two people of the English blindness
Doing each masterpiece the kindness
Of discovering it – from Baldovinetti
To Venice's most obscure jetty.
A true unfortunate traveller, I
Depend upon your nurse's eye
To pick the altars where no Grinner
Puts us off our tourists' dinner
And in hotels to bandy words
With Genevan girls and talking birds,
To wear your feet out following me
To night's end and true amity,
And call my rational fear of flying
A paradigm of Holy Dying –
And, oh my love, I wish you were
Once more with me, at night somewhere
In narrow streets applauding wines,
The moon above the Apennines
As large as logic and the stars,
Most middle-aged of avatars,
As bright as when they shone for truth
Upon untried and avid youth.

The rooms and days we wandered through
Shrink in my mind to one – there you

Lie quite absorbed by peace – the calm
Which life could not provide is balm
In death. Unseen by me, you look
Past bed and stairs and half-read book
Eternally upon your home,
The end of pain, the left alone.
I have no friend, or intercessor,
No psychopomp or true confessor
But only you who know my heart
In every cramped and devious part –
Then take my hand and lead me out,
The sky is overcast by doubt,
The time has come, I listen for
Your words of comfort at the door,
O guide me through the shoals of fear –
'*Fürchte dich nicht, ich bin bei dir.*'[1]

[1] Do not fear, I am with you.

The Exequy. To *his Matchless never to be forgotten Friend*[1]

HENRY KING

Accept thou Shrine of my dead Saint,
Instead of Dirges this complaint;
And for sweet flowers to crown thy hearse,
Receive a strew of weeping verse
From thy griev'd friend, whom thou might'st see
Quite melted into tears for thee.

Dear loss! since thy untimely fate
My task hath been to meditate
On thee, on thee: thou art the book,
The library whereon I look
Though almost blind. For thee (lov'd clay)
I languish out, not live the day,
Using no other exercise
But what I practise with mine eyes:
By which wet glasses I find out
How lazily time creeps about
To one that mourns: this, only this
My exercise and bus'ness is:
So I compute the weary hours
With sighs dissolvèd into showers.

Nor wonder if my time go thus
Backward and most preposterous;

---

[1] King married Anne Berkeley in 1617. She died in 1624, having borne him six children of whom only two survived infancy.

Thou hast benighted me, thy set
This Eve of blackness did beget,
Who was't my day, (though overcast
Before thou had'st thy Noon-tide past)
And I remember must in tears,
Thou scarce had'st seen so many years
As Day tells hours. By thy clear Sun
My life and fortune first did run;
But thou wilt never more appear
Folded within my Hemisphere,
Since both thy light and motion
Like a fled Star is fall'n and gone,
And twixt me and my soul's dear wish
The earth now interposed is,
Which such a strange eclipse doth make
As ne'er was read in Almanac.

I could allow thee for a time
To darken me and my sad Clime,
Were it a month, a year, or ten,
I would thy exile live till then;
And all that space my mirth adjourn,
So thou wouldst promise to return;
And putting off thy ashy shroud
At length disperse this sorrow's cloud.

But woe is me! the longest date
Too narrow is to calculate
These empty hopes: never shall I
Be so much blest as to descry
A glimpse of thee, till that day come
Which shall the earth to cinders doom,
And a fierce Fever must calcine
The body of this world like thine,
(My little World!). That fit of fire

Once off, our bodies shall aspire
To our souls' bliss: then we shall rise
And view our selves with clearer eyes
In that calm Region, where no night
Can hide us from each other's sight.

    Mean time, thou hast her, earth: much good
May my harm do thee. Since it stood
With Heaven's will I might not call
Her longer mine, I give thee all
My short-liv'd right and interest
In her, whom living I lov'd best:
With a most free and bounteous grief,
I give thee what I could not keep.
Be kind to her, and prithee look
Thou write into thy Doomsday book
Each parcel of this Rarity
Which in thy Casket shrin'd doth lie:
See that thou make thy reck'ning straight,
And yield her back again by weight;
For thou must audit on thy trust
Each grain and atom of this dust,
As thou wilt answer *Him* that lent,
Not gave thee, my dear Monument.

    So close the ground, and 'bout her shade
Black curtains draw, my *Bride* is laid.

    Sleep on my *Love* in thy cold bed
Never to be disquieted!
My last good night! Thou wilt not wake
Till I thy fate shall overtake:
Till age, or grief, or sickness must
Marry my body to that dust
It so much loves; and fill the room

My heart keeps empty in thy Tomb.
Stay for me there; I will not fail
To meet thee in that hollow Vale.
And think not much of my delay;
I am already on the way,
And follow thee with all the speed
Desire can make, or sorrows breed.
Each minute is a short degree,
And ev'ry hour a step towards thee.
At night when I betake to rest,
Next morn I rise nearer my West
Of life, almost by eight hours sail,
Than when sleep breath'd his drowsy gale.

Thus from the Sun my Bottom steers,
And my day's Compass downward bears:
Nor labour I to stem the tide
Through which to *Thee* I swiftly glide.

'Tis true, with shame and grief I yield,
Thou like the *Vann* first took'st the field,
And gotten hast the victory
In thus adventuring to die
Before me, whose more years might crave
A just precedence in the grave.
But hark! My pulse like a soft Drum
Beats my approach, tells *Thee* I come;
And slow howe'er my marches be,
I shall at last sit down by *Thee*.

The thought of this bids me go on,
And wait my dissolution
With hope and comfort. *Dear* (forgive
The crime) I am content to live
Divided, with but half a heart,
Till we shall meet and never part.

His Late Wife's Wedding-Ring

GEORGE CRABBE

The ring so worn, as you behold,
So thin, so pale, is yet of gold:
The passion such it was to prove;
Worn with life's cares, love yet was love.

3

Generations

One generation passeth away, and another
generation cometh: but the earth abideth for
ever.

The Bible, Authorized Version, Ecclesiastes 1:4

At My Father's Grave

HUGH MACDIARMID

The sunlicht still on me, you row'd in clood,
We look upon each ither noo like hills
Across a valley. I'm nae mair your son.
It is my mind, nae son o yours, that looks,
And the great darkness o your death comes up
And equals it across the way.
A livin man upon a deid man thinks
And ony sma'er thocht's impossible.

from *Absalom and Achitophel*

JOHN DRYDEN

But oh that yet he woud repent and live!
How easie 'tis for Parents to forgive!
With how few Tears a Pardon might be won
From Nature, pleading for a Darling Son!

The Last Hellos

LES MURRAY

Don't die, Dad –
but they die.

This last year he was wandery:
took off a new chainsaw blade
and cobbled a spare from bits.
Perhaps if I lay down
my head'll come better again.
His left shoulder kept rising
higher in his cardigan.

He could see death in a face.
Family used to call him in
to look at sick ones and say.
At his own time, he was told.

The knob found in his head
was duck-egg size. Never hurt.
Two to six months, Cecil.

I'll be right, he boomed
to his poor sister on the phone
I'll do that when I finish dyin.

*

Don't die, Cecil.
But they do.

Going for last drives
in the bush, odd massive
board-slotted stumps bony white
in whipstick second growth.
I could chop all day.

*I could always cash
a cheque, in Sydney or anywhere.
Any of the shops.*

Eating, still at the head
of the table, he now missed
food on his knife's side.

*Sorry, Dad, but like
have you forgiven your enemies?
Your father and all of them?*
All his lifetime of hurt.

I must have (grin). *I don't
think about that now.*

*

People can't say goodbye
any more. They say last hellos.

Going fast, over Christmas,
He'd still stumble out
of his room, where his photos
hang over the other furniture,
and play host to his mourners.

The courage of his bluster,
firm big voice of his confusion.

Two last days in the hospital:
his long forearms were still
red mahogany. His hands
gripped steel frame. *I'm dyin.*

On the second day:
*You're bustin to talk
but I'm too busy dyin.*

＊

Grief ended when he died,
the widower like soldiers who
won't live life their mates missed.

Good boy Cecil! No more Bluey dog.
No more cowtime. No more stories.
We're still using your imagination,
it was stronger than all ours.

Your grave's got littler
somehow, in the three months.
More pointy as the clay's shrivelled,
like a stuck zip in a coat.

Your cricket boots are in
the State museum! Odd letters
still come. Two more's died since you:
Annie, and Stewart. Old Stewart.

On your day there was a good crowd,
family, and people from away.
But of course a lot had gone
to their own funerals first.

Snobs mind us off religion
nowdays, if they can.
Fuck thém. I wish you God.

The Toys

COVENTRY PATMORE

My little Son, who look'd from thoughtful eyes
And moved and spoke in quiet grown-up wise,
Having my law the seventh time disobey'd,
I struck him, and dismiss'd
With hard words and unkiss'd,
His Mother, who was patient, being dead.
Then, fearing lest his grief should hinder sleep,
I visited his bed,
But found him slumbering deep,
With darken'd eyelids, and their lashes yet
From his late sobbing wet.
And I, with moan,
Kissing away his tears, left others of my own;
For, on a table drawn beside his head,
He had put, within his reach,
A box of counters and a red-vein'd stone,
A piece of glass abraded by the beach
And six or seven shells,
A bottle with bluebells
And two French copper coins, ranged there with careful art,
To comfort his sad heart.
So when that night I pray'd
To God, I wept, and said:
Ah, when at last we lie with tranced breath,
Not vexing Thee in death,
And Thou rememberest of what toys
We made our joys,
How weakly understood,

Thy great commanded good,
Then, fatherly not less
Than I whom Thou hast moulded from the clay,
Thou'lt leave Thy wrath, and say,
'I will be sorry for their childishness.'

Before the Birth of One of Her Children

ANNE BRADSTREET

All things within this fading world hath end,
Adversity doth still our joys attend;
No ties so strong, no friends so dear and sweet,
But with death's parting blow is sure to meet.
The sentence past is most irrevocable,
A common thing, yet oh, inevitable.
How soon, my Dear, death may my steps attend,
How soon't may be thy lot to lose thy friend,
We both are ignorant, yet love bids me
These farewell lines to recommend to thee,
That when that knot's untied that made us one,
I may seem thine, who in effect am none.
And if I see not half my days that's due,
What nature would, God grant to yours and you;
The many faults that well you know I have
Let be interred in my oblivious grave;
If any worth or virtue were in me,
Let that live freshly in thy memory
And when thou feel'st no grief, as I no harms,
Yet love thy dead, who long lay in thine arms.
And when thy loss shall be repaid with gains
Look to my little babes, my dear remains.
And if thou love thyself, or loved'st me,
These O protect from step-dame's injury.
And if chance to thine eyes shall bring this verse,
With some sad sighs honour my absent hearse;
And kiss this paper for thy love's dear sake,
Who with salt tears this last farewell did take.

The Turnstile

WILLIAM BARNES

Ah! sad wer we as we did peäce
The wold church road, wi' downcast feäce,
The while the bells, that mwoan'd so deep
Above our child a-left asleep,
Wer now a-zingen all alive
Wi' tother bells to meäke the vive.
But up at woone pleäce we come by,
'Twer hard to keep woone's two eyes dry:
On Steän-cliff road, 'ithin the drong,[1]
Up where, as vo'k do pass along,
The turnen stile, a-païnted white,
Do sheen by day an' show by night.
Vor always there, as we did goo
To church, thik stile did let us drough,
Wi' spreaden eärms that wheel'd to guide
Us each in turn to tother zide.
An' vu'st ov all the traïn he took
My wife, wi' winsome gaït an' look;
An' then zent on my little maïd,
A-skippen onward, overjaÿ'd
To reach ageän the pleäce o' pride,
Her comely mother's left han' zide.
An' then, a-wheelen roun', he took
On me, 'ithin his third white nook.
An' in the fourth, a-sheäkèn wild,
He zent us on our giddy child.

[1] drong: narrow way.

But eesterday he guided slow
My downcast Jenny, vull o' woe,
An' then my little maïd in black,
A-walken softly on her track;
An' after he'd a-turn'd ageän,
To let me goo along the leäne,
He had noo little bwoy to vill
His last white eärms, an' they stood still.[1]

---

[1] Barnes's son, John, died in 1837.

On the Receipt of My Mother's Picture out of Norfolk, the Gift of My Cousin Ann Bodham

WILLIAM COWPER

Oh that those lips had language! Life has passed
With me but roughly since I heard thee last.
Those lips are thine – thy own sweet smiles I see,
The same that oft in childhood solaced me;
Voice only fails, else how distinct they say,
'Grieve not, my child, chase all thy fears away!'
The meek intelligence of those dear eyes
(Blessed be the art that can immortalize,
The art that baffles time's tyrannic claim
To quench it) here shines on me still the same.
　　Faithful remembrancer of one so dear,
Oh welcome guest, though unexpected, here!
Who bidd'st me honour with an artless song,
Affectionate, a mother lost so long,
I will obey, not willingly alone,
But gladly, as the precept were her own;
And, while that face renews my filial grief,
Fancy shall weave a charm for my relief –
Shall steep me in Elysian reverie,
A momentary dream that thou art she.
　　My mother! when I learned that thou wast dead,
Say, wast thou conscious of the tears I shed?
Hovered thy spirit o'er thy sorrowing son,
Wretch even then, life's journey just begun?
Perhaps thou gav'st me, though unseen, a kiss;

Perhaps a tear, if souls can weep in bliss –
Ah that maternal smile! it answers – Yes.
I heard the bell tolled on thy burial day,
I saw the hearse that bore thee slow away,
And, turning from my nurs'ry window, drew
A long, long sigh, and wept a last adieu!
But was it such? – It was. – Where thou art gone
Adieus and farewells are a sound unknown.
May I but meet thee on that peaceful shore,
The parting sound shall pass my lips no more!
Thy maidens grieved themselves at my concern,
Oft gave me promise of a quick return.
What ardently I wished I long believed,
And, disappointed still, was still deceived;
By disappointment every day beguiled,
Dupe of *tomorrow* even from a child.
Thus many a sad tomorrow came and went,
Till, all my stock of infant sorrow spent,
I learned at last submission to my lot;
But, though I less deplored thee, ne'er forgot.

Where once we dwelt our name is heard no more,
Children not thine have trod my nurs'ry floor;
And where the gard'ner Robin, day by day,
Drew me to school along the public way,
Delighted with my bauble coach, and wrapped
In scarlet mantle warm, and velvet-capped,
'Tis now become a history little known,
That once we called the past'ral house our own.
Short-lived possession! but the record fair
That mem'ry keeps of all thy kindness there,
Still outlives many a storm that has effaced
A thousand other themes less deeply traced.
Thy nightly visits to my chamber made,
That thou might'st know me safe and warmly laid;
Thy morning bounties ere I left my home,

The biscuit, or confectionary plum;
The fragrant waters on my cheeks bestowed
By thy own hand, till fresh they shone and glowed;
All this, and more endearing still than all,
Thy constant flow of love, that knew no fall,
Ne'er roughened by those cataracts and brakes
That humour[1] interposed too often makes;
All this still legible in mem'ry's page,
And still to be so, to my latest age,
Adds joy to duty, makes me glad to pay
Such honours to thee as my numbers may;
Perhaps a frail memorial, but sincere,
Not scorned in heav'n, though little noticed here.
 Could time, his flight reversed, restore the hours,
When, playing with thy vesture's tissued flow'rs,
The violet, the pink and jessamine,
I pricked them into paper with a pin
(And thou wast happier than myself the while,
Would'st softly speak, and stroke my head and smile),
Could those few pleasant hours again appear,
Might one wish bring them, would I wish them here?
I would not trust my heart – the dear delight
Seems so to be desired, perhaps I might. –
But no – what here we call our life is such,
So little to be loved, and thou so much,
That I should ill requite thee to constrain
Thy unbound spirit into bonds again.
 Thou, as a gallant bark from Albion's coast
(The storms all weathered and the ocean crossed)
Shoots into port at some well-havened isle,
Where spices breathe and brighter seasons smile,
There sits quiescent on the floods that show
Her beauteous form reflected clear below,

[1] humour: mood or temper.

While airs impregnated with incense play
Around her, fanning light her streamers gay;
So thou, with sails how swift! hast reached the shore
'Where tempests never beat nor billows roar,'
And thy loved consort on the dang'rous tide
Of life, long since, has anchored at thy side.
But me, scarce hoping to attain that rest,
Always from port withheld, always distressed –
Me howling winds drive devious, tempest-tossed,
Sails ripped, seams op'ning wide, and compass lost,
And day by day some current's thwarting force
Sets me more distant from a prosp'rous course.
But oh the thought, that thou art safe, and he!
That thought is joy, arrive what may to me.
My boast is not that I deduce my birth
From loins enthroned, and rulers of the earth;
But higher far my proud pretensions rise –
The son of parents passed into the skies.
And now, farewell – time, unrevoked, has run
His wonted course, yet what I wished is done.
By contemplation's help, not sought in vain,
I seem t' have lived my childhood o'er again;
To have renewed the joys that once were mine,
Without the sin of violating thine:
And, while the wings of fancy still are free,
And I can view this mimic show of thee,
Time has but half succeeded in his theft –
Thyself removed, thy power to soothe me left.

Epistle to a Young Friend

ROBERT BURNS

I lang hae thought, my youthfu' friend,
   A Something to have sent you,
Tho' it should serve nae other end
   Than just a kind of memento;
But how the subject theme may gang,
   Let time and chance determine;
Perhaps it may turn out a Sang;
   Perhaps, turn out a Sermon.

Ye'll try the world soon my lad,
   And ANDREW dear believe me,
Ye'll find mankind an unco[1] squad,
   And muckle[2] they may grieve ye:
For care and trouble set your thought,
   Ev'n when your end's attained;
And a' your views may come to nought,
   Where ev'ry nerve is strained.

I'll no say, men are villains a';
   The real, harden'd wicked,
Wha[3] hae nae check but *human law*,
   Are to a few restricted:
But Och, mankind are unco weak,
   An' little to be trusted;

[1] unco: uncommon, unusual.
[2] muckle: much.
[3] wha: who.

If *Self* the wavering balance shake,
     It's rarely right adjusted!

Yet they wha fa'[1] in Fortune's strife,
     Their fate we should na censure,
For still th' *important end* of life,
     They equally may answer:
A man may hae an *honest heart*,
     Tho' Poortith[2] hourly stare him;
A man may tak a neebor's part,
     Yet hae nae *cash* to spare him.

Ay free, aff han', your story tell,
     When wi' a bosom crony;
But still keep something to yoursel
     Ye scarcely tell to ony.
Conceal yoursel as weel's ye can
     Frae critical dissection;
But keek[3] thro' ev'ry other man,
     Wi' sharpen'd, sly inspection.

The *sacred lowe*[4] o' weel plac'd love,
     Luxuriantly indulge it;
But never tempt th' *illicit rove*,
     Tho' naething should divulge it:
I wave the quantum o' the sin;
     The hazard of concealing;
But Och! it hardens *a' within*,
     And petrifies the feeling!

[1] fa': fall.
[2] Poortith: poverty.
[3] keek: look.
[4] lowe: flame.

To catch Dame Fortune's golden smile,
　　Assiduous wait upon her;
And gather gear by ev'ry wile,
　　That's justify'd by Honor:
Not for to *hide* it in a *hedge*,
　　Nor for a *train-attendant*;
But for the glorious priviledge
　　Of being *independant*.

The *fear o' Hell's* a hangman's whip,
　　To haud the wretch in order;
But where ye feel your *Honor* grip,
　　Let that ay be your border:
It's slightest touches, instant pause –
　　Debar a' side-pretences;
And resolutely keep its laws,
　　Uncaring consequences.

The great CREATOR to revere,
　　Must sure become the *Creature;*
But still the preaching cant forbear,
　　And ev'n the rigid feature:
Yet ne'er with Wits prophane to range,
　　Be complaisance extended;
An *athiest-laugh's* a poor exchange
　　For *Deity offended!*

When ranting round in Pleasure's ring,
　　Religion may be blinded;
Or if she gie a *random-sting*,
　　It may be little minded;
But when on Life we're tempest-driv'n,
　　A Conscience but a canker –
A correspondence fix'd wi' Heav'n,
　　Is sure a noble *anchor!*

Adieu, dear, amiable Youth!
    Your *heart* can ne'er be wanting!
May Prudence, Fortitude and Truth
    Erect your brow undaunting!
In *ploughman phrase* 'GOD send you speed,
    Still daily to grow wiser;
And may ye better reck the *rede*,[1]
    Than ever did th' *Adviser!*

[1] reck the rede: pay attention to the advice.

To Daphne and Virginia[1]

WILLIAM CARLOS WILLIAMS

The smell of the heat is boxwood
          when rousing us
                  a movement of the air
stirs our thoughts
          that had no life in them
                  to a life, a life in which
two women agonize:
          to live and to breathe is no less.
                  Two young women.
The box odor
          is the odour of that of which
                  partaking separately,
each to herself
          I partake also
                  .separately.

Be patient that I address you in a poem,
          there is no other
                  fit medium.
The mind
          lives there. It is uncertain,
                  can trick us and leave us
agonized. But for resources
          what can equal it?
                  There is nothing. We
should be lost

[1] The poet's daughters-in-law.

without its wings to
            fly off upon.

The mind is the cause of our distresses
            but of it we can build anew.
                        Oh something more than
it flies off to:
            a woman's world,
                        of crossed sticks, stopping
thought. A new world
            is only a new mind.
                        And the mind and the poem
are all apiece.
            Two young women
                        to be snared,
odor of box,
            to bind and hold them
                        for the mind's labors.

All women are fated similarly
            facing men
                        and there is always
another, such as I,
            who loves them,
                        loves all women, but
finds himself, touching them,
            like other men,
                        often confused.

I have two sons,
            the husbands of these women,
                        who live also
in a world of love,
            apart.
                        Shall this odor of box in

the heat
not also touch them
                    fronting a world of women
                              from which they are
debarred
              by the very scents which draw them on
                        against easy access?
In our family we stammer unless,
              half mad,
                        we come to speech at last

And I am not
              a young man.
                        My love encumbers me.
It is a love
              less than
                        a young man's love but,
like this box odor
              more penetrant, infinitely
                        more penetrant,
in that sense not to be resisted.

There is, in the hard
              give and take
                        of a man's life with
                        a woman
a thing which is not the stress itself
              but beyond
                        and above
that,
              something that wants to rise
                        and shake itself
free. We are not chickadees
              on a bare limb
                        with a worm in the mouth.

The worm is in our brains
          and concerns them
                    and not food for our
offspring, wants to disrupt
          our thought
                    and throw it
to the newspapers
          or anywhere.
                    There is, in short,
a counter stress,
          born of the sexual shock,
                    which survives it
consonant with the moon,
          to keep its own mind.
                    There is, of course,
more.
          Women
                    are not alone
in that. At least
          while this healing odor is abroad
                    one can write a poem.

Staying here in the country
          on an old farm
                    we eat our breakfasts
on a balcony under an elm.
          The shrubs below us
                    are neglected. And
there, penned in,
          or he would eat the garden,
                    lives a pet goose who
tilts his head
          sidewise
                    and looks up at us,
a very quiet old fellow

who writes no poems.
Fine mornings we sit there
while birds
come and go.
A pair of robins
is building a nest
for the second time
this season. Men
against their reason
speak of love, sometimes,
when they are old. It is
all they can do
or watch a heavy goose
who waddles, slopping
noisily in the mud of
his pool.

The Young that Died in Beauty

WILLIAM BARNES

If souls should only sheen so bright
In heaven as in e'thly light,
An' nothèn better wer the ceäse,
How comely still, in sheäpe an' feäce,
Would many reach thik happy pleäce, –
The hopeful souls that in their prime
Ha' seem'd a-took avore their time –
The young that died in beauty.

But when woone's lim's ha' lost their strength
A-twilèn drough[1] a lifetime's langth,
An' auver cheäks a-growèn wold
The slowly-weästen years ha' rolled,
The deep'nèn wrinkle's hollor vwold;[2]
When life is ripe, then death do call
Vor less ov thought, than when do vall[3]
On young vo'ks in their beauty.

But pinèn souls, wi' heads a-hung
In heavy sorrow vor the young,
The sister or the brother dead,
The father wi' a child a-vled,
The husband when his bride ha' laid
Her head at rest, noo mwore to turn,

---

[1] A-twilèn drough: having toiled through.
[2] vwold: fold.
[3] vall: fall. (v = f in Dorset dialect.)

Have all a-vound the time to murn
Vor youth that died in beauty.

An' yeet the church, where praÿer do rise
Vrom thoughtvul souls, wi' downcast eyes,
An' village greens, a-beät half beäre
By dancers that do meet, an' weär
Such merry looks at feäst an' feäir,
Do gather under leätest skies,
Their bloomèn cheäks an' sparklèn eyes,
Though young ha' died in beauty.

But still the dead shall mwore than keep
The beauty ov their eärly sleep;
Where comely looks shall never weär
Uncomely, under twile an' ceäre.
The feär[1] to livers' thought an' love,
An' feäirer still to God above,
Than when they died in beauty.

---

[1] feär or feäir: fair.

Long Distance (ii)

TONY HARRISON

Though my mother was already two years dead
Dad kept her slippers warming by the gas,
put hot water bottles her side of the bed
and still went to renew her transport pass.

You couldn't just drop in. You had to phone.
He'd put you off an hour to give him time
to clear away her things and look alone
as though his still raw love were such a crime.

He couldn't risk my blight of disbelief
though sure that very soon he'd hear her key
scrape in the rusted lock and end his grief.
He *knew* she'd just popped out to get the tea.

I believe life ends with death, and that is all.
You haven't both gone shopping; just the same,
in my new black leather phone book there's your name
and the disconnected number I still call.

Grant, I thee pray, such heat into mine heart

SIR THOMAS MORE

Grant, I thee pray, such heat into mine heart
That to this love of thine may be equàl;
Grant me from Satan's service to astart,
With whom me rueth so long to have been thrall;
Grant me, good Lord and Creator of all,
The flame to quench of all sinful desire
And in thy love set all mine heart afire.

That when the journey of this deadly life
My silly ghost hath finished, and thence
Departen must without his fleshly wife,
Alone into his Lordes high presènce,
He may thee find, O well of indulgènce,
In thy lordship not as a lord, but rather
As a very tender, loving father.

Well of Sorrows in Purple Tinctures

DOUGLAS OLIVER

These thoughts in purple knots of cloud
dash down false lightning flashes like
neon signs above the glistening
Grands Boulevards, illuminating streetwise
melodramas not without beauty when
the will grows weary of the nightlong life
and you go walking.

I keep returning to Paris from scenes of death;
each time a problem with the plumbing
lets out the teary waters.
Plumber came to plumb my flat
on the rue des Messageries just now,
disjointed the pipes behind the bath tiles,
refilled the ancient well of sorrows
dried up since the baroque years,
drenched Boehringer's ceiling down below,
his concert office closed at Pentecost.
A frog with immense white limbs
swims in the well.

And I'm walking with a gospel tune in mind
which Eddie sent over from the States.
Says life's a burden you can lay down.

Lay my-ah
burden down, go walking
go walking on the other side

of the Grands Boulevards;
neon silently barks at a pigeon
sends it up in flurries like a bat;
let it rest. See my-ah
dressed in his golf leathers
father there,
see my-ah
dressed in white hair
mother there,
see my-ah
dressed in her Pentecost
sister there,
see my-ah
dressed in stained feathers
baby son there.
No side on the other side.

See my father falling on the fairway
of his life. Light goes out,
but darkness won't descend
on featureless houses,
absence of mood,
golf course grass greying and serious,
the whack gone out of the game,
the blood gone out of the brain,
trees coming alive with night
but not releasing it.
No passion yet in this childhood of a thought.
Past time's a heron once
in the course pond:
straw leg dislocated in water clear to the bottom.

A lot is loaded down, settled for good.
But who's uneasy there no more?
Who's in trouble there no more?

See my mother lay her head,
flakes of soap on a transparent pillow
an empty memory fringed with lace
(the snow fell
on such a resting place),
an elderly woman lies down there
dressed in her last cardigan,
in her coma,
the watery pillow whirls with lights
and heart-beat oscillograph blips.
I will her soul to go if it wants to.
'Please go, wherever you are.'
If flurries upwards like a white bat.
Who took the soap flakes packet,
let the flakes float down?
I was thinking of Jean Cocteau.

Emotions stagger forwards
in these distracted counsels.
I turn my head:
a gate had fallen away in her face.
And I continue walking.

See my sister; when her mouth was
morphine-dry, God sent saliva,
so she could sing her valediction hymn.
My-ah burden down.
Her belief a fixed acquittal
in the *cause célèbre* of our lives,
and I had thoughts on another side
of my mind. Mine the pale legs

like a huge white frog, went swimming
off Grenada's Grande Anse jetty
in the Caribbean Sea. Journalists floated
round about; it was thunderous
night above truffled green waters
welling onto beach of palm shadows.
Dressed in stained leathers,
a bat flew low on the wave, up
sidelong through a lightning flash
and I was hot shit in that flash romance.
Back in Surrey there
saw my sister who revealed her face
brimming with mysterious fortune
the face of one who justly assumed
in her dying that she earned a heaven.
Something very God-like rose within her;
she was immeasurably superior to me then,
interrupted the purpled lightning.
Bade me goodbye from her armchair;
I withdrew with a curious grimace.

A lot is loaded down now, I say,
halfway become my nature.
And I go walking on the boulevards,
bail à céder, soldes,
a price is no price unless a sale price;
my elbows are itchier than in the old days,
each time in Paris I'm more settled in habit,
a journeyman of innocence:
behold this Faustian innocent,
shedding deaths of others
as he goes walking.

See my baby lay his head on a down pillow,
pigeons flurrying on the boulevards.

Lay my bird in down.
Well, Tom's long in his coffin, inside his altar,
in some cathedral I've made for him
lit by summer photographic flashes.
I scarcely dare cross those cracked flags.
Why do I see instead the electric figure
of a black abbot
flitting along the galleries like a bat
and into high doors?
You'll never know where he'll appear next
in these galleries of my unbelief.
I don't know where the abbot is now,
for I'm casting the deaths of others
like disjointed stones into the cathedral well.

I continue walking towards what remains.
The trail I have left is the trail left behind.
On this, my third time of living in Paris,
I know these memories as
the mere same endroits;
the voice that used to speak for me is still there,
but I'm learning to speak over it, catching
it up like an under-air
on the Grands Boulevards
pigeons high against empurpling clouds.

Holocaust 1944

To my mother
ANNE RANASINGHE

I do not know
In what strange far off earth
They buried you;
Nor what harsh northern winds
Blow through the stubble,
The dry, hard stubble
Above your grave.

And did you think of me
That frost-blue December morning,
Snow-heavy and bitter,
As you walked naked and shivering
Under the leaden sky,
In that last moment
When you knew it was the end,
The end of nothing
And the beginning of nothing,
Did you think of me?

Oh I remember you my dearest,
Your pale hands spread
In the ancient blessing
Your eyes bright and shining
Above the candles
Intoning the blessing
Blessed be the Lord ...

And therein lies the agony,
The agony and the horror
That after all there was no martyrdom
But only futility –
The futility of dying
The end of nothing
And the beginning of nothing.
I weep red tears of blood.
Your blood.

Part Two

HERE AND NOW

Day, Night ...

I will lift up mine eyes unto the hills, from
whence cometh my help.
My help cometh from the Lord, which made
heaven and earth.
He will not suffer thy foot to be moved: he
that keepeth thee will not slumber.
Behold, he that keepeth Israel shall neither
slumber nor sleep.
The Lord is thy keeper: the Lord is thy shade
upon thy right hand.
The sun shall not smite thee by day, nor the
moon by night.
The Lord shall preserve thee from all evil: he
shall preserve thy soul.
The Lord shall preserve thy going out and
thy coming in from this time forth, and even
for evermore.

The Bible, Authorized Version, Psalm 121

from *Horae Canonicae*[1]

I. Prime

W. H. AUDEN

Simultaneously, as soundlessly,
  Spontaneously, suddenly
As, at the vaunt of the dawn, the kind
  Gates of the body fly open
To its world beyond, the gates of the mind,
  The horn gate and the ivory gate
Swing to, swing shut, instantaneously
  Quell the nocturnal rummage
Of its rebellious fronde, ill-favoured,
  Ill-natured and second-rate,
Disenfranchised, widowed and orphaned
  By an historical mistake:
Recalled from the shades to be a seeing being,
  From absence to be on display,
Without a name or history I wake
  Between my body and the day.

Holy this moment, wholly in the right,
  As, in complete obedience
To the light's laconic outcry, next
  As a sheet, near as a wall,
Out there as a mountain's poise of stone,
  The world is present, about,
And I know that I am, here, not alone
  But with a world and rejoice

---

[1] The (seven) canonical hours of the Christian church.

143

Unvexed, for the will has still to claim
    This adjacent arm as my own,
The memory to name me, resume
    Its routine of praise and blame,
And smiling to me is this instant while
    Still the day is intact, and I
The Adam sinless in our beginning,
Adam still previous to any act.

I draw breath; that is of course to wish
    No matter what, to be wise,
To be different, to die and the cost,
    No matter how, is Paradise
Lost of course and myself owing a death:
    The eager ridge, the steady sea,
The flat roofs of the fishing village
    Still asleep in its bunny,
Though as fresh and sunny still are not friends
    But things to hand, this ready flesh
No honest equal, but my accomplice now,
    My assassin to be, and my name
Stands for my historical share of care
    For a lying self-made city,
Afraid of our living task, the dying
    Which the coming day will ask.

Living

HAROLD MONRO

Slow bleak awakening from the morning dream
Brings me in contact with the sudden day.
I am alive – this I.
I let my fingers move along my body.
Realization warns them, and my nerves
Prepare their rapid messages and signals.
While Memory begins recording, coding,
Repeating: all the time Imagination
Mutters: You'll only die.

Here's a new day. O Pendulum move slowly!
My usual clothes are waiting on their peg.
I am alive – this I.
And in a moment Habit, like a crane,
Will bow its neck and dip its pulleyed cable,
Gathering me, my body, and our garment,
And swing me forth, oblivious of my question,
Into the daylight – why?

I think of all the others who awaken,
And wonder if they go to meet the morning
More valiantly than I;
Nor asking of this Day they will be living:
What have I done that I should be alive?
O, can I not forget that I am living?
How shall I reconcile the two conditions:
Living, and yet – to die?

Between the curtains the autumnal sunlight
With lean and yellow finger points me out;
The clock moans: Why? Why? Why?

But suddenly, as if without a reason,
Heart, Brain and Body, and Imagination
All gather in tumultuous joy together,
Running like children down the path of morning
To fields where they can play without a quarrel:
A country I'd forgotten, but remember,
And welcome with a cry.

O cool glad pasture; living tree, tall corn,
Great cliff, or languid sloping sand, cold sea,
Waves; rivers curving: you, eternal flowers,
Give me content, while I can think of you:
Give me your living breath!
Back to your rampart, Death.

In Earliest Morning

JAMES SCHUYLER

an orange devours
the crusts of clouds and you,
getting up, put on
your daily life
grown somewhat shabby, worn
but comfortable, like old jeans: at the least,
familiar. Water
boils, coffee
scents the air
and level light plunges
among the layering boughs of a balsam fir
and enflames its trunk.
Other trees are scratched
lightly on the west.
A purposeful mutt
makes dark marks
in blue dew. The day
offers so much, holds
so little or is it
simply you who
asking too much take
too little? It is
merely morning
so always marvelously
gratuitous and undemanding,
freighted with messages
and meaning: such
as, day

is different from the night
for some; see
the south dazzle
in an effulgence
thrown out by an ocean;
a myriad iridescence
of green;
the shape
of the cold egg
you break
and with a fork
again break
and stir and pour
into a pan, where it lightly hisses.
The sediment
in your mind sinks
as something rises
in it, a thought
perhaps, like a tree when it
is just two green
crumpled bits of tape
secured to grit; a
memory – beyond
a box of Gold Dust
laundry soap a cherry
in full flower and
later full of fruit;
a face, a name
without a face,
water with a name:
Mediterranean, Cazenovia, or
iced, or
to be flushed
away; a
flash of

good humor, no
more than a
wink; and the sun
dims its light
behind a morning
Times of cloud.

I *wake and feel the fell of dark*

GERARD MANLEY HOPKINS

I wake and feel the fell of dark, not day.
What hours, O what black hours we have spent
This night! what sights you, heart, saw; ways you went!
And more must, in yet longer light's delay.
    With witness I speak this. But where I say
Hours I mean years, mean life. And my lament
Is cries countless, cries like dead letters sent
To dearest him that lives alas! away.

I am gall, I am heartburn. God's most deep decree
Bitter would have me taste: my taste was me;
Bones built in me, flesh filled, blood brimmed the curse.
    Selfyeast of spirit a dull dough sours. I see
The lost are like this, and their scourge to be
As I am mine, their sweating selves; but worse.

No *worst, there is none*

GERARD MANLEY HOPKINS

No worst, there is none. Pitched past pitch of grief,
More pangs will, schooled at forepangs, wilder wring.
Comforter, where, where is your comforting?
Mary, mother of us, where is your relief?
My cries heave, herds-long; huddle in a main, a chief
Woe, world-sorrow; on an age-old anvil wince and sing –
Then lull, then leave off. Fury had shrieked 'No ling-
ering! Let me be fell: force I must be brief.'

O the mind, mind has mountains; cliffs of fall
Frightful, sheer, no-man-fathomed. Hold them cheap
May who ne'er hung there. Nor does long our small
Durance deal with that steep or deep. Here! creep,
Wretch, under a comfort serves in a whirlwind: all
Life death does end and each day dies with sleep.

Abide with me

HENRY FRANCIS LYTE

Abide with me; fast falls the eventide;
The darkness deepens; Lord, with me abide:
When other helpers fail, and comforts flee,
Help of the helpless, oh abide with me.

Swift to its close ebbs out life's little day;
Earth's joys grow dim, its glories pass away;
Change and decay in all around I see;
O thou who changest not, abide with me.

I need thy presence every passing hour;
What but thy grace can foil the tempter's power?
Who like thyself my guide and stay can be?
Through cloud and sunshine, Lord, abide with me.

I fear no foe with thee at hand to bless;
Ills have no weight, and tears no bitterness;
Where is death's sting? where, grave, thy victory?
I triumph still, if thou abide with me.

Hold thou thy cross before my closing eyes;
Shine through the gloom, and point me to the skies;
Heaven's morning breaks, and earth's vain shadows flee;
In life, in death, O Lord, abide with me.

Now *winter nights enlarge*

THOMAS CAMPION

Now winter nights enlarge
The number of their hours;
And clouds their storms discharge
Upon the airy towers.
Let now the chimneys blaze
And cups o'erflow with wine,
Let well-tuned words amaze
With harmony divine!
Now yellow waxen lights
Shall wait on honey love
While youthful revels, masques, and Courtly sights,
Sleep's leaden spells remove.

   This time doth well dispense[1]
   With lovers' long discourse;
Much speech hath some defence,
   Though beauty no remorse.
All do not all things well;
   Some measures comely tread
Some knotted riddles tell,
   Some poems smoothly read.
The summer hath his joys,
   And winter his delights;
Though love and all his pleasures are but toys,
   They shorten tedious nights.

[1] dispense with: allow of.

A Nocturnal upon S. Lucy's Day, Being the Shortest Day[1]

JOHN DONNE

'Tis the year's midnight, and it is the day's,
Lucy's, who scarce seven hours herself unmasks,
 The sun is spent, and now his flasks[2]
 Send forth light squibs, no constant rays;
  The world's whole sap is sunk:
The general balm th' hydroptic[3] earth hath drunk,
Whither, as to the bed's-feet, life is shrunk,
Dead and interred; yet all these seem to laugh,
Compared with me, who am their epitaph.

Study me then, you who shall lovers be
At the next world, that is, at the next spring:
 For I am every dead thing,
 In whom love wrought new alchemy.[4]
  For his art did express[5]
A quintessence[6] even from nothingness,
From dull privations, and lean emptiness
He ruined me, and I am re-begot
Of absence, darkness, death; things which are not.

---

[1] 13 December, the winter solstice, though the name Lucy signifies light.

[2] flasks: the stars, storing the sun's light.

[3] hydroptic: insatiably thirsty.

[4] alchemy: usually the transmutation of other metals into gold or to produce the elixir of love, but here the chemistry of loss produces an elixir of death and extreme negation.

[5] express: distill by crushing.

[6] quintessence: the first principle, the pure concentrated essence.

All others, from all things, draw all that's good,
Life, soul, form, spirit, whence they being have;
   I, by love's limbeck,[1] am the grave
   Of all, that's nothing. Oft a flood
      Have we two wept, and so
Drowned the whole world, us two; oft did we grow
To be two chaoses, when we did show
Care to aught else; and often absences
Withdrew our souls, and made us carcases.

But I am by her death (which word wrongs her)
Of the first nothing, the elixir grown;
   Were I a man, that I were one,
   I needs must know; I should prefer,
      If I were any beast,
Some ends, some means; yea plants, yea stones detest,
And love; all, all some properties invest;
If I an ordinary nothing were,
As shadow, a light, and body must be here.

But I am none; nor will my sun renew.
You lovers, for whose sake, the lesser sun
   At this time to the Goat[2] is run
   To fetch new lust, and give it you,
      Enjoy your summer all;
Since she enjoys her long night's festival,
Let me prepare towards her, and let me call
This hour her vigil, and her eve, since this
Both the year's, and the day's deep midnight is.

[1] limbeck: alembic, useful for distillation.
[2] Goat: Capricorn, the constellation of sexual energy.

Frost at Midnight

SAMUEL TAYLOR COLERIDGE

The Frost performs its secret ministry,
Unhelped by any wind. The owlet's cry
Came loud – and hark, again! loud as before.
The inmates of my cottage, all at rest,
Have left me to that solitude, which suits
Abstruser musings: save that at my side
My cradled infant slumbers peacefully.
'Tis calm indeed! so calm, that it disturbs
And vexes meditation with its strange
And extreme silentness. Sea, hill, and wood,
This populous village! Sea, and hill, and wood,
With all the numberless goings-on of life,
Inaudible as dreams! the thin blue flame
Lies on my low-burnt fire, and quivers not;
Only that film, which fluttered on the grate,
Still flutters there, the sole unquiet thing.
Methinks, its motion in this hush of nature
Gives it dim sympathies with me who live,
Making it a companionable form,
Whose puny flaps and freaks the idling Spirit
By its own moods interprets, everywhere
Echo or mirror seeking of itself,
And makes a toy of Thought.

                              But O! how oft,
How oft, at school, with most believing mind,
Presageful, have I gazed upon the bars,

To watch that fluttering *stranger*![1] and as oft
With unclosed lids, already had I dreamt
Of my sweet birth-place, and the old church-tower,
Whose bells, the poor man's only music, rang
From morn to evening, all the hot Fair-day,
So sweetly, that they stirred and haunted me
With a wild pleasure, falling on mine ear
Most like articulate sounds of things to come!
So gazed I, till the soothing things I dreamt,
Lulled me to sleep, and sleep prolonged my dreams!
And so I brooded all the following morn,
Awed by the stern preceptor's face, mine eye
Fixed with mock study on my swimming book:
Save if the door half opened, and I snatched
A hasty glance, and still my heart leapt up,
For still I hoped to see the *stranger's* face,
Townsman, or aunt, or sister more beloved,
My play-mate when we both were clothed alike!

   Dear Babe, that sleepest cradled by my side,
Whose gentle breathings, heard in this deep calm,
Fill up the interspersèd vacancies
And momentary pauses of the thought!
My babe so beautiful! it thrills my heart
With tender gladness, thus to look at thee,
And think that thou shalt learn far other lore,
And in far other scenes! For I was reared
In the great city, pent 'mid cloisters dim,
And saw nought lovely but the sky and stars.
But *thou*, my babe! shalt wander like a breeze
By lakes and sandy shores, beneath the crags
Of ancient mountain, and beneath the clouds,

---

[1] The common superstition that the flames betoken the coming of a stranger.

Which image in their bulk both lakes and shores
And mountain crags: so shalt thou see and hear
The lovely shapes and sounds intelligible
Of that eternal language, which thy God
Utters, who from eternity doth teach
Himself in all, and all things in himself.
Great universal Teacher! he shall mould
Thy spirit, and by giving make it ask.

Therefore all seasons shall be sweet to thee,
Whether the summer clothe the general earth
With greenness, or the redbreast sit and sing
Betwixt the tufts of snow on the bare branch
Of mossy apple-tree, while the nigh thatch
Smokes in the sun-thaw; whether the eave-drops fall
Heard only in the trances of the blast,
Or if the secret ministry of frost
Shall hang them up in silent icicles,
Quietly shining to the quiet Moon.

Hesperus

JOHN CLARE

Hesperus the day is gone
Soft falls the silent dew
A tear is now on many a flower
And heaven lives in you

Hesperus the evening mild
Falls round us soft and sweet
'Tis like the breathings of a child
When day and evening meet

Hesperus the closing flower
Sleeps on the dewy ground
While dews fall in a silent shower
And heaven breathes around

Hesperus thy twinkling ray
Beams in the blue of heaven
And tells the traveller on his way
That earth shall be forgiven

The Night

John 3:2[1]

HENRY VAUGHAN

Through that pure *Virgin-shrine*,
That sacred veil drawn o'er thy glorious noon
That men might look and live as glow-worms shine,
    And face the moon:
  Wise *Nicodemus* saw such light
  As made him know his God by night.

  Most blest believer he!
Who in that land of darkness and blind eyes
Thy long expected healing wings could see,
    When thou didst rise,
  And what can never more be done,
  Did at mid-night speak with the Sun!

  O who will tell me, where
He found thee at that dead and silent hour!
What hallowed solitary ground did bear
    So rare a flower,
  Within whose sacred leaves did lie
  The fullness of the Deity.

  No mercy-seat of gold,
No dead and dusty *Cherub*, nor carved stone,
But his own living works did my Lord hold
    And lodge alone;

[1] Nicodemus came to Jesus by night.

Where *trees* and *herbs* did watch and peep
And wonder, while the *Jews* did sleep.

    Dear night! this world's defeat;
The stop to busy fools; care's check and curb;
The day of Spirits; my soul's calm retreat
      Which none disturb!
    Christ's progress, and his prayer time;
    The hours to which high Heaven doth chime.

    God's silent, searching flight:
When my Lord's head is filled with dew, and all
His locks are wet with the clear drops of night;
      His still, soft call;
    His knocking time; the soul's dumb watch,
    When Spirits their fair kindred catch.

    Were all my loud, evil days
Calm and unhaunted as is thy dark Tent,
Whose peace but by some *Angel's* wing or voice
      Is seldom rent;
    Then I in Heaven all the long year
    Would keep, and never wander here.

    But living where the sun
Doth all things wake, and where all mix and tire
Themselves and others, I consent and run
      To every mire,
    And by this world's ill-guiding light,
    Err more than I can do by night.

    There is in God (some say)
A deep, but dazzling darkness; as men here
Say it is late and dusky, because they

See not all clear;
O for that night! where I in him
Might live invisible and dim.

Aubade

PHILIP LARKIN

I work all day, and get half-drunk at night.
Waking at four to soundless dark, I stare.
In time the curtain-edges will grow light.
Till then I see what's really always there:
Unresting death, a whole day nearer now,
Making all thought impossible but how
And where and when I shall myself die.
Arid interrogation: yet the dread
Of dying, and being dead,
Flashes afresh to hold and horrify.

The mind blanks at the glare. Not in remorse
– The good not done, the love not given, time
Torn off unused – nor wretchedly because
An only life can take so long to climb
Clear of its wrong beginnings, and may never;
But at the total emptiness for ever,
The sure extinction that we travel to
And shall be lost in always. Not to be here,
Not to be anywhere,
And soon; nothing more terrible, nothing more true.

This is a special way of being afraid
No trick dispels. Religion used to try,
That vast moth-eaten musical brocade
Created to pretend we never die,
And specious stuff that says *No rational being
Can fear a thing it will not feel*, not seeing

That this is what we fear – no sight, no sound,
No touch or taste or smell, nothing to think with,
Nothing to love or link with,
The anaesthetic from which none come round.

And so it stays just on the edge of vision,
A small unfocused blur, a standing chill
That slows each impulse down to indecision.
Most things may never happen: this one will,
And realization of it rages out
In furnace-fear when we are caught without
People or drink. Courage is no good:
It means not scaring others. Being brave
Lets no one off the grave.
Death is no different whined at than withstood.

Slowly light strengthens, and the room takes shape.
It stands plain as a wardrobe, what we know,
Have always known, know that we can't escape,
Yet can't accept. One side will have to go.
Meanwhile telephones crouch, getting ready to ring
In locked-up offices, and all the uncaring
Intricate rented world begins to rouse.
The sky is white as clay, with no sun.
Work has to be done.
Postmen like doctors go from house to house.

Shadows

D. H. LAWRENCE

And if tonight my soul may find her peace
in sleep, and sink in good oblivion,
and in the morning wake like a new-opened flower
then I have been dipped again in God, and new-created.

And if, as weeks go round, in the dark of the moon
my spirit darkens and goes out, and soft, strange gloom
pervades my movements and my thoughts and words
then I shall know that I am walking still
with God, we are close together now the moon's in shadow.

And if, as autumn deepens and darkens
I feel the pain of falling leaves, and stems that break in
    storms
and trouble and dissolution and distress
and then the softness of deep shadows folding, folding
around my soul and spirit, around my lips
so sweet, like a swoon, or more like the drowse of a low,
    sad song
singing darker than the nightingale, on, on to the solstice
and the silence of short days, the silence of the year, the
    shadow,
then I shall know that my life is moving still
with the dark earth, and drenched
with the deep oblivion of earth's lapse and renewal.

And if, in the changing phases of man's life
I fall in sickness and in misery

my wrists seem broken and my heart seems dead
and strength is gone, and my life
is only the leavings of a life:

and still, among it all, snatches of lovely oblivion, and
    snatches of renewal
odd, wintry flowers upon the withered stem, yet new strange
    flowers
such as my life has not brought forth before, new blossoms
    of me –

then I must know that still
I am in the hands of the unknown God,
he is breaking me down to his own oblivion
to send me forth on a new morning, a new man.

2

Being

' "To be or not to be." Ere I decide
I should be glad to know that which is being'

Lord Byron
Don Juan IX. 16

The Salutation

THOMAS TRAHERNE

These little limbs,
These eyes and hands which here I find,
This panting heart wherewith my life begins,
Where have ye been? Behind
What curtain were ye from me hid so long?
Where was, in what abyss, my new-made tongue?

When silent I
So many thousand thousand years
Beneath the dust did in a *Chaos* lie,
How could I *Smiles*, or *Tears*,
Or *Lips*, or *Hands*, or *Eyes*, or *Ears* perceive?
Welcome ye treasures which I now receive.

I that so long
Was *Nothing* from eternity
Did little think such joys as ear and tongue
To celebrate or see;
Such sounds to hear, such hands to feel, such feet,
Such eyes and objects, on the ground to meet.

New burnished joys!
Which finest gold and pearl excel!
Such sacred treasures are the limbs of boys
In which a soul doth dwell;
Their organizèd joints and azure veins
More wealth include than the dead world contains.

From dust I rise
And out of Nothing now awake.
These brighter regions which salute mine eyes
A gift from God I take.
The earth, the seas, the light, the lofty skies,
The sun and stars are mine; if these I prize.

A stranger here
Strange things doth meet, strange glory see,
Strange treasures lodg'd in this fair world appear,
Strange all and new to me;
But that they *mine* should be who Nothing was,
That strangest is of all; yet brought to pass.

The Little Black Boy

WILLIAM BLAKE

My mother bore me in the southern wild,
And I am black, but oh! my soul is white.
White as an angel is the English child;
But I am black as if bereaved of light.

My mother taught me underneath a tree,
And sitting down before the heat of day
She took me on her lap and kissed me,
And pointing to the east began to say:

'Look on the rising sun! There God does live,
And gives his light and gives his heat away;
And flowers and trees and beasts and men receive
Comfort in morning, joy in the noon day.

'And we are put on earth a little space,
That we may learn to bear the beams of love;
And these black bodies and this sun-burnt face
Is but a cloud, and like a shady grove.

'For when our souls have learned the heat to bear
The cloud will vanish; we shall hear his voice,
Saying: "Come out from the grove my love and care,
And round my golden tent like lambs rejoice." '

Thus did my mother say and kissed me,
And thus I say to little English boy.

When I from black and he from white cloud free,
And round the tent of God like lambs we joy,

I'll shade him from the heat till he can bear
To lean in joy upon our father's knee,
And then I'll stand and stroke his silver hair
And be like him, and he will then love me.

I Am

JOHN CLARE

I AM – yet what I am, none cares or knows;
  My friends forsake me like a memory lost: –
I am the self-consumer of my woes; –
  They rise and vanish in oblivion's host,
Like shadows in love's frenzied stifled throes: –
And yet I am, and live – like vapours tost

Into the nothingness of scorn and noise, –
  Into the living sea of waking dreams,
Where there is neither sense of life or joys,
  But the vast shipwreck of my lifes esteems;
Even the dearest, that I love the best
Are strange – nay, rather stranger than the rest.

I long for scenes, where man hath never trod
  A place where woman never smiled or wept
There to abide with my Creator, God;
  And sleep as I in childhood, sweetly slept,
Untroubling, and untroubled where I lie,
The grass below – above the vaulted sky.

Who Shall Deliver Me?

CHRISTINA ROSSETTI

God strengthen me to bear myself,
That heaviest weight of all to bear,
Inalienable weight of care.

All others are outside myself;
I lock my door and bar them out,
The turmoil, tedium, gad-about.

I lock my door upon myself,
And bar them out; but who shall wall
Self from myself, most loathed of all?

If I could once lay down myself,
And start self-purged upon the race
That all must run! Death runs apace.

If I could set aside myself,
And start with lightened heart upon
The road by all men overgone!

God harden me against myself,
This coward with pathetic voice
Who craves for ease, and rest, and joys:

Myself, arch-traitor to myself;
My hollowest friend, my deadliest foe,
My clog whatever road I go.

Yet One there is can curb myself,
Can roll the strangling load from me,
Break off the yoke and set me free.

Upon Absence[1]

KATHERINE PHILIPS

'Tis now since I began to die
   Four months, and more yet gasping live.
Wrapp'd up in sorrows, do I lie
   Hoping, yet doubting a reprieve.
Adam from Paradise expell'd
Just such a wretched being held.

'Tis not thy love I fear to lose
   That will in spite of absence hold;
But 'tis the benefit and use
   Is lost, as in imprison'd Gold:
Which though the sum be ne'er so great,
Enriches nothing but conceit.[2]

What angry star then governs me
   That I must feel a double smart?
Pris'ner to fate as well as thee,
   Kept from thy face, link'd to thy heart
Because my Love, all Love excels
Must my griefs have no parallels.

Hapless and dead as winter here
   I now remain and all I see
Copies of my wild 'state appear,

---

[1] To her husband, James. She died of smallpox in 1664, aged thirty-three.
[2] conceit: thought.

But I am their epitome.
Love me no more! for I am grown
Too dead and dull for thee to own.

Narcissus

corpus putat esse, quod umbra est[1]

C. H. SISSON

If I could only find a little stream
Which leapt out of the ground over black pebbles
And wore a hat of light on every ripple,
I should not care for the imaginary
Problems of I and Me, or Who or Why.
This corner of the world would be my mind;
What it saw I would say, if it were cloud,
Blue sky or even wind told by an eddy:
But what I would not see is this body,
Aged, severe, and, written on it, REFUSE.
If that came back into my little stream
It might be I should wake shrieking from my dream.
To what? Ah, what is there for us to wake to?
When pain is past, that is our hope or pleasure.
But nail that nothing now, keep me in vain
Beside the water, not seeing any shadow,
Only translucence, only the pebbles and earth,
A weed swaying, a fish, but nothing human
Or bearing any resemblance to man or woman,
Nothing compels our nature to this shape
For a stone will resemble the friends we make.
The mind is not peculiarly under skin
But might lie loose upon a high mountain.
A corner of a cloud would do for mind,
The bright border perhaps, with the moon behind,

[1] Narcissus considers to be body that which is shadow.

The wind, recognized by its wandering billow
Scattering to surf as the moon comes and goes.
I thought I was a man because I was taught so.

from *Jubilate Agno*

CHRISTOPHER SMART

For I will consider my Cat Jeoffry.

For he is the servant of the Living God duly and daily
serving him.

For at the first glance of the glory of God in the East he
worships in his way.

For is this done by wreathing his body seven times round
with elegant quickness.

For then he leaps up to catch the musk, which is the blessing
of God upon his prayer.

For he rolls upon prank to work it in.

For having done duty and received blessing he begins to
consider himself.

For this he performs in ten degrees.

For first he looks upon his fore-paws to see if they are clean.

For secondly he kicks up behind to clear away there.

For thirdly he works it upon stretch with the fore-paws
extended.

For fourthly he sharpens his paws by wood.

For fifthly he washes himself.

For sixthly he rolls upon wash.

For seventhly he fleas himself, that he may not be interrupted
upon the beat.

For eighthly he rubs himself against a post.

For ninthly he looks up for his instructions.

For tenthly he goes in quest of food.

For having consider'd God and himself he will consider his
neighbour.

For if he meets another cat he will kiss her in kindness.

For when he takes his prey he plays with it to give it chance.

For one mouse in seven escapes by his dallying.

For when his day's work is done his business more properly begins.

For he keeps the Lord's watch in the night against the adversary.

For he counteracts the powers of darkness by his electrical skin and glaring eyes.

For he counteracts the Devil, who is death, by brisking about the life.

For in his morning orisons he loves the sun and the sun loves him.

For he is of the tribe of Tiger.

For the Cherub Cat is a term of the Angel Tiger.

For he has the subtlety and hissing of a serpent, which in goodness he suppresses.

For he will not do destruction, if he is well-fed, neither will he spit without provocation.

For he purrs in thankfulness, when God tells him he's a good Cat.

For he is an instrument for the children to learn benevolence upon.

For every house is incompleat without him and a blessing is lacking in the spirit.

For the Lord commanded Moses concerning the cats at the departure of the Children of Israel from Egypt.

For every family had one cat at least in the bag.

For the English Cats are the best in Europe.

For he is the cleanest in the use of his fore-paws of any quadrupede.

For the dexterity of his defence is an instance of the love of God to him exceedingly.

For he is the quickest to his mark of any creature.

For he is tenacious of his point.

For he is a mixture of gravity and waggery.

For he knows that God is his Saviour.

For there is nothing sweeter than his peace when at rest.

For there is nothing brisker than his life when in motion.

For he is of the Lord's poor and so indeed is he called by benevolence perpetually – Poor Jeoffry! poor Jeoffry! the rat has bit thy throat.

For I bless the name of the Lord Jesus that Jeoffry is better.

For the divine spirit comes about his body to sustain it in compleat cat.

For his tongue is exceeding pure so that it has in purity what it wants in musick.

For he is docile and can learn certain things.

For he can set up with gravity which is patience upon approbation.

For he can fetch and carry, which is patience in employment.

For he can jump over a stick which is patience upon proof positive.

For he can spraggle upon waggle at the word of command.

For he can jump from an eminence into his master's bosom.

For he can catch the cork and toss it again.

For he is hated by the hypocrite and miser.

For the former is afraid of detection.

For the latter refuses the charge.

For he camels his back to bear the first notion of business.

For he is good to think on, if a man would express himself neatly.

For he made a great figure in Egypt for his signal services.

For he killed the Ichneumon-rat very pernicious by land.

For his ears are so acute that they sting again.

For from this proceeds the passing quickness of his attention.

For by stroaking of him I have found out electricity.

For I perceived God's light about him both wax and fire.

For the Electrical fire is the spiritual substance, which God sends from heaven to sustain the bodies both of man and beast.

For God has blessed him in the variety of his movements.
For, though he cannot fly, he is an excellent clamberer.
For his motions upon the face of the earth are more than
any other quadrupede.
For he can tread to all the measures upon the musick.
For he can swim for life.
For he can creep.

A Misremembered Lyric

DENISE RILEY

A misremembered lyric: a soft catch of its song
whirrs in my throat. 'Something's gotta hold of my heart
tearing my' soul and my conscience apart, long after
presence is clean gone and leaves unfurnished no
shadow. Rain lyrics. Yes, then the rain lyrics fall.
I don't want absence to be this beautiful.
It shouldn't be; in fact I know it wasn't, while
'everything that consoles is false' is off the point –
you get no consolation anyway until your memory's
dead: or something never had gotten hold of
your heart in the first place, and that's the fear thought.
Do shrimps make good mothers? Yes they do.
There is no beauty out of loss; can't do it –
and once the falling rain starts on the upturned
leaves, and I listen to the rhythm of unhappy pleasure
what I hear is bossy death telling me which way to
go, what I see is a pool with an eye in it. Still let
me know. Looking for a brand-new start. Oh and never
notice yourself ever. As in life you don't.

Stanzas

EMILY JANE BRONTË (*or possibly*
CHARLOTTE BRONTË)

Often rebuked, yet always back returning
  To those first feelings that were born with me,
And leaving busy chase of wealth and learning
  For idle dreams of things which cannot be:

Today, I will not seek the shadowy region;
  Its unsustaining vastness waxes drear;
And visions rising, legion after legion,
  Bring the unreal world too strangely near.

I'll walk, but not in old heroic traces,
  And not in paths of high morality,
And not among the half-distinguished faces
  The clouded forms of long-past history.

I'll walk where my own nature would be leading:
  It vexes me to choose another guide:
Where the grey flocks in ferny glens are feeding;
  Where the wild wind blows on the mountain side.

What have those lonely mountains worth revealing?
  More glory and more grief than I can tell:
The earth that wakes one human heart to feeling
  Can centre both the worlds of Heaven and Hell.

The Rain

ROBERT CREELEY

All night the sound had
come back again,
and again falls
this quiet, persistent rain.

What am I to myself
that must be remembered,
insisted upon,
so often? Is it

that never the ease,
even the hardness,
of rain falling
will have for me

something other than this,
something not so insistent –
am I to be locked in this
final uneasiness.

Love, if you love me,
lie next to me.
Be for me, like rain,
the getting out

of the tiredness, the fatuousness, the semi-
lust of intentional indifference.
Be wet
with a decent happiness.

There's a certain Slant of light

EMILY DICKINSON

There's a certain Slant of light,
Winter Afternoons –
That oppresses, like the Heft
Of Cathedral Tunes –

Heavenly Hurt, it gives us –
We can find no scar,
But internal difference,
Where the Meanings, are –

None may teach it – Any –
'Tis the Seal Despair –
An imperial affliction
Sent us of the Air –

When it comes, the Landscape listens –
Shadows – hold their breath –
When it goes, 'tis like the Distance
On the look of Death –

Stepping Westward

WILLIAM WORDSWORTH

While my Fellow-traveller and I were walking by the side of
Loch Ketterine, one fine evening after sunset, in our road to a
Hut where, in the course of our Tour, we had been hospitably
entertained some weeks before, we met, in one of the loneliest
parts of that solitary region, two well-dressed Women, one of
whom said to us, by way of greeting, 'What, you are
stepping westward?'

> '*What, you are stepping westward?*' – 'Yea.'
> – 'Twould be a *wildish* destiny,
> If we, who thus together roam
> In a strange Land, and far from home,
> Were in this place the guests of Chance:
> Yet who would stop, or fear to advance,
> Though home or shelter he had none,
> With such a sky to lead him on?
>
> The dewy ground was dark and cold;
> Behind, all gloomy to behold;
> And stepping westward seemed to be
> A kind of *heavenly* destiny:
> I liked the greeting; 'twas a sound
> Of something without place or bound;
> And seemed to give me spiritual right
> To travel through that region bright.
>
> The voice was soft, and she who spake
> Was walking by her native lake:

The salutation had to me
The very sound of courtesy:
Its power was felt; and while my eye
Was fixed upon the glowing Sky,
The echo of the voice enwrought
A human sweetness with the thought
Of travelling through the world that lay
Before me in my endless way.

Under the Waterfall

THOMAS HARDY

'Whenever I plunge my arm, like this,
In a basin of water, I never miss
The sweet sharp sense of a fugitive day
Fetched back from its thickening shroud of gray.
  Hence the only prime
  And real love-rhyme
  That I know by heart,
  And that leaves no smart,
Is the purl of a little valley fall
About three spans wide and two spans tall
Over a table of solid rock,
And into a scoop of the self-same block;
The purl of a runlet that never ceases
In stir of kingdoms, in wars, in peaces;
With a hollow boiling voice it speaks
And has spoken since hills were turfless peaks.'

'And why gives this the only prime
Idea to you of a real love-rhyme?
And why does plunging your arm in a bowl
Full of spring water, bring throbs to your soul?'

'Well, under the fall, in a crease of the stone,
Though where precisely none ever has known,
Jammed darkly, nothing to show how prized,
And by now with its smoothness opalized,
  Is a drinking-glass:
  For, down that pass

My lover and I
Walked under a sky
Of blue with a leaf-wove awning of green,
In the burn of August, to paint the scene,
And we placed our basket of fruit and wine
By the runlet's rim, where we sat to dine;
And when we had drunk from the glass together,
Arched by the oak-copse from the weather,
I held the vessel to rinse in the fall,
Where it slipped, and sank, and was past recall,
Though we stooped and plumbed the little abyss
With long bared arms. There the glass still is.
And, as said, if I thrust my arm below
Cold water in basin or bowl, a throe
From the past awakens a sense of that time,
And the glass we used, and the cascade's rhyme.
The basin seems the pool, and its edge
The hard smooth face of the brook-side ledge,
And the leafy pattern of china-ware
The hanging plants that were bathing there.

'By night, by day, when it shines or lours,
There lies intact that chalice of ours,
And its presence adds to the rhyme of love
Persistently sung by the fall above.
No lip has touched it since his and mine
In turns therefrom sipped lovers' wine.'

The Water-fall

HENRY VAUGHAN

With what deep murmurs through time's silent stealth
Doth thy transparent, cool and watery wealth
      Here flowing fall,
      And chide, and call,
As if his liquid, loose retinue stayed
Ling'ring, and were of this steep place afraid,
      The common pass
      Where, clear as glass,
      All must descend
      Not to an end:
But quickened by this deep and rocky grave,
Rise to a longer course more bright and brave.
Dear stream! dear bank, where often I
Have sat, and pleased my pensive eye,
Why, since each drop of thy quick store
Runs thither, whence it flowed before,
Should poor souls fear a shade or night,
Who came (sure) from a sea of light?
Or since those drops are all sent back
So sure to thee, that none doth lack,
Why should frail flesh doubt any more
That what God takes, he'll not restore?
O useful element and clear!
My sacred wash and cleanser here,
My first consigner unto those
Fountains of life, where the Lamb goes?
What sublime truths, and wholesome themes,
Lodge in thy mystical, deep streams!

Such as dull man can never find
Unless that Spirit lead his mind,
Which first upon thy face did move,
And hatched all with his quickening love.
As this loud brook's incessant fall
In streaming rings restagnates all,
Which reach by course the bank, and then
Are no more seen, just so pass men.
O my invisible estate,
My glorious liberty, still late!
Thou art the channel my soul seeks,
Not this with cataracts and creeks.

The Signals

THEODORE ROETHKE

Often I meet, on walking from a door,
A flash of objects never seen before.

As known particulars come wheeling by,
They dart across a corner of the eye.

They flicker faster than a blue-tailed swift,
Or when dark follows dark in lightning rift.

They slip between the fingers of my sight.
I cannot put my glance upon them tight.

Sometimes the blood is privileged to guess
The things the eye or hand cannot possess.

Old Man Travelling

Animal Tranquillity and Decay, a Sketch
WILLIAM WORDSWORTH

The little hedgerow birds,
That peck along the road, regard him not.
He travels on, and in his face, his step,
His gait, is one expression: every limb,
His look and bending figure, all bespeak
A man who does not move with pain, but moves
With thought – He is insensibly subdued
To settled quiet: he is one by whom
All effort seems forgotten; one to whom
Long patience has such mild composure given,
That patience now doth seem a thing of which
He hath no need. He is by nature led
To peace so perfect, that the young behold
With envy, what the Old Man hardly feels.[1]

[1] In the original version Wordsworth had six final lines which he
later deleted:

– I asked him whither he was bound, and what
The object of his journey; he replied
'Sir! I am going many miles to take
A last leave of my son, a mariner,
Who from a sea-fight has been brought to Falmouth,
And there is dying in an hospital.'

Blue Sonata

JOHN ASHBERY

Long ago was the then beginning to seem like now
As now is but the setting out on a new but still
Undefined way. *That* now, the one once
Seen from far away, is our destiny
No matter what else may happen to us. It is
The present past of which our features,
Our opinions are made. We are half it and we
Care nothing about the rest of it. We
Can see far enough ahead for the rest of us to be
Implicit in the surroundings that twilight is.
We know that this part of the day comes every day
And we feel that, as it has its rights, so
We have our right to be ourselves in the measure
That we are in it and not some other day, or in
Some other place. The time suits us
Just as it fancies itself, but just so far
As we not give up that inch, breath
Of becoming before becoming may be seen,
Or come to seem all that it seems to mean now.

The things that were coming to be talked about
Have come and gone and are still remembered
As being recent. There is a grain of curiosity
At the base of some new thing, that unrolls
Its question mark like a new wave on the shore.
In coming to give, to give up what we had,
We have, we understand, gained or been gained
By what was passing through, bright with the sheen

Of things recently forgotten and revived.
Each image fits into place, with the calm
Of not having too much, of having just enough.
We live in the sigh of our present.

If that was all there was to have
We could re-imagine the other half, deducing it
From the shape of what is seen, thus
Being inserted into its idea of how we
Ought to proceed. It would be tragic to fit
Into the space created by our not having arrived yet,
To utter the speech that belongs there,
For progress occurs through re-inventing
These words from a dim recollection of them,
In violating that space in such a way as
To leave it intact. Yet we do after all
Belong here, and have moved a considerable
Distance; our passing is a facade.
But our understanding of it is justified.

3

In Midst of All

My soul, sit thou a patient looker-on;
Judge not the play before the play is done:
Her plot has many changes; every day
Speaks a new scene; the last act crowns the
play.

Francis Quarles, 'Epigram'

An Essay on Man

from *Epistle I*

ALEXANDER POPE

The bliss of man (could pride that blessing find)
Is not to act or think beyond mankind;
No pow'rs of body or of soul to share,
But what his nature and his state can bear.
Why has not man a microscopic eye?
For this plain reason, man is not a fly.
Say what the use, were finer optics giv'n,
T' inspect a mite, not comprehend the heav'n?
Or touch, if tremblingly alive all o'er,
To smart and agonize at ev'ry pore?
Or quick effluvia darting through the brain,
Die of a rose in aromatic pain?
If nature thundered in his opening ears,
And stunned him with the music of the spheres,
How would he wish that heav'n had left him still
The whisp'ring zephyr, and the purling rill?
Who finds not Providence all good and wise,
Alike in what it gives, and what denies?
　　Far as creation's ample range extends,
The scale of sensual, mental pow'rs ascends:
Mark how it mounts to man's imperial race,
From the green myriads in the peopled grass:
What modes of sight betwixt each wide extreme,
The mole's dim curtain, and the lynx's beam:
Of smell, the headlong lioness between,
And hound sagacious on the tainted green:
Of hearing, from the life that fills the flood,

To that which warbles through the vernal wood:
The spider's touch, how exquisitely fine!
Feels at each thread, and lives along the line:
In the nice bee, what sense so subtly true
From pois'nous herbs extracts the healing dew:
How instinct varies in the grov'ling swine,
Compared, half-reas'ning elephant, with thine:
'Twixt that, and reason, what a nice barrier,
For ever sep'rate, yet for ever near!
Remembrance and reflection how allied;
What thin partitions sense from thought divide;
And middle natures, how they long to join,
Yet never pass th' insuperable line!
Without this just gradation could they be
Subjected, these to those, or all to thee?
The pow'rs of all subdued by thee alone,
Is not thy reason all these pow'rs in one?

  See, through this air, this ocean, and this earth,
All matter quick, and bursting into birth.
Above, how high progressive life may go!
Around, how wide! how deep extend below!
Vast chain of being, which from God began,
Natures ethereal, human, angel, man,
Beast, bird, fish, insect! what no eye can see,
No glass can reach! from infinite to thee,
From thee to nothing! – On superior pow'rs
Were we to press, inferior might on ours;
Or in the full creation leave a void,
Where, one step broken, the great scale's destroyed:
From nature's chain whatever link you strike,
Tenth or ten thousandth, breaks the chain alike.

   And, if each system in gradation roll,
Alike essential to th' amazing whole,
The least confusion but in one, not all
That system only, but the whole must fall.

Let earth unbalanced from her orbit fly,
Planets and suns run lawless through the sky;
Let ruling angels from their spheres be hurled,
Being on being wrecked, and world on world,
Heav'ns whole foundations to their centre nod,
And nature tremble to the throne of God:
All this dread order break – for whom? for thee?
Vile worm! – oh madness, pride, impiety!

What if the foot, ordained the dust to tread,
Or hand to toil, aspired to be the head?
What if the head, the eye, or ear repined
To serve mere engines to the ruling mind?
Just as absurd for any part to claim
To be another, in this gen'ral frame;
Just as absurd, to mourn the tasks or pains
The great directing Mind of All ordains.

All are but parts of one stupendous whole,
Whose body nature is, and God the soul;
That, changed through all, and yet in all the same,
Great in the earth, as in the ethereal frame,
Warms in the sun, refreshes in the breeze,
Glows in the stars, and blossoms in the trees,
Lives through all life, extends through all extent,
Spreads undivided, operates unspent,
Breathes in our soul, informs our mortal part,
As full, as perfect, in a hair as heart;
As full, as perfect, in vile man that mourns,
As the rapt seraph that adores and burns;
To him no high, no low, no great, no small;
He fills, he bounds, connects, and equals all.

Cease then, nor order imperfection name:
Our proper bliss depends on what we blame.
Know thy own point: this kind, this due degree
Of blindness, weakness, heav'n bestows on thee.
Submit – in this, or any other sphere,

Secure to be as blest as thou canst bear:
Safe in the hand of one disposing pow'r,
Or in the natal, or the mortal hour.
All nature is but art, unknown to thee;
All chance, direction, which thou canst not see;
All discord, harmony not understood;
All partial evil, universal good.
And, spite of pride, in erring reason's spite,
One truth is clear, 'Whatever is, is right.'

Wit Wonders

ANONYMOUS (fifteenth century)

A God and yet a man,
A maid and yet a mother:
Wit wonders what wit can
Conceive this or the other.

A God and can he die?
A dead man, can he live?
What wit can well reply?
What reason reason give?

God, Truth itself, doth teach it.
Man's wit sinks too far under
By reason's power to reach it:
Believe and leave to wonder.

The Say-but-the-word Centurion Attempts a Summary

LES MURRAY

That numinous healer who preached Saturnalia and paradox
has died a slave's death. We were manoeuvred into it by
    priests
and by the man himself. To complete his poem.

He was certainly dead. The pilum guaranteed it. His
    message,
unwritten except on his body, like anyone's, was wrapped
like a scroll and despatched to our liberated selves, the gods.

If he has now risen, as our infiltrators gibber,
he has outdone Orpheus, who went alive to the Shades.
Solitude may be stronger than embraces. Inventor of the
    mustard tree,

he mourned one death, perhaps all, before he reversed it.
He forgave the sick to health, disregarded the sex of the
    Furies
when expelling them from minds. And he never speculated.

If he is risen, all are children of a most high real God
or something even stranger called by that name
who knew to come and be punished for the world.

To have knowledge of right, after that, is to be in the wrong.
Death came through the sight of law. His people's oldest
    wisdom.

If death is now the birth-gate into things unsayable

in language of death's era, there will be wars about religion
as there never were about the death-ignoring Olympians.
Love, too, his new universal, so far ahead of you it has died

for you before you meet it, may seem colder than the favours
    of gods
who are our poems, good and bad. But there never was a
    bad baby.
Half of his worship will be grinding his face in the dirt

then lifting it to beg, in private. The low will rule, and curse
    by him.
Divine bastard, soul-usurer, eros-frightener, he is out to
    monopolize hatred.
Whole philosophies will be devised for their brief snubbings
    of him.

But regained excels kept, he taught. Thus he has done the
    impossible
to show us it is there. To ask it of us. It seems we are to be
    the poem
and live the impossible. As each time we have, with mixed
    cries.

Chorus Sacerdotum[1]

FULKE GREVILLE

Oh wearisome Condition of Humanity!
Born under one Law, to another bound:
Vainly begot, and yet forbidden vanity,
Created sick, commanded to be sound:
What meaneth Nature by these diverse Laws?
Passion and Reason, self-division cause:
Is it the mark, or Majesty of Power
To make offences that it may forgive?
Nature herself, doth her own self deflower,
To hate those errors she her self doth give.
For how should man think that he may not do,
If Nature did not fail, and punish too?
Tyrant to others, to her self unjust,
Only commands things difficult and hard.
Forbids us all things, which it knows is lust,[2]
Makes easy pains, unpossible reward.
If Nature did not take delight in blood,
She would have made more easy ways to good.
We that are bound by vows, and by Promotion,
With pomp of holy Sacrifice and rites,
To teach belief in good and still devotion,
To preach of Heaven's wonders, and delights:
Yet when each of us, in his own heart looks,
He finds the God there, far unlike his Books.

[1] Chorus of the Priests.
[2] lust: pleasure.

Brahma

RALPH WALDO EMERSON

If the red slayer thinks he slays,
  Or if the slain think he is slain,
They know not well the subtle ways
  I keep, and pass, and turn again.

Far or forgot to me is near;
  Shadow and sunlight are the same;
The vanished gods to me appear;
  And one to me are shame and fame.

They reckon ill who leave me out;
  When me they fly I am the wings;
I am the doubter and the doubt,
  And I the hymn the Brahmin sings.

The strong gods pine for my abode,
  And pine in vain the sacred Seven;
But thou, meek lover of the good!
  Find me, and turn thy back on heaven.

What is Our Life?

SIR WALTER RALEGH

What is our life? a play of passion,
Our mirth the music of division,
Our mothers wombs the tyring houses be,
Where we are dressed for this short Comedy,
Heaven the Judicious sharp spectator is,
That sits and marks still who doth act amiss,
Our graves that hide us from the searching Sun,
Are like drawn curtains when the play is done,
Thus march we playing to our latest rest,
Only we die in earnest, that's no Jest.

An Essay on Man
from *Epistle II*
ALEXANDER POPE

Know then thyself, presume not God to scan;
The proper study of mankind is man.
Placed on this isthmus of a middle state,
A being darkly wise, and rudely great:
With too much knowledge for the sceptic side,
With too much weakness for the stoic's pride,
He hangs between; in doubt to act, or rest,
In doubt to deem himself a god, or beast;
In doubt his mind or body to prefer,
Born but to die, and reas'ning but to err;
Alike in ignorance, his reason such,
Whether he thinks too little, or too much:
Chaos of thought and passion, all confused;
Still by himself abused, or disabused;
Created half to rise, and half to fall;
Great lord of all things, yet a prey to all;
Sole judge of truth, in endless error hurled:
The glory, jest, and riddle of the world!

Before the Beginning

CHRISTINA ROSSETTI

Before the beginning Thou hast foreknown the end,
   Before the birthday the death-bed was seen of Thee:
Cleanse what I cannot cleanse, mend what I cannot mend.
   O Lord All-Merciful, be merciful to me.

While the end is drawing near I know not mine end:
   Birth I recall not, my death I cannot foresee:
O God, arise to defend, arise to befriend,
   O Lord All-Merciful, be merciful to me.

Old Man

EDWARD THOMAS

Old Man, or Lad's-love, – in the name there's nothing
To one that knows not Lad's-love, or Old Man,
The hoar-green feathery herb, almost a tree,
Growing with rosemary and lavender.
Even to one that knows it well, the names
Half decorate, half perplex, the thing it is:
At least, what that is clings not to the names
In spite of time. And yet I like the names.

The herb itself I like not, but for certain
I love it, as some day the child will love it
Who plucks a feather from the door-side bush
Whenever she goes in or out of the house.
Often she waits there, snipping the tips and shrivelling
The shreds at last on to the path, perhaps
Thinking, perhaps of nothing, till she sniffs
Her fingers and runs off. The bush is still
But half as tall as she, though it is as old;
So well she clips it. Not a word she says;
And I can only wonder how much hereafter
She will remember, with that bitter scent,
Of garden rows, and ancient damson-trees
Topping a hedge, a bent path to a door,
A low thick bush beside the door, and me
Forbidding her to pick.

As for myself,
Where first I met the bitter scent is lost.

I, too, often shrivel the grey shreds,
Sniff them and think and sniff again and try
Once more to think what it is I am remembering,
Always in vain. I cannot like the scent,
Yet I would rather give up others more sweet,
With no meaning, than this bitter one.

I have mislaid the key. I sniff the spray
And think of nothing; I see and I hear nothing;
Yet seem, too, to be listening, lying in wait
For what I should, yet never can, remember:
No garden appears, no path, no hoar-green bush
Of Lad's-love, or Old Man, no child beside,
Neither father nor mother, nor any playmate;
Only an avenue, dark, nameless, without end.

The Temper[1] (i)

GEORGE HERBERT

How should I praise thee, Lord! how should my rhymes
    Gladly engrave thy love in steel,
    If what my soul doth feel sometimes,
      My soul might ever feel!

Although there were some forty heav'ns, or more,
    Sometimes I peer above them all;
    Sometimes I hardly reach a score,
      Sometimes to hell I fall.

O rack me not to such a vast extent;
    Those distances belong to thee:
    The world's too little for thy tent,
      A grave too big for me.

Wilt thou meet[2] arms with man, that thou dost stretch
    A crumb of dust from heav'n to hell?
    Will great God measure with a wretch?
      Shall he thy stature spell?

O let me, when thy roof my soul hath hid,
    O let me roost and nestle there:
    Then of a sinner thou art rid,
      And I of hope and fear.

[1] Temper: frame of mind of various kinds (including tempering steel
and tuning instruments).
[2] meet: measure, as in sword fight.

Yet take thy way; for sure thy way is best:
　　Stretch or contract me, thy poor debtor:
　This is but tuning of my breast,
　　To make the music better.

Whether I fly with angels, fall with dust,
　　Thy hands made both, and I am there:
　Thy power and love, my love and trust
　　Make one place ev'ry where.

Of *Many* Worlds *in this* World

MARGARET CAVENDISH, DUCHESS OF NEWCASTLE

Just like unto a *Nest* of *Boxes* round,
Degrees of *sizes* within each *Box* are found.
So in this *World*, may many *Worlds* more be,
Thinner, and less, and less still by degree;
Although they are not subject to our *Sense*,
A *World* may be no bigger than *two-pence*.
Nature is curious, and such *work* may make,
That our dull *Sense* can never find, but scape.
For *Creatures*, small as *Atoms*, may be there,
If every *Atom* a *Creature's Figure* bear.
If four *Atoms* a *World* can make,[1] then see,
What several *Worlds* might in an *Earring* be.
For *Millions* of these *Atoms* may be in
The *Head* of one *small*, little, *single Pin*.
And if thus *small*, then *Ladies* well may wear
A *World* of *Worlds*, as *Pendants* in each *Ear*.

[1] It was argued that the four main atoms made the four elements, 'square, round, long and sharp'.

On a Drop of Dew

ANDREW MARVELL

See how the Orient Dew,
Shed from the Bosom of the Morn
  Into the blowing Roses,
Yet careless of its Mansion new,
For the clear Region where 'twas born,
  Round in its self incloses,
  And in its little Globe's Extent,
Frames as it can its native Element.
How it the purple flow'r does slight,
  Scarce touching where it lies,
But gazing back upon the Skies,
  Shines with a mournful Light;
    Like its own Tear,
Because so long divided from the Sphere.
  Restless it rolls and unsecure,
    Trembling lest it grow impure:
  Till the warm Sun pity its Pain,
And to the Skies exhale it back again.
  So the Soul, that Drop, that Ray
Of the clear Fountain of Eternal Day,
Could it within the human flow'r be seen,
  Remembring still its former height,
  Shuns the sweet leaves and blossoms green;
  And, recollecting its own Light,
Does, in its pure and circling thoughts, express
The greater Heaven in an Heaven less.
  In how coy a Figure wound,
  Every way it turns away:

So the World excluding round,
Yet receiving in the Day.
Dark beneath, but bright above:
Her disdaining, there in Love,
How loose and easy hence to go:
How girt and ready to ascend,
Moving but on a point below,
It all about does upwards bend.
Such did the Manna's sacred Dew distill;
White, and entire, though congeal'd and chill.
Congeal'd on Earth: but does, dissolving, run
Into the Glories of th' Almighty Sun.

To a Mouse

on turning her up in her nest, with the plough,
November 1785

ROBERT BURNS

Wee, sleekit, cowrin, tim'rous beastie,
O, what a panic's in thy breastie!
Thou need na start awa sae hasty,[1]
       Wi' bickering brattle![2]
I wad be laith[3] to rin an' chase thee,
       Wi' murd'ring pattle![4]

I'm truly sorry Man's dominion
Has broken Nature's social union,
An' justifies that ill opinion,
       Which makes thee startle,
At me, thy poor, earth-born companion,
       An' fellow-mortal!

I doubt na, whyles,[5] but thou may thieve;
What then? poor beastie, thou maun live!
A daimen icker[6] in a thrave[7]
       'S a sma' request.
I'll get a blessin wi' the lave,[8]
       An' never miss't!

[1] hasty: hurrying.
[2] brattle: scamper.
[3] laith: loath.
[4] pattle: plough-staff.
[5] whyles: sometimes.
[6] daimen icker: odd ear.
[7] thrave: twenty-four sheaves.
[8] lave: what's left.

Thy wee-bit housie, too, in ruin!
It's silly[1] wa's the win's are strewin!
An' naething, now to big[2] a new ane,
        O' foggage[3] green!
An' bleak December's winds ensuin,
        Baith snell[4] an' keen!

Thou saw the fields laid bare an' waste,
An' weary Winter comin fast,
An' cozie here, beneath the blast,
        Thou thought to dwell,
Till crash! the cruel coulter past
        Out thro' thy cell.

That wee-bit heap o' leaves an stibble[5]
Has cost thee monie a weary nibble!
Now thou's turn'd out, for a' thy trouble,
        But[6] house or hald,[7]
To thole[8] the Winter's sleety dribble,
        An' cranreuch[9] cauld!

But, Mousie, thou art no thy lane,[10]
In proving foresight may be vain:
The best-laid schemes o' Mice an' Men
        Gang aft a-gley,[11]
An' lea'e us nought but grief an' pain,
        For promis'd joy!

[1] silly: feeble.
[2] big: build.
[3] foggage: moss.
[4] snell: biting.
[5] stibble: stubble.
[6] But: without.
[7] hald: holding.
[8] thole: endure.
[9] cranreuch: hoar-frost.
[10] lane: alone.
[11] a-gley: awry.

Still thou art blest, compar'd wi' me!
The present only toucheth thee:
But, Och! I backward cast my e'e
            On prospects drear!
An' forward, tho' I cannot see,
            I guess an' fear!

from *To the Immortal Memory and Friendship of that Noble Pair, Sir Lucius Cary and Sir Henry Morison*

BEN JONSON

I. iii

For what is life, if measured by the space,
Not by the act?
Or maskèd man, if valued by his face,
Above his fact?
Here's one out-lived his peers,
And told forth fourscore years;
He vexèd time, and busied the whole State,
Troubled both foes and friends;
But ever to no ends:
What did this stirrer but die late?
How well at twenty had he fallen or stood!
For three of his fourscore he did no good.

II. i

He entered well, by virtuous parts,
Got up and thrived with honest arts:
He purchased friends and fame and honours then,
And had his noble name advanced with men;
But, weary of that flight,
He stooped in all men's sight
To sordid flatteries, acts of strife,
And sunk in that dead sea of life
So deep as he did then death's waters sup;
But that the cork of Title buoyed him up.

II. ii

Alas, but Morison fell young:
He never fell, thou fall'st, my tongue.
He stood, a soldier to the last right end,
A perfect patriot, and a noble friend,
But most, a virtuous son.
All offices were done
By him, so ample, full, and round,
In weight, in measure, number, sound,
As, though his age imperfect might appear,
His life was of humanity the sphere.

II. iii

Go now, and tell out days summed up with fears,
And make them years;
Produce thy mass of miseries on the stage,
To swell thine age;
Repeat of things a throng,
To shew thou hast been long,
Not lived; for life doth her great actions spell
By what was done and wrought
In season, and so brought
To light: her measures are – how well
Each syllable answered, and was formed, how fair:
These make the lines of life, and that's her air.

III. i

It is not growing like a tree
In bulk, doth make man better be;
Or standing long an oak, three hundred year,
To fall a log at last, dry, bald, and sere:
A lily of a day
Is fairer far in May,

Although it fall and die that night,
It was the plant and flower of light.
In small proportions we just beauty see,
And in short measures life may perfect be.

The World

John 2:16–17[1]

HENRY VAUGHAN

I saw Eternity the other night
Like a great *Ring* of pure and endless light,
    All calm, as it was bright,
And round beneath it, Time in hours, days, years
        Driven by the spheres
Like a vast shadow moved, in which the world
      And all her train were hurled;
The doting lover in his quaintest strain
                mplain,
Near hi   fancy, and his flights,
              ghts,
With gloves, an   s the silly snares of pleasure
      Yet his   treasure
All scattered la   'e he his eyes did pour
      Upon   er.

The darkso   sman hung with weights and woe
Like a thic   ght-fog moved there so slow
    He di   stay, nor go;
Condemning thoughts (like sad eclipses) scowl
        Upon his soul,
And clouds of crying witnesses without
    Pursued him with one shout.

[1] All that is in the world, the lust of the flesh, the lust of the eyes, and the pride of life, is not of the father but is of the world.
    And the world passeth away, and the lusts thereof, but he that doth the will of God abideth for ever.

Yet digged the mole, and lest his ways be found
      Worked under ground,
Where he did clutch his prey, but one did see
      That policy,
Churches and altars fed him, perjuries
      Were gnats and flies,
It rained about him blood and tears, but he
      Drank them as free.

The fearful miser on a heap of rust
Sat pining all his life there, did scarce trust
      His own hands with the dust,
Yet would not place one piece above, but lives
      In fear of thieves.
Thousands there were as frantic as himself
      And hugged each one his pelf
The down-right epicure placed   nse
      And scorned preten
While others slipped into a
      Said little less;
The weaker sort slight, trivial v   enslave
      Who think them bra
And poor, despised truth sat c   by
      Their victory.

Yet some, who all this while did w   nd sing,
And sing, and weep, soared up into *ing*,
      But most would use no wing.
O fools (said I,) thus to prefer dark night
      Before true light,
To live in grots, and caves, and hate the day
      Because it shows the way,
The way which from this dead and dark abode
      Leads up to God.
A way where you might tread the Sun, and be

More bright than he.
But as I did their madness so discuss
    One whispered thus,
This ring the bride-groom did for none provide
    But for his bride.

Psalm 8

THE BIBLE, AUTHORIZED VERSION

O Lord our Lord, how excellent is thy name in all the
  earth! who hast set thy glory above the heavens.
Out of the mouth of babes and sucklings hast thou
  ordained strength because of thine enemies, that thou
  mightest still the enemy and the avenger.
When I consider thy heavens, the work of thy fingers,
  the moon and the stars, which thou hast ordained;
What is man, that thou art mindful of him? and the son
  of man, that thou visitest him?
For thou hast made him a little lower than the angels,
  and hast crowned him with glory and honour.
Thou madest him to have dominion over the works of
  thy hands; thou hast put all things under his feet:
All sheep and oxen, yea, and the beasts of the field;
The fowl of the air, and the fish of the sea, and
  whatsoever passeth through the paths of the seas.
O Lord our Lord, how excellent is thy name in all the
  earth!

Hymn to the Creator

JOHN CLARE

Almighty creator and ruler as well
Of the earth and the heaven and darkness and hell
We adore thee – and worship as simple as when
Adam knelt in the garden the first of all men
The God of that sun that yet brings the broad day
When Eve the first flower in the first garden lay
That mercy that yet ever falls from the sky
Says that the meanest of beings never shall die

Almighty creator of all we behold
The mountains bare rock and the meadows all gold
The wilderness old and the desert of sand
Are his in his glory and wild barren land
To cheer and to cherish in wonder and love
The earth well as heaven, his dwellings above
Almighty creator to seek and to save
We need from the cradle thy help to the grave

We need thee and fear thee so ought we to fear
When thou hast no mercy none other will hear
And mercy thou shewest every day to our land
In keeping us all as the work of thy hand
In helping the feeble in seeking the lost
For man neither springs from a pillar or post
But breath[e]s from his father eternally yet
His hell or his heaven in mercy is met

Almighty creator of heaven and earth
Creations protector its life and its birth
In thee all began and in thee all have end
Our father at first and at last the one friend
We love and adore thee or ought so to do
From the sunrise of morning to evenings bright dew
Through morning and evening and blackest midnight
Thou'rt our faith in nights darkness and love in morns light

The Slip[1]

WENDELL BERRY

The river takes the land, and leaves nothing.
Where the great slip gave way in the bank
and an acre disappeared, all human plans
dissolve. An awful clarification occurs
where a place was. Its memory breaks
from what is known now, and begins to drift.
Where cattle grazed and trees stood, emptiness
widens the air for birdflight, wind, and rain.
As before the beginning, nothing is there.
Human wrong is in the cause, human
ruin in the effect – but no matter;
all will be lost, no matter the reason.
Nothing, having arrived, will stay.
The earth, even, is like a flower, so soon
passeth it away. And yet this nothing
is the seed of all – heaven's clear
eye, where all the worlds appear.
Where the imperfect has departed, the perfect
begins its struggle to return. The good gift
begins again its descent. The maker moves
in the unmade, stirring the water until
it clouds, dark beneath the surface,
stirring and darkening the soul until pain
perceives new possibility. There is nothing
to do but learn and wait, return to work
on what remains. Seed will sprout in the scar.
Though death is in the healing, it will heal.

[1] A landslip on the poet's farm.

Lines Composed a Few Miles above Tintern Abbey, on Revisiting the Banks of the Wye during a Tour. July 13 1798

WILLIAM WORDSWORTH

Five years have past; five summers, with the length
Of five long winters! and again I hear
These waters, rolling from their mountain-springs
With a soft inland murmur. – Once again
Do I behold these steep and lofty cliffs,
That on a wild secluded scene impress
Thoughts of more deep seclusion; and connect
The landscape with the quiet of the sky.
The day is come when I again repose
Here, under this dark sycamore, and view
These plots of cottage-ground, these orchard-tufts,
Which at this season, with their unripe fruits,
Are clad in one green hue, and lose themselves
'Mid groves and copses. Once again I see
These hedge-rows, hardly hedge-rows, little lines
Of sportive wood run wild: these pastoral farms,
Green to the very door; and wreaths of smoke
Sent up, in silence, from among the trees!
With some uncertain notice, as might seem
Of vagrant dwellers in the houseless woods,
Or of some Hermit's cave, where by his fire
The Hermit sits alone.

                  These beauteous forms,
Through a long absence, have not been to me
As is a landscape to a blind man's eye:

But oft, in lonely rooms, and 'mid the din
Of towns and cities, I have owed to them
In hours of weariness, sensations sweet,
Felt in the blood, and felt along the heart;
And passing even into my purer mind,
With tranquil restoration: – feelings too
Of unremembered pleasure: such, perhaps,
As have no slight or trivial influence
On that best portion of a good man's life,
His little, nameless, unremembered, acts
Of kindness and of love. Nor less, I trust,
To them I may have owed another gift,
Of aspect more sublime; that blessed mood,
In which the burden of the mystery,
In which the heavy and the weary weight
Of all this unintelligible world,
Is lightened: – that serene and blessed mood,
In which the affections gently lead us on, –
Until, the breath of this corporeal frame
And even the motion of our human blood
Almost suspended, we are laid asleep
In body, and become a living soul:
While with an eye made quiet by the power
Of harmony, and the deep power of joy,
We see into the life of things.
                                                    If this
Be but a vain belief, yet, oh! how oft –
In darkness and amid the many shapes
Of joyless daylight; when the fretful stir
Unprofitable, and the fever of the world,
Have hung upon the beatings of my heart –
How oft, in spirit, have I turned to thee,
O sylvan Wye! thou wanderer through the woods,
How often has my spirit turned to thee!

And now, with gleams of half-extinguished thought,
With many recognitions dim and faint,
And somewhat of a sad perplexity,
The picture of the mind revives again:
While here I stand, not only with the sense
Of present pleasure, but with pleasing thoughts
That in this moment there is life and food
For future years. And so I dare to hope,
Though changed, no doubt, from what I was when first
I came among these hills; when like a roe
I bounded o'er the mountains, by the sides
Of the deep rivers, and the lonely streams,
Wherever nature led: more like a man
Flying from something that he dreads, than one
Who sought the thing he loved. For nature then
(The coarser pleasures of my boyish days,
And their glad animal movements all gone by)
To me was all in all. – I cannot paint
What then I was. The sounding cataract
Haunted me like a passion: the tall rock,
The mountain, and the deep and gloomy wood,
Their colours and their forms, were then to me
An appetite; a feeling and a love,
That had no need of a remoter charm,
By thought supplied, nor any interest
Unborrowed from the eye. – That time is past,
And all its aching joys are now no more,
And all its dizzy raptures. Not for this
Faint I, nor mourn nor murmur; other gifts
Have followed; for such loss, I would believe,
Abundant recompense. For I have learned
To look on nature, not as in the hour
Of thoughtless youth; but hearing oftentimes
The still, sad music of humanity,
Nor harsh nor grating, though of ample power

To chasten and subdue. And I have felt
A presence that disturbs me with the joy
Of elevated thoughts; a sense sublime
Of something far more deeply interfused,
Whose dwelling is the light of setting suns,
And the round ocean and the living air,
And the blue sky, and in the mind of man:
A motion and a spirit, that impels
All thinking things, all objects of all thought,
And rolls through all things. Therefore am I still
A lover of the meadows and the woods,
And mountains; and of all that we behold
From this green earth; of all the mighty world
Of eye, and ear, – both what they half create,
And what perceive; well pleased to recognize
In nature and the language of the sense,
The anchor of my purest thoughts, the nurse,
The guide, the guardian of my heart, and soul
Of all my moral being.

                Nor perchance,
If I were not thus taught, should I the more
Suffer my genial spirits to decay:
For thou art with me here upon the banks
Of this fair river; thou my dearest Friend,
My dear, dear Friend; and in thy voice I catch
The language of my former heart, and read
My former pleasures in the shooting lights
Of thy wild eyes. Oh! yet a little while
May I behold in thee what I was once,
My dear, dear Sister! and this prayer I make,
Knowing that Nature never did betray
The heart that loved her; 'tis her privilege,
Through all the years of this our life, to lead
From joy to joy: for she can so inform
The mind that is within us, so impress

With quietness and beauty, and so feed
With lofty thoughts, that neither evil tongues,
Rash judgements, nor the sneers of selfish men,
Nor greetings where no kindness is, nor all
The dreary intercourse of daily life,
Shall e'er prevail against us, or disturb
Our cheerful faith, that all which we behold
Is full of blessings. Therefore let the moon
Shine on thee in thy solitary walk;
And let the misty mountain-winds be free
To blow against thee; and, in after years,
When these wild ecstasies shall be matured
Into a sober pleasure; when thy mind
Shall be a mansion for all lovely forms,
Thy memory be as a dwelling-place
For all sweet sounds and harmonies; oh! then,
If solitude, or fear, or pain, or grief,
Should be thy portion, with what healing thoughts
Of tender joy wilt thou remember me,
And these my exhortations! Nor, perchance –
If I should be where I no more can hear
Thy voice, nor catch from thy wild eyes these gleams
Of past existence – wilt thou then forget
That on the banks of this delightful stream
We stood together; and that I, so long
A worshipper of Nature, hither came
Unwearied in that service: rather say
With warmer love – oh! with far deeper zeal
Of holier love. Nor wilt thou then forget,
That after many wanderings, many years
Of absence, these steep woods and lofty cliffs,
And this green pastoral landscape, were to me
More dear, both for themselves and for thy sake!

Part Three

'OUT OF THE DEPTHS'

The Bible, Authorized Version, Psalm 130

I

Trouble

'Yet man is born unto trouble as the sparks fly
upward.'

The Bible, Authorized Version, Job 5:7

Psalm 130

De profundis clamavi

SIR THOMAS WYATT

From depth of sin and from a deep despair,
  From depth of death, from depth of heart's sorrow,
  From this deep cave of darkness' deep repair,
Thee have I called, O Lord, to be my borrow.
  Thou in my voice, O Lord, perceive and hear
  My heart, my hope, my plaint, my overthrow,
My will to rise, and let by grant appear
  That to my voice thine ears do well intend.
  No place so far that to thee is not near;
No depth so deep that thou ne mayst extend
  Thine ear thereto. Hear then my woeful plaint.
  For, Lord, if thou do observe what men offend
And put thy native mercy in restraint,
  If just exaction demand recompense,
  Who may endure, O Lord? Who shall not faint
At such account? Dread and not reverence
  Should so reign large. But thou seeks rather love
  For in thy hand is mercy's residence
By hope whereof thou dost our hearts move.
  I in thee, Lord, have set my confidence;
  My soul such trust doth evermore approve.
Thy holy word of eterne excellence,
  Thy mercy's promise that is always just,
  Have been my stay, my pillar, and pretence.
My soul in God hath more desirous trust
  Than hath the watchman looking for the day
  By the relief to quench of sleep the thrust.

Let Israel trust unto the Lord alway
  For grace and favour arn his property.
  Plenteous ransom shall come with him, I say,
And shall redeem all our iniquity.

Psalm 91

THE BIBLE, AUTHORIZED VERSION

He that dwelleth in the secret place of the most High shall
   abide under the shadow of the Almighty.
I will say of the Lord, He is my refuge and my fortress:
   my God; in him will I trust.
Surely he shall deliver thee from the snare of the fowler,
   and from the noisome pestilence.
He shall cover thee with his feathers, and under his wings
   shalt thou trust: his truth shall be thy shield and buckler.
Thou shalt not be afraid for the terror by night; *nor* for the
   arrow that flieth by day;
Nor for the pestilence that walketh in darkness; *nor* for the
   destruction that wasteth at noonday.
A thousand shall fall at thy side, and ten thousand at thy
   right hand; but it shall not come nigh thee.
Only with thine eyes shalt thou behold and see the reward
   of the wicked.
Because thou hast made the Lord, which is my refuge, even
   the most High, thy habitation;
There shall no evil befall thee, neither shall any plague
   come nigh thy dwelling.
For he shall give his angels charge over thee, to keep thee
   in all thy ways.
They shall bear thee up in their hands, lest thou dash thy
   foot against a stone.
Thou shalt tread upon the lion and adder: the young lion
   and the dragon shalt thou trample under feet.
Because he hath set his love upon me, therefore will I

deliver him: I will set him on high, because he hath known
my name.

He shall call upon me, and I will answer him: I will be
with him in trouble; I will deliver him, and honour him.

With long life will I satisfy him, and shew him my
salvation.

Psalm 102

JOHN CLARE

Lord, hear my prayer when trouble glooms,
Let sorrow find a way,
And when the day of trouble comes,
Turn not thy face away:
My bones like hearthstones burn away,
My life like vapoury smoke decays.

My heart is smitten like the grass,
That withered lies and dead,
And I, so lost to what I was,
Forget to eat my bread.
My voice is groaning all the day,
My bones prick through this skin of clay.

The wilderness's pelican,
The desert's lonely owl –
I am their like, a desert man
In ways as lone and foul.
As sparrows on the cottage top
I wait till I with fainting drop.

I hear my enemies reproach,
All silently I mourn;
They on my private peace encroach,
Against me they are sworn.
Ashes as bread my trouble shares,
And mix my food with weeping cares.

Yet not for them is sorrow's toil,
I fear no mortal's frowns –
But thou hast held me up awhile
And thou hast cast me down.
My days like shadows waste from view,
I mourn like withered grass in dew.

But thou, Lord, shalt endure for ever,
All generations through;
Thou shalt to Zion be the giver
Of joy and mercy too.
Her very stones are in thy trust,
Thy servants reverence her dust.

Heathens shall hear and fear thy name,
All kings of earth thy glory know
When thou shalt build up Zion's fame
And live in glory there below.
He'll not despise their prayers, though mute,
But still regard the destitute.

Sonnet 44

WILLIAM SHAKESPEARE

If the dull substance of my flesh were thought,
Injurious distance should not stop my way;
For then despite of space I would be brought,
From limits far remote, where thou dost stay.
No matter then although my foot did stand
Upon the farthest earth removed from thee;
For nimble thought can jump both sea and land
As soon as think the place where he would be.
But ah, thought kills me that I am not thought,
To leap large lengths of miles when thou art gone,
But that, so much of earth and water wrought,
I must attend time's leisure with my moan;
   Receiving naught by elements so slow
   But heavy tears, badges of either's woe.

A Song of Grief

ANNE FINCH, COUNTESS OF WINCHILSEA

Oh grief! why hast thou so much pow'r?
   Why do the ruling fates decree
No state should e'er without thee be?
   Why dost thou joys and hopes devour,
And clothe ev'n love himself in thy dark livery?

Thou, and cold fear, thy close ally,
   Do not alone on life attend,
But following mortals to their end,
   Do wrack the wretches whilst they die,
And to eternal shades too often with them fly.

To thee, great monarch, I submit,
   Thy sables and thy cypress bring,
I own thy power, I own thee king,
   Thy title in my heart is writ,
And till that breaks, I ne'er shall freedom get.

Forc'd smiles thy rigour will allow,
   And whilst thy seat is in the soul,
And there all mirth thou dost control,
   Thou canst admit to outward show
The smooth appearance and dissembled brow.

An Absolutely Ordinary Rainbow

LES MURRAY

The word goes round Repins,
the murmur goes round Lorenzinis.
At Tattersalls, men look up from sheets of numbers,
the Stock Exchange scribblers forget the chalk in their hands
and men with bread in their pockets leave the Greek Club:
There's a fellow crying in Martin Place. They can't stop him.

The traffic in George Street is banked up for half a mile
and drained of motion. The crowds are edgy with talk
and more crowds come hurrying. Many run in the back
     streets
which minutes ago were busy main streets, pointing:
There's a fellow weeping down there. No one can stop him.

The man we surround, the man no one approaches
simply weeps, and does not cover it, weeps
not like a child, not like the wind, like a man
and does not declaim it, nor beat his breast, nor even
sob very loudly – yet the dignity of his weeping

holds us back from his space, the hollow he makes about
     him
in the midday light, in his pentagram of sorrow,
and uniforms back in the crowd who tried to seize him
stare out at him, and feel, with amazement, their minds
longing for tears as children for a rainbow.

Some will say, in the years to come, a halo
or force stood around him. There is no such thing.
Some will say they were shocked and would have stopped
    him
but they will not have been there. The fiercest manhood,
the toughest reserve, the slickest wit amongst us

trembles with silence, and burns with unexpected
judgements of peace. Some in the concourse scream
who thought themselves happy. Only the smallest children
and such as look out of Paradise come near him
and sit at his feet, with dogs and dusty pigeons.

Ridiculous, says a man near me, and stops
his mouth with his hands, as if it uttered vomit –
and I see a woman, shining, stretch her hand
and shake as she receives the gift of weeping;
as many as follow her also receive it

and many weep for sheer acceptance, and more
refuse to weep for fear of all acceptance,
but the weeping man, like the earth, requires nothing,
the man who weeps ignores us, and cries out
of his writhen face and ordinary body

not words, but grief, not messages, but sorrow
hard as the earth, sheer, present as the sea –
and when he stops, he simply walks between us
mopping his face with the dignity of one
man who has wept, and now has finished weeping.

Evading believers, he hurries off down Pitt Street.

Tears, Idle Tears

ALFRED, LORD TENNYSON

Tears, idle tears, I know not what they mean,
Tears from the depth of some divine despair
Rise in the heart, and gather to the eyes,
In looking on the happy Autumn-fields,
And thinking of the days that are no more.

Fresh as the first beam glittering on a sail,
That brings our friends up from the underworld,
Sad as the last which reddens over one
That sinks with all we love below the verge;
So sad, so fresh, the days that are no more.

Ah, sad and strange as in dark summer dawns
The earliest pipe of half-awakened birds
To dying ears, when unto dying eyes
The casement slowly grows a glimmering square;
So sad, so strange, the days that are no more.

Dear as remembered kisses after death,
And sweet as those by hopeless fancy feigned
On lips that are for others; deep as love,
Deep as first love, and wild with all regret;
O Death in Life, the days that are no more.

Drop, drop, slow tears

PHINEAS FLETCHER

Drop, drop, slow tears
  and bathe those beauteous feet,
Which brought from heaven
  the news and Prince of peace:
Cease not, wet eyes,
  his mercies to entreat;
To cry for vengeance
  sin doth never cease:
In your deep floods
  drown all my faults and fears;
Nor let his eye
  see sin, but through my tears.

Me, Lord? Canst thou mispend

PHINEAS FLETCHER

Me, Lord? Canst thou mispend
One word, misplace one look on me?
Call'st me thy Love, thy Friend?
Can this poor soul the object be
Of these love-glances, those life-kindling eyes?
What? I the centre of thy arms' embraces?
Of all thy labour I the prize?
Love never mocks, Truth never lies.
Oh how I quake: Hope fear, fear hope displaces:
I would, but cannot hope: such wondrous love amazes.

See, I am black as night,
See, I am darkness: dark as hell.
Lord, thou more fair than light;
Heaven's sun thy shadow: can suns dwell
With shades? 'twixt light and darkness what commerce?
True: thou art darkness, I thy Light: my ray
Thy mists and hellish fogs shall pierce.
With me, black soul, with me converse;
I make the foul December flowery May.
Turn thou thy night to me: I'll turn thy night to day.

See, Lord, see, I am dead:
Tombed in myself: myself my grave.
A drudge: so born, so bred:
Myself even to myself a slave.
Thou Freedom, Life: can Life and Liberty
Love bondage, death? *Thy Freedom I: I tied*

To loose thy bonds: be bound to me:
My yoke shall ease, my bonds shall free.
Dead soul, thy Spring of life, my dying side:
There die with me to live: to live in thee I died.

I'll come when thou art saddest

EMILY JANE BRONTË

I'll come when thou art saddest,
Laid alone in the darkened room;
When the mad day's mirth has vanished,
And the smile of joy is banished
From evening's chilly gloom.

I'll come when the heart's real feeling
Has entire, unbiased sway,
And my influence o'er thee stealing,
Grief deepening, joy congealing,
Shall bear thy soul away.

Listen, 'tis just the hour,
The awful time for thee;
Dost thou not feel upon thy soul
A flood of strange sensations roll,
Forerunners of a sterner power,
Heralds of me?

Dejection

SAMUEL TAYLOR COLERIDGE

Well! If the Bard was weather-wise who made
The grand old ballad of Sir Patrick Spence,
This night, so tranquil now, will not go hence
Unroused by winds, that ply a busier trade
Than those which mould yon cloud in lazy flakes,
Or the dull sobbing draft, that moans and rakes
Upon the strings of this Aeolian lute,
  Which better far were mute.
 For lo! the New-moon winter-bright!
 And overspread with phantom light,
 (With swimming phantom light o'erspread
 But rimmed and circled by a silver thread)
I see the old Moon in her lap, foretelling
 The coming-on of rain and squally blast.
And oh! that even now the gust were swelling,
 And the slant night-shower driving loud and fast!
Those sounds which oft have raised me, whilst they awed
 And sent my soul abroad,
Might now perhaps their wonted impulse give,
Might startle this dull pain, and make it move and live!

A grief without a pang, void, dark, and drear,
 A stifled, drowsy, unimpassioned grief,
 Which finds no natural outlet, no relief,
  In word or sigh or tear –
 O Lady! in this wan and heartless mood,
To other thoughts by yonder throstle wooed,
 All this long eve, so balmy and serene,

Have I been gazing on the western sky,
    And its peculiar tint of yellow green:
And still I gaze – and with how blank an eye!
And those thin clouds above, in flakes and bars,
That give away their motion to the stars;
Those stars, that glide behind them or between,
Now sparkling, now bedimmed, but always seen:
Yon crescent Moon, as fixed as if it grew
In its own cloudless, starless lake of blue,
I see them all so excellently fair,
I see, not feel, how beautiful they are!

    My genial spirits fail;
    And what can these avail
To lift the smothering weight from off my breast?
    It were a vain endeavour,
    Though I should gaze for ever
On that green light that lingers in the west:
I may not hope from outward forms to win
The passion and the life, whose fountains are within.

O Lady! we receive but what we give
And in our life alone does Nature live:
Ours is her wedding garment, ours her shroud!
    And would we aught behold of higher worth,
Than that inanimate cold world allowed
To the poor loveless ever-anxious crowd,
    Ah! from the soul itself must issue forth
A light, a glory, a fair luminous cloud
    Enveloping the Earth –
And from the soul itself must there be sent
    A sweet and potent voice, of its own birth,
Of all sweet sounds the life and element!

O pure of heart! thou need'st not ask of me
What this strong music in the soul may be!
What, and wherein it doth exist,
This light, this glory, this fair luminous mist,
This beautiful and beauty-making power.

      Joy, virtuous Lady! Joy that ne'er was given,
Save to the pure, and in their purest hour,
Life, and Life's effluence, cloud at once and shower,
Joy, Lady! is the spirit and the power,
Which wedding Nature to us gives in dower
      A new Earth and new Heaven,
Undreamt of by the sensual and the proud –
Joy is the sweet voice, Joy the luminous cloud –
        We in ourselves rejoice!
And thence flows all that charms or ear or sight,
      All melodies the echoes of that voice,
All colours a suffusion from that light.

There was a time when, though my path was rough,
      This joy within me dallied with distress,
And all misfortunes were but as the stuff
      Whence Fancy made me dreams of happiness:
For hope grew round me, like the twining vine,
And fruits and foliage, not my own, seemed mine.
But now afflictions bow me down to earth:
Nor care I that they rob me of my mirth;
      But oh! each visitation
Suspends what nature gave me at my birth,
      My shaping spirit of Imagination.
For not to think of what I needs must feel,
      But to be still and patient, all I can;
And haply by abstruse research to steal
      From my own nature all the natural man –
      This was my sole resource, my only plan:
Till that which suits a part infects the whole,
And now is almost grown the habit of my soul.

Hence, viper thoughts, that coil around my mind,
   Reality's dark dream!
I turn from you, and listen to the wind,
  Which long has raved unnoticed. What a scream
Of agony by torture lengthened out
That lute sent forth! Thou Wind, that rav'st without,
  Bare crag, or mountain-tairn, or blasted tree,
Or pine-grove whither woodman never clomb,
Or lonely house, long held the witches' home,
  Methinks were fitter instruments for thee,
Mad Lutanist, who in this month of showers,
Of dark brown gardens and of peeping flowers,
Mak'st Devils' yule, with worse than wintry song,
The blossoms, buds, and timorous leaves among.
  Thou Actor, perfect in all tragic sounds!
Thou mighty Poet, e'en to frenzy bold!
   What tell'st thou now about?
   'Tis of the rushing of a host in rout,
  With groans of trampled men with smarting wounds –
At once they groan with pain and shudder with the cold!
But hush! there is a pause of deepest silence!
  And all that noise, as of a rushing crowd,
With groans and tremulous shudderings – all is over –
  It tells another tale, with sounds less deep and loud!
    A tale of less affright,
    And tempered with delight,
As Otway's self had framed the tender lay, –
    'Tis of a little child
    Upon a lonesome wild,
Not far from home, but she hath lost her way:
And now moans low in bitter grief and fear,
And now screams loud, and hopes to make her mother hear.

'Tis midnight, but small thoughts have I of sleep:
Full seldom may my friend such vigils keep!

Visit her, gentle sleep! with wings of healing,
And may this storm be but a mountain-birth,
May all the stars hang bright above her dwelling,
Silent as though they watched the sleeping Earth!
With light heart may she rise,
Gay fancy, cheerful eyes,
Joy lift her spirit, joy attune her voice;
To her may all things live from pole to pole,
Their life the eddying of her living soul!
O simple spirit, guided from above,
Dear lady! friend devoutest of my choice,
Thus mayest thou ever, evermore rejoice.

My life closed twice before its close

EMILY DICKINSON

My life closed twice before its close –
It yet remains to see
If Immortality unveil
A third event to me

So huge, so hopeless to conceive
As these that twice befell.
Parting is all we know of heaven,
And all we need of hell.

Dining[1]

DOUGLAS DUNN

No more in supermarkets will her good taste choose
 Her favourite cheese and lovely things to eat,
Or, hands in murmuring tubs, sigh as her fingers muse
 Over the mundane butter, mundane meat.
Nor round the market stalls of France will Lesley stroll
 Appraising aubergines, *langoustes*, *patisseries*
And artichokes, or hear the poultry vendors call,
 Watch merchants slicing spokes in wheels of Brie.
My lady loved to cook and dine, but never more
 Across starched linen and the saucy pork
Can we look forward to *Confit de Périgord*.
 How well my lady used her knife and fork!
Happy together – ah, my lady loved to sport
 And love. She loved the good; she loved to laugh
And loved so many things, infallible in art
 That pleased her, water, oil or lithograph,
With her own talent to compose the world in light.
 And it is hard for me to cook my meals
From recipes she used, without that old delight
 Returning, masked in sadness, until it feels
As if I have become a woman hidden in me –
 familiar with each kitchen-spotted page,
Each stain, each note in her neat hand a sight to spin me
 Into this grief, this kitchen pilgrimage.
O my young wife, how sad I was, yet pleased, to see
 And help you eat the soup that Jenny made

[1] Lesley, the poet's wife, was a painter who died of cancer, tended by
her husband.

On your last night, who all that day had called for tea,
    And only that, or slept your unafraid,
Serene, courageous sleeps, then woke, and asked for tea –
    'Nothing to eat. Tea. Please' – lucid and polite.
Eunice, Daphne, Cresten, Sandra, how you helped me,
    To feed my girl and keep her kitchen bright.
Know that I shake with gratitude, as, Jenny, when
    My Lesley ate your soup on her last night,
That image of her as she savoured rice and lemon
    Refused all grief, but was alight
    With nature, courage, friendship, appetite.

Reading Pascal in the Lowlands

DOUGLAS DUNN

His aunt has gone astray in her concern
And the boy's mum leans across his wheelchair
To talk to him. She points to the river.
An aged angler and a boy they know
Cast lazily into the rippled sun.
They go there, into the dappled grass, shadows
Bickering and falling from the shaken leaves.

His father keeps apart from them, walking
On the beautiful grass that is bright green
In the sunlight of July at 7 p.m.
He sits on the bench beside me, saying
It is a lovely evening, and I rise
From my sorrows, agreeing with him.
His large hand picks tobacco from a tin;

His smile falls at my feet, on the baked earth
Shoes have shuffled over and ungrassed.
It is discourteous to ask about
Accidents, or of the sick, the unfortunate.
I do not need to, for he says 'Leukaemia'.
We look at the river, his son holding a rod,
The line going downstream in a cloud of flies.

I close my book, the *Pensées* of Pascal.
I am light with meditation, religiose
And mystic with a day of solitude.
I do not tell him of my own sorrows.

He is bored with misery and premonition.
He has seen the limits of time, asking 'Why?'
Nature is silent on that question.

A swing squeaks in the distance. Runners jog
Round the perimeter. He is indiscreet.
His son is eight years old, with months to live.
His right hand trembles on his cigarette.
He sees my book, and then he looks at me,
Knowing me for a stranger. I have said
I am sorry. What more is there to say?

He is called over to the riverbank.
I go away, leaving the Park, walking through
The Golf Course, and then a wood, climbing,
And then bracken and gorse, sheep pasturage.
From a panoptic hill I look down on
A little town, its estuary, its bridge,
Its houses, churches, its undramatic streets.

Simon Lee, the Old Huntsman

With an incident in which he was concerned

WILLIAM WORDSWORTH

In the sweet shire of Cardigan,
Not far from pleasant Ivor-hall,
An old Man dwells, a little man, –
'Tis said he once was tall.
Full five-and-thirty years he lived
A running huntsman merry;
And still the centre of his cheek
Is red as a ripe cherry.

No man like him the horn could sound,
And hill and valley rang with glee
When Echo bandied, round and round,
The halloo of Simon Lee.
In those proud days, he little cared
For husbandry or tillage;
To blither tasks did Simon rouse
The sleepers of the village.

He all the country could outrun,
Could leave both man and horse behind;
And often, ere the chase was done,
He reeled, and was stone-blind.
And still there's something in the world
At which his heart rejoices;
For when the chiming hounds are out,
He dearly loves their voices!

But, oh the heavy change! – bereft
Of health, strength, friends, and kindred, see!
Old Simon to the world is left
In liveried poverty.
His Master's dead, – and no one now
Dwells in the Hall of Ivor;
Men, dogs, and horses, all are dead;
He is the sole survivor.

And he is lean and he is sick;
His body, dwindled and awry,
Rests upon ankles swoln and thick;
His legs are thin and dry.
One prop he has, and only one,
His wife, an aged woman,
Lives with him, near the waterfall,
Upon the village Common.

Beside their moss-grown hut of clay,
Not twenty paces from the door,
A scrap of land they have, but they
Are poorest of the poor.
This scrap of land he from the heath
Enclosed when he was stronger;
But what to them avails the land
Which he can till no longer?

Oft, working by her Husband's side,
Ruth does what Simon cannot do;
For she, with scanty cause for pride,
Is stouter of the two.
And, though you with your utmost skill
From labour could not wean them,
'Tis little, very little – all
That they can do between them.

Few months of life has he in store
As he to you will tell,
For still, the more he works, the more
Do his weak ankles swell.
My gentle Reader, I perceive
How patiently you've waited,
And now I fear that you expect
Some tale will be related.

O Reader! had you in your mind
Such stores as silent thought can bring,
O gentle Reader! you would find
A tale in everything.
What more I have to say is short,
And you must kindly take it:
It is no tale; but, should you think,
Perhaps a tale you'll make it.

One summer-day I chanced to see
This old Man doing all he could
To unearth the root of an old tree,
A stump of rotten wood.
The mattock tottered in his hand;
So vain was his endeavour,
That at the root of the old tree
He might have worked for ever.

'You're overtasked, good Simon Lee,
Give me your tool,' to him I said;
And at the word right gladly he
Received my proffered aid.
I struck, and with a single blow
The tangled root I severed,
At which the poor old Man so long
And vainly had endeavoured.

The tears into his eyes were brought,
And thanks and praises seemed to run
So fast out of his heart, I thought
They never would have done.
– I've heard of hearts unkind, kind deeds
With coldness still returning;
Alas! the gratitude of men
Hath oftener left me mourning.

My song is love unknown

SAMUEL CROSSMAN

My song is love unknown,
　My Saviour's love to me,
Love to the loveless shown,
　That they might lovely be.
　　O who am I,
　　　That for my sake
　　　My Lord should take
　　Frail flesh, and die?

He came from his blest throne,
　Salvation to bestow;
But men made strange, and none
　The longed-for Christ would know.
　　But O, my friend,
　　　My friend indeed,
　　　Who at my need
　　His life did spend!

Sometimes they strew his way,
　And his sweet praises sing;
Resounding all the day
　Hosannas to their king.
　　Then 'Crucify!'
　　　Is all their breath,
　　　And for his death
　　They thirst and cry.

Why, what hath my Lord done?
　　What makes this rage and spite?
He made the lame to run,
　　He gave the blind their sight.
　　　Sweet injuries!
　　　　Yet they at these
　　　　Themselves displease,
　　And 'gainst him rise.

They rise, and needs will have
　　My dear Lord made away;
A murderer they save,
　　The Prince of Life they slay.
　　　Yet cheerful he
　　　　To suffering goes,
　　　　That he his foes
　　From thence might free.

In life, no house, no home
　　My Lord on earth might have;
In death, no friendly tomb
　　But what a stranger gave.
　　　What may I say?
　　　　Heaven was his home;
　　　　But mine the tomb
　　Wherein he lay.

Here might I stay and sing,
　　No story so divine;
Never was love, dear King,
　　Never was grief like thine.
　　　This is my Friend,
　　　　In whose sweet praise
　　　　I all my days
　　Could gladly spend.

After great pain a formal feeling comes

EMILY DICKINSON

After great pain a formal feeling comes –
The nerves sit ceremonious like tombs:
The stiff Heart questions – was it He that bore?
And yesterday – or centuries before?

The feet mechanical
Go round a wooden way
Of ground or air or Ought, regardless grown.
A quartz contentment like a stone.

This is the hour of lead
Remembered if outlived.
As freezing persons recollect the snow –
First chill, then stupor, then the letting go.

Psalm 27

THE BIBLE, AUTHORIZED VERSION

The Lord is my light and my salvation; whom shall I fear? the Lord is the strength of my life; of whom shall I be afraid?

When the wicked, even mine enemies and my foes, came upon me to eat up my flesh, they stumbled and fell.

Though an host should encamp against me, my heart shall not fear: though war should rise against me, in this will I be confident.

One thing have I desired of the Lord, that will I seek after; that I may dwell in the house of the Lord all the days of my life, to behold the beauty of the Lord, and to inquire in his temple.

For in the time of trouble he shall hide me in his pavilion: in the secret of his tabernacle shall he hide me; he shall set me up upon a rock.

And now shall mine head be lifted up above mine enemies round about me: therefore will I offer in his tabernacle sacrifices of joy; I will sing, yea, I will sing praises unto the Lord.

Hear, O Lord, when I cry with my voice: have mercy also upon me, and answer me.

When thou saidst, Seek ye my face; my heart said unto thee, Thy face, Lord, will I seek.

Hide not thy face far from me; put not thy servant away in anger: thou hast been my help; leave me not, neither forsake me, O God of my salvation.

When my father and my mother forsake me, then the Lord will take me up.

Teach me thy way, O Lord, and lead me in a plain path, because of mine enemies.

Deliver me not over unto the will of mine enemies: for false witnesses are risen up against me, and such as breathe out cruelty.

I had fainted, unless I had believed to see the goodness of the Lord in the land of the living.

Wait on the Lord: be of good courage, and he shall stengthen thine heart: wait, I say, on the Lord.

Man Frail, and God Eternal

ISAAC WATTS

O God, our help in ages past,
   Our hope for years to come,
Our shelter from the stormy blast,
   And our eternal home.

Under the shadow of thy throne
   Thy saints have dwelt secure;
Sufficient is thine arm alone,
   And our defence is sure.

Before the hills in order stood,
   Or earth receiv'd her frame,
From everlasting thou art God,
   To endless years the same.

Thy word commands our flesh to dust,
   'Return, ye sons of men':
All nations rose from earth at first,
   And turn to earth again.

A thousand ages in thy sight
   Are like an evening gone;
Short as the watch that ends the night
   Before the rising sun.

The busy tribes of flesh and blood,
   With all their lives and cares,
Are carried downwards by thy flood,
   And lost in following years.

Time like an ever-rolling stream
　　Bears all its sons away;
They fly forgotten as a dream
　　Dies at the opening day.

Like flowering fields the nations stand
　　Pleas'd with the morning light;
The flowers beneath the mower's hand
　　Lie withering ere 'tis night.

Our God, our help in ages past,
　　Our hope for years to come,
Be thou our guard while troubles last,
　　And our eternal home.

Psalm 46

THE BIBLE, AUTHORIZED VERSION

God is our refuge and strength, a very present help in
  trouble.
Therefore will not we fear, though the earth be removed,
  and though the mountains be carried into the midst of the
  sea;
Though the waters thereof roar and be troubled, though
  the mountains shake with the swelling thereof. Sē-läh.
There is a river, the streams whereof shall make glad the
  city of God, the holy place of the tabernacles of the most
  High.
God is in the midst of her; she shall not be moved: God
  shall help her, and that right early.
The heathen raged, the kingdoms were moved: he uttered
  his voice, the earth melted.
The Lord of hosts is with us; the God of Jacob is our
  refuge. Sē-läh.
Come, behold the works of the Lord, what desolations he
  hath made in the earth.
He maketh wars to cease unto the end of the earth; he
  breaketh the bow, and cutteth the spear in sunder; he
  burneth the chariot in the fire.
Be still, and know that I am God: I will be exalted
  among the heathen, I will be exalted in the earth.
The Lord of hosts is with us; the God of Jacob is our
  refuge. Sē-läh.

Lost

Almighty and most merciful Father; We have
erred, and strayed from thy ways like lost
sheep. We have followed too much the devices
and desires of our own hearts. We have
offended against thy holy laws. We have left
undone those things which we ought to have
done; And we have done those things which we
ought not to have done; And there is no health
in us. But thou, O Lord, have mercy upon us,
miserable offenders. Spare thou them, O God,
which confess their faults. Restore thou them
that are penitent; According to thy promises,
declared unto mankind in Christ Jesu our Lord.
And grant, O most merciful Father, for his
sake; That we may hereafter live a godly,
righteous, and sober life, To the glory of thy
holy Name. Amen.

Book of Common Prayer

Later Life 6

CHRISTINA ROSSETTI

We lack, yet cannot fix upon the lack:
　　Not this, nor that; yet somewhat, certainly.
　　We see the things we do not yearn to see
Around us: and what see we glancing back?
Lost hopes that leave our hearts upon the rack,
　　Hopes that were never ours yet seemed to be,
　　For which we steered on life's salt stormy sea
Braving the sunstroke and the frozen pack.
If thus to look behind is all in vain,
　　And all in vain to look to left or right,
Why face we not our future once again,
Launching with hardier hearts across the main,
　　Straining dim eyes to catch the invisible sight,
And strong to bear ourselves in patient pain?

Later Life 17

CHRISTINA ROSSETTI

Something this foggy day, a something which
   Is neither of this fog nor of today,
   Has set me dreaming of the winds that play
Past certain cliffs, along one certain beach,
   And turn the topmost edge of waves to spray:
   Ah pleasant pebbly strand so far away,
So out of reach while quite within my reach,
   As out of reach as India or Cathay!
I am sick of where I am and where I am not.
   I am sick of foresight and of memory,
   I am sick of all I have and all I see,
     I am sick of self, and there is nothing new;
Oh weary impatient patience of my lot! –
     Thus with myself: how fares it, Friends, with you?

The Porch

R. S. THOMAS

Do you want to know his name?
It is forgotten. Would you learn
what he was like? He was like
anyone else, a man with ears
and eyes. Be it sufficient
that in a church porch on an evening
in winter, the moon rising, the frost
sharp, he was driven
to his knees and for no reason
he knew. The cold came at him;
his breath was carved angularly
as the tombstones; an owl screamed.

He had no power to pray.
His back turned on the interior
he looked out on a universe
that was without knowledge
of him and kept his place
there for an hour on that lean
threshold, neither outside nor in.

In Tenebris (I)

Percussus sicut foenum, et aruit cor meum – Ps. CI
THOMAS HARDY

Wintertime nighs;
But my bereavement-pain
It cannot bring again:
    Twice no one dies.

Flower-petals flee;
But, since it once hath been,
No more that severing scene
    Can harrow me.

Birds faint in dread:
I shall not lose old strength
In the lone frost's black length:
    Strength long since fled!

Leaves freeze to dun;
But friends can not turn cold
This season as of old
    For him with none.

Tempests may scathe;
But love can not make smart
Again this year his heart
    Who no heart hath.

Black is night's cope;
But death will not appal
One who, past doubtings all,
    Waits in unhope.

Affliction (iv)

GEORGE HERBERT

Broken in pieces all asunder,
   Lord, hunt me not,
   A thing forgot,
Once a poor creature, now a wonder,
   A wonder tortur'd in the space
   Betwixt this world and that of grace.

My thoughts are all a case of knives,
   Wounding my heart
   With scatter'd smart,
As watring pots give flowers their lives.
   Nothing their fury can control,
   While they do wound and prick[1] my soul.

All my attendants[2] are at strife,
   Quitting their place
   Unto my face:
Nothing performs the task of life:
   The elements are let loose to fight,
   And while I live, try out their right.

Oh help, my God! let not their plot
   Kill them and me,
   And also thee,
Who art my life: dissolve the knot,

---

[1] prick: stab as in fencing.
[2] attendants: faculties.

As the sun scatters by his light
All the rebellions of the night.

Then shall those powers, which work for grief,
           Enter thy pay,
           And day by day
Labour thy praise, and my relief;
      With care and courage building me,
      Till I reach heav'n, and much more, thee.

Non sum qualis eram bonae sub regno Cynarae[1]

ERNEST DOWSON

Last night, ah yesternight, betwixt her lips and mine
There fell thy shadow, Cynara! thy breath was shed
Upon my soul between the kisses and the wine;
And I was desolate and sick of an old passion,
      Yea, I was desolate and bowed my head:
I have been faithful to thee, Cynara! in my fashion.

All night upon my heart I felt her warm heart beat,
Night-long within my arms in love and sleep she lay;
Surely the kisses of her bought red mouth were sweet;
But I was desolate and sick of an old passion,
      When I awoke and found the dawn was gray:
I have been faithful to thee, Cynara! in my fashion.

I have forgot much, Cynara! gone with the wind,
Flung roses, roses riotously with the throng.
Dancing, to put thy pale, lost lilies out of mind;
But I was desolate and sick of an old passion,
      Yea, all the time, because the dance was long:
I have been faithful to thee, Cynara! in my fashion.

I cried for madder music and for stronger wine,
But when the feast is finished and the lamps expire,
Then falls thy shadow, Cynara! the night is thine;

[1] 'I am not as I was under the reign of good Cynara.'

And I am desolate and sick of an old passion,
    Yea, hungry for the lips of my desire;
I have been faithful to thee, Cynara! in my fashion.

Sonnet *129*

WILLIAM SHAKESPEARE

Th'expense of spirit in a waste of shame
Is lust in action, and, till action, lust
Is perjured, murd'rous, bloody, full of blame,
Savage, extreme, rude, cruel, not to trust,
Enjoyed no sooner but despisèd straight,
Past reason hunted, and no sooner had,
Past reason hated as a swallowed bait
On purpose laid to make the taker mad;
Mad in pursuit, and in possession so,
Had, having, and in quest to have, extreme,
A bliss in proof, and proved, a very woe,
Before, a joy proposed, behind, a dream.
   All this the world well knows, yet none knows well
   To shun the heaven that leads men to this hell.

Thou art indeed just, Lord

GERARD MANLEY HOPKINS

Thou art indeed just, Lord, if I contend[1]
With thee; but, sir, so what I plead is just.
Why do sinners' ways prosper? and why must
Disappointment all I endeavour end?
   Wert thou my enemy, O thou my friend,
How wouldst thou worse, I wonder, than thou dost
Defeat, thwart me? Oh, the sots and thralls of lust
Do in spare hours more thrive than I that spend,
Sir, life upon thy cause. See, banks and brakes
Now, leaved how thick! laced they are again
With fretty chervil, look, and fresh wind shakes
Them; birds build – but not I build; no, but strain,
Time's eunuch, and not breed one work that wakes.
Mine, O thou lord of life, send my roots rain.

[1] See Psalm 119:137–60.

Caelica XCVIII

FULKE GREVILLE

Wrapp'd up, O Lord, in man's degeneration;
The glories of thy truth, thy joys eternal,
Reflect upon my soul dark desolation,
And ugly prospects o'er the sprites infernal.
   Lord, I have sinn'd, and mine iniquity,
   Deserves this hell; yet Lord deliver me.

Thy power and mercy never comprehended,
Rest lively-imag'd in my conscience wounded;
Mercy to grace, and power to fear extended,
Both infinite, and I in both confounded;
   Lord, I have sinn'd, and mine iniquity,
   Deserves this hell, yet Lord deliver me.

If from this depth of sin, this hellish grave,
And fatal absence from my Saviour's glory,
I could implore his mercy, who can save,
And for my sins, not pains of sin, be sorry:
   Lord, from this horror of iniquity,
   And hellish grave, thou would'st deliver me.

Carrion Comfort

GERARD MANLEY HOPKINS

Not, I'll not, carrion comfort, Despair, not feast on thee;
Not untwist – slack they may be – these last strands of man
In me ór, most weary, cry *I can no more.* I can;
Can something, hope, wish day come, not choose not to be.

But ah, but O thou terrible, why wouldst thou rude on me
Thy wring-world right foot rock? lay a lionlimb against me?
   scan
With darksome devouring eyes my bruisèd bones? and fan,
O in turns of tempest, me heaped there; me frantic to avoid
   thee and flee?

Why? That my chaff might fly; my grain lie, sheer and clear.
Nay in all that toil, that coil, since (seems) I kissed the rod,
Hand rather, my heart lo! lapped strength, stole joy, would
   laugh, chéer.
Cheer whom though? The hero whose heaven-handling flung
   me, fóot tród
Me? or me that fought him? O which one? is it each one?
   That night, that year
Of now done darkness I wretch lay wrestling with (my God!)
   my God.

Caelica XCIX

FULKE GREVILLE

Down in the depth of mine iniquity,
That ugly centre of infernal spirits;
Where each sin feels her own deformity,
In those peculiar torments she inherits,
  Depriv'd of human graces, and divine,
  Even there appears this saving God of mine.

And in this fatal mirror of transgression,
Shows man as fruit of his degeneration,
The error's ugly infinite impression,
Which bears the faithless down to desperation;
  Depriv'd of human graces and divine,
  Even there appears this saving God of mine.

In power and truth, almighty and eternal,
Which on the sin reflects strange desolation,
With glory scouring all the sprites infernal,
And uncreated hell with unprivation;
  Depriv'd of human graces, not divine,
  Even there appears this saving God of mine.

For on this sp'ritual cross condemnèd lying,
To pains infernal by eternal doom,
I see my Saviour for the same sins dying,
And from that hell I fear'd, to free me, come;
  Depriv'd of human graces, not divine,
  Thus hath his death rais'd up this soul of mine.

It may be good, like it who list

SIR THOMAS WYATT

It may be good, like it who list.
But I do doubt: who can me blame?
For oft assured yet have I missed
And now again I fear the same.
The windy words, the eyes' quaint game
Of sudden change maketh me aghast.
For dread to fall I stand not fast.

Alas, I tread an endless maze
That seek to accord two contraries;
And hope still, and nothing haze,[1]
Imprisoned in liberties;
As one unheard and still that cries;
Always thirsty yet naught I taste.
For dread to fall I stand not fast.

Assured I doubt I be not sure.
And should I trust to such surety
That oft hath put the proof in ure[2]
And never hath found it trusty?
Nay, sir, in faith it were great folly.
And yet my life thus I do waste:
For dread to fall I stand not fast.

---

[1] haze: hazard, venture (or possibly 'has').
[2] ure: use.

Yet a Little While

CHRISTINA ROSSETTI

I dreamed and did not seek: today I seek
    Who can no longer dream;
But now am all behindhand, waxen weak,
   And dazed amid so many things that gleam
    Yet are not what they seem.

I dreamed and did not work: today I work
    Kept wide awake by care
And loss, and perils dimly guessed to lurk;
   I work and reap not, while my life goes bare
    And void in wintry air.

I hope indeed; but hope itself is fear
    Viewed on the sunny side;
I hope, and disregard the world that's here,
   The prizes drawn, the sweet things that betide;
    I hope, and I abide.

On His Blindness

JOHN MILTON

When I consider how my light is spent,
  Ere half my days, in this dark world and wide,
  And that one talent which is death to hide
  Lodged with me useless, though my soul more bent
To serve therewith my Maker, and present
  My true account, lest he returning chide,
  'Doth God exact day-labour, light denied?'
  I fondly ask. But Patience, to prevent
That murmur, soon replies: 'God doth not need
  Either man's work or his own gifts; who best
  Bear his mild yoke, they serve him best. His state
Is kingly: thousands at his bidding speed,
  And post o'er land and ocean without rest;
  They also serve who only stand and wait.'

from *In Memoriam*

ALFRED, LORD TENNYSON

LV

The wish, that of the living whole
    No life may fail beyond the grave,
    Derives it not from what we have
The likest God within the soul?

Are God and Nature then at strife,
    That Nature lends such evil dreams?
    So careful of the type she seems,
So careless of the single life;

That I, considering everywhere
    Her secret meaning in her deeds,
    And finding that of fifty seeds
She often brings but one to bear,

I falter where I firmly trod,
    And falling with my weight of cares
    Upon the great world's altar-stairs
That slope thro' darkness up to God,

I stretch lame hands of faith, and grope,
    And gather dust and chaff, and call
    To what I feel is Lord of all,
And faintly trust the larger hope.

Dialogue

GEORGE HERBERT

Sweetest Saviour, if my soul
 Were but worth the having,
Quickly should I then control
 Any thought of waiving.
But when all my care and pains
Cannot give the name of gains
To thy wretch so full of stains,
What delight or hope remains?

What (child) is the balance thine,
 Thine the poise and measure?
If I say, Thou shalt be mine,
 Finger not my treasure.
What the gains in having thee
Do amount to, only he,
Who for man was sold,[1] can see;
That transferr'd th' accounts to me.

But as I can see no merit,
 Leading to this favour:
So the way to fit me for it,
 Is beyond my savour.
As the reason then is thine,
So the way is none of mine:
I disclaim the whole design:
Sin disclaims and I resign.

[1] Christ was sold by Judas for thirty pieces of silver.

That is all, if that I could
  Get without repining;
And my clay, my creature, would
  Follow my resigning.[1]
That as I did freely part
With my glory and desert,
Left all joys to feel all smart –
  Ah! no more: thou break'st my heart.

[1] resigning divine status through the Incarnation.

The Collar

GEORGE HERBERT

I struck the board,[1] and cry'd, No more.
                    I will abroad.
What? shall I ever sigh and pine?
My lines and life are free; free as the road,
    Loose as the wind, as large as store.
            Shall I be still in suit?
        Have I no harvest but a thorn
        To let me blood, and not restore
What I have lost with cordial fruit?
                    Sure there was wine
        Before my sighs did dry it: there was corn
        Before my tears did drown it.
    Is the year only lost to me?
        Have I no bays to crown it?
No flowers, no garlands gay? all blasted?
                    All wasted?
    Not so, my heart: but there is fruit,
                And thou hast hands.

        Recover all thy sigh-blown age
On double pleasures: leave thy cold dispute
Of what is fit, and not; forsake thy cage,
            Thy rope of sands,
Which petty thoughts have made, and made to thee
    Good cable, to enforce and draw,
                And be thy law,

---

[1] board: table, also possibly communion table.

While thou didst wink and wouldst not see.
Away; take heed:
I will abroad.
Call in thy death's head there: tie up thy fears.
He that forbears
To suit and serve his need,
Deserves his load.
But as I rav'd and grew more fierce and wild
At every word,
Me thoughts I heard one calling, *Child*:
And I reply'd, *My Lord*.

To *learn the transport by the pain*

EMILY DICKINSON

To learn the transport by the pain
As blind men learn the sun,
To die of thirst suspecting
That brooks in meadows run,

To stay the homesick, homesick feet
Upon a foreign shore,
Haunted by native lands the while,
And blue, beloved air –

This is the sovreign anguish,
This the signal woe.
These are the patient laureates
Whose voices, trained below,

Ascend in ceaseless carol,
Inaudible indeed
To us, the duller scholars
Of the mysterious bard.

ὕμνοςἄϋμνος

'Hymnos ahmynos': a hymn, yet not a hymn
ARTHUR HUGH CLOUGH

O thou whose image in the shrine
Of human spirits dwells divine
Which from that precinct once conveyed
To be to outer day displayed
Doth vanish, part, and leave behind
Mere blank and void of empty mind
Which wilful fancy seeks in vain
With casual shapes to fill again –

O thou that in our bosoms' shrine
Dost dwell because unknown divine
I thought to speak, I thought to say
'The light is here,' 'behold the way'
'The voice was thus' and 'thus the word,'
And 'thus I saw' and 'that I heard,'
But from the lips but half essayed
The imperfect utterance fell unmade.

O thou in that mysterious shrine
Enthroned, as we must say, divine.
I will not frame one thought of what
Thou mayest either be or not.
I will not prate of 'thus' and 'so'
And be profane with 'yes' and 'no,'
Enough that in our soul and heart
Thou whatsoe'er thou may'st be art.

Unseen, secure in that high shrine
Acknowledged present and divine
I will not ask some upper air,
Some future day, to place thee there.
Nor say nor yet deny, Such men
Or women saw thee thus and then;
Thy name was such, and there or here
To him or her thou didst appear.

Do only thou in that dim shrine
Unknown or known remain divine.
There or if not, at least in eyes
That scan the fact that round them lies.
– The hand to sway, the judgment guide
In sight and sense thyself divide
Be thou but there; in soul and heart,
I will not ask to feel thou art.

The Haunter[1]

THOMAS HARDY

He does not think that I haunt here nightly:
    How shall I let him know
That whither his fancy sets him wandering
    I, too, alertly go? –
Hover and hover a few feet from him
    Just as I used to do,
But cannot answer the words he lifts me –
    Only listen thereto!

When I could answer he did not say them:
    When I could let him know
How I would like to join in his journeys
    Seldom he wished to go.
Now that he goes and wants me with him
    More than he used to do,
Never he sees my faithful phantom
    Though he speaks thereto.

Yes, I companion him to places
    Only dreamers know,
Where the shy hares print long paces,
    Where the night rooks go;
Into old aisles where the past is all to him,
    Close as his shade can do,
Always lacking the power to call to him,
    Near as I reach thereto!

[1] The imagined speaker is Hardy's late wife, Emma, as ghost
unseen.

What a good haunter I am, O tell him!
    Quickly make him know
If he but sigh since my loss befell him
    Straight to his side I go.
Tell him a faithful one is doing
    All that love can do
Still that his path may be worth pursuing,
    And to bring peace thereto.

from *In Memoriam*

ALFRED, LORD TENNYSON

LIV

Oh yet we trust that somehow good
    Will be the final goal of ill,
    To pangs of nature, sins of will,
Defects of doubt, and taints of blood;

That nothing walks with aimless feet;
    That not one life shall be destroy'd,
    Or cast as rubbish to the void,
When God hath made the pile complete;

That not a worm is cloven in vain;
    That not a moth with vain desire
    Is shrivell'd in a fruitless fire,
Or but subserves another's gain.

Behold, we know not anything;
    I can but trust that good shall fall
    At last – far off – at last, to all,
And every winter change to spring.

So runs my dream: but what am I?
    An infant crying in the night:
    An infant crying for the light:
And with no language but a cry.

from *In Memoriam*

ALFRED, LORD TENNYSON

CXXIV

That which we dare invoke to bless;
　　Our dearest faith; our ghastliest doubt;
　　He, They, One, All; within, without;
The Power in darkness whom we guess;

I found Him not in world or sun,
　　Or eagle's wing, or insect's eye;
　　Nor through the questions men may try,
The petty cobwebs we have spun:

If e'er when faith had fall'n asleep,
　　I heard a voice 'believe no more'
　　And heard an ever-breaking shore
That tumbled in the Godless deep;

A warmth within the breast would melt
　　The freezing reason's colder part,
　　And like a man in wrath the heart
Stood up and answered 'I have felt.'

No, like a child in doubt and fear:
　　But that blind clamour made me wise;
　　Then was I as a child that cries,
But, crying, knows his father near;

And what I am beheld again
　　What is, and no man understands:
　　And out of darkness came the hands
That reach through nature, moulding men.

from *Four Quartets: 'East Coker'*

T. S. ELIOT

III

O dark dark dark. They all go into the dark,
The vacant interstellar spaces, the vacant into the vacant,
The captains, merchant bankers, eminent men of letters.
The generous patrons of art, the statesmen and the rulers,
Distinguished civil servants, chairmen of many committees,
Industrial lords and petty contractors, all go into the dark,
And dark the Sun and Moon, and the Almanach de Gotha
And the Stock Exchange Gazette, the Directory of Directors,
And cold the sense and lost the motive of action.
And we all go with them, into the silent funeral,
Nobody's funeral, for there is no one to bury.
I said to my soul, be still, and let the dark come upon you
Which shall be the darkness of God. As, in a theatre,
The lights are extinguished, for the scene to be changed
With a hollow rumble of wings, with a movement of
    darkness on darkness,
And we know that the hills and the trees, the distant
    panorama
And the bold imposing façade are all being rolled away –
Or as, when an underground train, in the tube, stops too
    long between stations
And the conversation rises and slowly fades into silence
And you see behind every face the mental emptiness deepen
Leaving only the growing terror of nothing to think about;
Or when, under ether, the mind is conscious but conscious of
    nothing –

I said to my soul, be still, and wait without hope
For hope would be hope for the wrong thing; wait without
   love
For love would be love of the wrong thing; there is yet faith
But the faith and the love and the hope are all in the
   waiting.
Wait without thought, for you are not ready for thought:
So the darkness shall be the light, and the stillness the
   dancing.
Whisper of running streams, and winter lightning.
The wild thyme unseen and the wild strawberry,
The laughter in the garden, echoed ecstasy
Not lost, but requiring, pointing to the agony
Of death and birth.

Psalm 130

BOOK OF COMMON PRAYER

Out of the deep have I called unto thee, O Lord: Lord, hear
my voice.

O let thine ears consider well: the voice of my complaint.

If thou, Lord, wilt be extreme to mark what is done amiss:
O lord, who may abide it?

For there is mercy with thee: therefore shalt thou be
feared.

I look for the Lord; my soul doth wait for him: in his
word is my trust.

My soul fleeth unto the Lord: before the morning watch, I
say, before the morning watch.

O Israel, trust in the Lord, for with the Lord there is
mercy: and with him is plenteous redemption.

And he shall redeem Israel: from all his sins.

Part Four

OF GOOD

Finally, brethren, whatsoever things are true,
whatsoever things are just, whatsoever things
are pure, whatsoever things are lovely,
whatsoever things are of good report; if there
be any virtue, and if there be any praise, think
on these things.

The Bible, Authorized Version, Philippians 4:8

Joy

I see something of God each hour of the twenty-four, and
  each moment then,
In the faces of men and women I see God, and in my own
  face in the glass,
I find letters from God dropt in the street, and every one is
  sign'd by God's name,
And I leave them where they are, for I know that
  wheresoe'er I go,
Others will punctually come for ever and ever.

Walt Whitman, 'Song of Myself'

Blank

D. H. LAWRENCE

At present I am a blank, and I admit it.
In feeling I am just a blank.
My mind is fairly nimble, and is not blank.
My body likes its dinner and the warm sun, but otherwise is
    blank.
My soul is almost blank, my spirit quite.
I have a certain amount of money, so my anxieties are blank.
And I can't do anything about it, even there I am blank.
So I am just going to go on being a blank, till something
    nudges me from within,
and makes me know I am not blank any longer.

The Morning-Watch

HENRY VAUGHAN

O joys! Infinite sweetness! with what flowers,
And shoots of glory, my soul breaks, and buds!
   All the long hours
   Of night, and rest
   Through the still shrouds
   Of sleep, and clouds,
  This dew fell on my breast;
   O how it *bloods*,
And *spirits* all my earth! hark! In what rings,
And *hymning circulations* the quick world
   Awakes, and sings;
   The rising winds,
   And falling springs,
   Birds, beasts, all things
  Adore him in their kinds.
   Thus all is hurled
In sacred *hymns*, and *order*, the great *chime*
And *symphony* of nature. Prayer is
   The world in tune,
   A spirit-voice,
   And vocal joys
  Whose *echo* is heaven's bliss.
   O let me climb
When I lie down! The pious soul by night
Is like a clouded star, whose beams though said
   To shed their light
   Under some cloud
   Yet are above,

And shine, and move
Beyond that misty shroud.
So in my bed
That curtained grave, though sleep, like ashes, hide
My lamp, and life, both shall in thee abide.

Meeting Point

LOUIS MACNEICE

Time was away and somewhere else,
There were two glasses and two chairs
And two people with the one pulse
(Somebody stopped the moving stairs):
Time was away and somewhere else.

And they were neither up nor down,
The stream's music did not stop
Flowing through heather, limpid brown,
Although they sat in a coffee shop
And they were neither up nor down.

The bell was silent in the air
Holding its inverted poise –
Between the clang and clang a flower,
A brazen calyx of no noise:
The bell was silent in the air.

The camels crossed the miles of sand
That stretched around the cups and plates;
The desert was their own, they planned
To portion out the stars and dates:
The camels crossed the miles of sand.

Time was away and somewhere else.
The waiter did not come, the clock
Forgot them and the radio waltz

Came out like water from a rock:
Time was away and somewhere else.

Her fingers flicked away the ash
That bloomed again in tropic trees:
Not caring if the markets crash
When they had forests such as these,
Her fingers flicked away the ash.

God or whatever means the Good
Be praised that time can stop like this,
That what the heart has understood
Can verify in the body's peace
God or whatever means the Good.

Time was away and she was here
And life no longer what it was,
The bell was silent in the air
And all the room a glow because
Time was away and she was here.

from *A Dialogue of Self and Soul*

W. B. YEATS

My Self. A living man is blind and drinks his drop.
What matter if the ditches are impure?
What matter if I live it all once more?
Endure that toil of growing up;
The ignominy of boyhood; the distress
Of boyhood changing into man;
The unfinished man and his pain
Brought face to face with his own clumsiness;

The finished man among his enemies? –
How in the name of Heaven can he escape
That defiling and disfigured shape
The mirror of malicious eyes
Casts upon his eyes until at last
He thinks that shape must be his shape?
And what's the good of an escape
If honour find him in the wintry blast?

I am content to live it all again
And yet again, if it be life to pitch
Into the frog-spawn of a blind man's ditch,
A blind man battering blind men;
Or into that most fecund ditch of all,
The folly that man does
Or must suffer, if he woos
A proud woman not kindred of his soul.

I am content to follow to its source
Every event in action or in thought;
Measure the lot; forgive myself the lot!
When such as I cast out remorse
So great a sweetness flows into the breast
We must laugh and we must sing,
We are blest by everything,
Everything we look upon is blest.

Shadows

SAMUEL DANIEL

Are they shadows that we see?
  And can shadows pleasure give?
Pleasures only shadows be,
  Cast by bodies we conceive,
    And are made the things we deem
    In those figures which they seem.

But these pleasures vanish fast,
  Which by shadows are expressed;
Pleasures are not, if they last;
  In their passing is their best.
    Glory is most bright and gay
    In a flash and so away.

Feed apace, then, greedy eyes
  On the wonder you behold;
Take it sudden as it flies,
  Though you take it not to hold.
    When your eyes have done their part,
    Thought must length it in the heart.

News

THOMAS TRAHERNE

News from a foreign country came,
As if my treasure and my wealth lay there:
   So much it did my heart inflame,
'Twas wont to call my Soul into mine ear;
     Which thither went to meet
      The approaching Sweet,
     And on the threshold stood,
   To entertain the unknown Good.
      It hovered there
     As if 'twould leave mine ear,
   And was so eager to embrace
   The joyful tidings as they came,
'Twould almost leave its dwelling-place,
    To entertain the same.

As if the tidings were the things,
My very Joys themselves, my foreign treasure,
   Or else did bear them on their wings,
With so much joy they came, with so much pleasure.
     My Soul stood at the gate
      To recreate
     Itself with Bliss, and to
   Be pleased with speed. A fuller view
      It fain would take,
     Yet journeys back would make
   Unto my heart; as if 'twould fain
   Go out to meet, yet stay within

To fit a place, to entertain
And bring the tidings in.

What sacred instinct did inspire
My Soul in childhood with a hope so strong?
What secret force moved my desire
To expect my Joys beyond the seas, so young?
Felicity I knew
Was out of view:
And being here alone,
I saw that happiness was gone,
From me! For this,
I thirsted absent Bliss,
And thought that sure beyond the seas,
Or else in something near at hand
I knew not yet – since naught did please
I knew – my Bliss did stand.

But little did the infant dream
That all the treasures of the world were by;
And that himself was so the cream
And crown of all which round about did lie.
Yet thus it was. The Gem,
The Diadem,
The Ring enclosing all
That stood upon this earthly ball,
The Heavenly Eye,
Much wider than the sky,
Wherein they all included were,
The glorious Soul that was the King
Made to possess them, did appear
A small and little thing.

Hope

ANNE FINCH, COUNTESS OF WINCHILSEA

The tree of knowledge we in Eden prov'd;
The tree of life was thence to heav'n remov'd:
Hope is the growth of earth, the only plant
Which either heav'n or paradise could want.

Hell knows it not, to us alone confin'd,
And cordial only to the human mind.
Receive it then, t' expel these mortal cares,
Nor waive a med'cine which thy God prepares.

True Riches

ISAAC WATTS

I am not concern'd to know
What to morrow Fate will do:
'Tis enough that I can say
I've possest my self to day:
Then if haply Midnight-Death
Seize my Flesh and stop my Breath,
Yet to morrow I shall be
Heir to the best Part of Me.
    Glittering Stones and Golden things,
Wealth and Honours that have Wings,
Ever fluttering to be gone
I could never call my own:
Riches that the World bestows
She can take and I can lose;
But the Treasures that are mine
Lie afar beyond her Line.
When I view my spacious Soul,
And survey my self awhole,
And enjoy my self alone,
I'm a Kingdom of my own.
    I've a mighty Part within
That the World hath never seen,
Rich as *Eden*'s happy Ground,
And with choicer Plenty crown'd.
Here on all the shining Boughs
Knowledge fair and useful grows;
On the same young flow'ry Tree
All the Seasons you may see;

Notions in the Bloom of Light,
Just disclosing to the Sight;
Here are Thoughts of larger Growth,
Rip'ning into solid Truth;
Fruits refin'd, of noble Taste;
Seraphs feed on such Repast.
Here in a green and shady Grove
Streams of Pleasure mix with Love:
There beneath the smiling Skies
Hills of Contemplation rise;
Now upon some shining Top
Angels light, and call me up;
I rejoice to raise my Feet,
Both rejoice when there we meet.

There are endless Beauties more
Earth hath no Resemblance for;
Nothing like them round the Pole,
Nothing can describe the Soul:
'Tis a Region half unknown,
That has Treasures of its own,
More remote from public View
Than the Bowels of *Peru*;
Broader 'tis and brighter far
Than the Golden *Indies* are;
Ships that trace the watry Stage
Cannot coast it in an Age;
Harts or Horses, strong and fleet,
Had they Wings to help their Feet,
Could not run it half way o'er
In ten thousand Days and more.

Yet the silly wandring Mind
Loath to be too much confin'd
Roves and takes her daily Tours,
Coasting round the narrow Shores,
Narrow Shores of Flesh and Sense,

Picking Shells and Pebbles thence:
Or she sits at Fancy's Door,
Calling Shapes and Shadows to her,
Foreign Visits still receiving,
And t' her self a Stranger living.
Never, never would she buy
Indian Dust or *Tyrian* Dye,
Never trade abroad for more
If she saw her native Store,
If her inward Worth were known
She might ever live alone.

Love (iii)

GEORGE HERBERT

Love bade me welcome: yet my soul drew back,
   Guilty of dust and sin.
But quick-ey'd Love, observing me grow slack
   From my first entrance in,
Drew nearer to me, sweetly questioning,
   If I lack'd any thing.

A guest, I answer'd, worthy to be here:
   Love said, you shall be he.
I the unkind, ungrateful? Ah my dear,
   I cannot look on thee.
Love took my hand, and smiling did reply,
   Who made the eyes but I?

Truth Lord, but I have marr'd them: let my shame
   Go where it doth deserve.
And know you not, says Love, who bore the blame?
   My dear, then I will serve
You must sit down, says Love, and taste my meat:[1]
   So I did sit and eat.

[1] 'Jesus took bread and blessed it ... Take, eat: this is my body'
Matthew 26:26.

from *Sonnets from the Portuguese*[1]

ELIZABETH BARRETT BROWNING

V

I lift my heavy heart up solemnly,
As once Electra her sepulchral urn,
And, looking in thine eyes, I overturn
The ashes at thy feet. Behold and see
What a great heap of grief lay hid in me,
And how the red wild sparkles dimly burn
Through the ashen greyness. If thy foot in scorn
Could tread them out to darkness utterly,
It might be well perhaps. But if instead
Thou wait beside me for the wind to blow
The grey dust up, ... those laurels on thine head,
O my Belovèd, will not shield thee so,
That none of all the fires shall scorch and shred
The hair beneath. Stand further off then! go.

VI

Go from me. Yet I feel that I shall stand
Henceforward in thy shadow. Nevermore
Alone upon the threshold of my door
Of individual life, I shall command

---

[1] The Portuguese was Robert Browning's nickname for his beloved.
These courtship poems from his wife Elizabeth to Robert mark
Elizabeth Barrett's struggle to overcome bereavement (at the loss of
her brothers Samuel and Edward) and lung disorder in her
confinement within the house of her strict widowed father. Cf.
Samuel Crossman 'Love to the loveless shown/That they might lovely
be' ('My Song is Love Unknown').

The uses of my soul, nor lift my hand
Serenely in the sunshine as before,
Without the sense of that which I forbore –
Thy touch upon the palm. The widest land
Doom takes to part us, leaves thy heart in mine
With pulses that beat double. What I do
And what I dream include thee, as the wine
Must taste of its own grapes. And when I sue
God for myself, He hears that name of thine,
And sees within my eyes the tears of two.

XIV

If thou must love me, let it be for nought
Except for love's sake only. Do not say
'I love her for her smile ... her look ... her way
Of speaking gently, ... for a trick of thought
That falls in well with mine, and certes brought
A sense of pleasant ease on such a day' –
For these things in themselves, Belovèd, may
Be changed, or change for thee, – and love, so wrought
May be unwrought so. Neither love me for
Thine own dear pity's wiping my cheeks dry, –
A creature might forget to weep, who bore
Thy comfort long, and lose thy love thereby!
But love me for love's sake, that evermore
Thou may'st love on, through love's eternity.

XXXV

If I leave all for thee, wilt thou exchange
And be all to me? Shall I never miss
Home-talk and blessing and the common kiss
That comes to each in turn, nor count it strange,
When I look up, to drop on a new range
Of walls and floors, ... another home than this?

Nay, wilt thou fill that place by me which is
Filled by dead eyes too tender to know change?
That's hardest. If to conquer love, has tried,
To conquer grief, tries more ... as all things prove,
For grief indeed is love and grief beside.
Alas, I have grieved so I am hard to love.
Yet love me – wilt thou? Open thine heart wide,
And fold within, the wet wings of thy dove.

John Anderson My Jo[1]

ROBERT BURNS

John Anderson my jo, John,
    When we were first Acquent;[2]
Your locks were like the raven,
    Your bony brow was brent;[3]
But now your brow is beld,[4] John,
    Your locks are like the snaw;
But blessings on your frosty pow,[5]
    John Anderson my Jo.

John Anderson my jo, John,
    We clamb the hill the gither;[6]
And mony a canty[7] day John,
    We've had wi' ane anither:
Now we maun totter down, John,
    And hand in hand we'll go;
And sleep the gither at the foot,
    John Anderson my Jo.

[1] Jo: dear.
[2] Acquent: acquainted.
[3] brent: smooth.
[4] beld: bald.
[5] pow: head.
[6] the gither: together.
[7] canty: cheerful.

from *Sonnets from the Portuguese*

ELIZABETH BARRET BROWNING

X

Yet, love, mere love, is beautiful indeed
And worthy of acceptation. Fire is bright,
Let temple burn, or flax. An equal light
Leaps in the flame from cedar-plank or weed.
And love is fire. And when I say at need
I love thee ... mark! ... *I love thee* – in thy sight
I stand transfigured, glorified aright,
With conscience of the new rays that proceed
Out of my face toward thine. There's nothing low
In love, when love the lowest: meanest creatures
Who love God, God accepts while loving so.
And what I *feel*, across the inferior features
Of what I *am*, doth flash itself, and show
How that great work of Love enhances Nature's.

Lightenings

SEAMUS HEANEY

viii

The annals say: when the monks of Clonmacnoise
Were all at prayers inside the oratory
A ship appeared above them in the air.

The anchor dragged along behind so deep
It hooked itself into the altar rails
And then, as the big hull rocked to a standstill,

A crewman shinned and grappled down the rope
And struggled to release it. But in vain.
'This man can't bear our life here and will drown,'

The abbot said, 'unless we help him.' So
They did, the freed ship sailed, and the man climbed back
Out of the marvellous as he had known it.

Of the Last Verses in the Book

EDMUND WALLER

When we for age could neither read nor write,
The subject made us able to indite;
The soul, with nobler resolutions decked,
The body stooping, does herself erect.
No mortal parts are requisite to raise
Her that, unbodied, can her Maker praise.

The seas are quiet when the winds give o'er;
So, calm are we when passions are no more!
For then we know how vain it was to boast
Of fleeting things, so certain to be lost.
Clouds of affection from our younger eyes
Conceal that emptiness which age descries.

The soul's dark cottage, battered and decayed,
Lets in new light through chinks that time has made;
Stronger by weakness, wiser men become,
As they draw near to their eternal home.
Leaving the old, both worlds at once they view,
That stand upon the threshold of the new.

The New Cemetery

NORMAN NICHOLSON

Now that the town's dead
Amount to more than its calculable future,
They are opening a new graveyard

In the three-hedged field where once
Horses of the L.M.S. delivery wagons
Were put to grass. Beside the fence

Of the cricket-ground, we'd watch
On Saturday afternoon, soon after the umpires
Laid the bails to the stumps and the match

Had begun. They'd lead them
Then between railway and St. George's precinct – huge
Beasts powerful as the steam

Engines they were auxiliary to:
Hanked muscles oscillating slow and placid as pistons,
Eyes blinkered from all view

Of the half-acre triangle of green,
Inherited for Sunday. But once they'd slipped the harness,
And the pinched field was seen

With its blue lift of freedom,
Those haunches heaved like a sub-continental earthquake
Speeded up in film.

Half a ton of horse-flesh
Rose like a balloon, gambolled like a week-old lamb;
Hind legs lashed

Out at inoffensive air,
Capsized a lorryful of weekdays, stampeded down
Fifty yards of prairie.

We heard the thump
Of hoof on sun-fired clay in the hush between
The bowler's run-up

And the click of the late
Cut. And when, one end-of-season day, they lead me
Up through the churchyard gate

To that same
Now consecrated green – unblinkered and at last delivered
Of a lifetime's

Load of parcels – let me fling
My hooves at the boundary wall and bang them down again,
Making the thumped mud ring.

Psalm 126

THE BIBLE, AUTHORIZED VERSION

When the Lord turned again the captivity of Zion, we were like them that dream.

Then was our mouth filled with laughter, and our tongue with singing: then said they among the heathen, The Lord hath done great things for them.

The Lord hath done great things for us; whereof we are glad.

Turn against our captivity, O Lord, as the streams in the south.

They that sow in tears shall reap in joy.

He that goeth forth and weepeth, bearing precious seed, shall doubtless come again with rejoicing, bringing his sheaves with him.

The Flower

GEORGE HERBERT

How fresh, O Lord, how sweet and clean
Are thy returns! ev'n as the flowers in spring;
    To which, besides their own demean,[1]
The late-past frosts tributes of pleasure bring.
        Grief melts away
        Like snow in May,
    As if there were no such cold thing.

    Who would have thought my shrivel'd heart
Could have recover'd greenness? It was gone
    Quite under ground; as flowers depart
To see their mother-root, when they have blown;
        Where they together
        All the hard weather,
    Dead to the world, keep house unknown.

    These are thy wonders, Lord of power,
Killing and quickning, bringing down to hell
    And up to heaven in an hour;
Making a chiming of a passing-bell.
        We say amiss,
        This or that is:
    Thy word is all, if we could spell.

    O that I once past changing were,
Fast in thy Paradise, where no flower can wither!

---

[1] demean: demeanour and estate (domain).

Many a spring I shoot up fair,
Offring at heav'n, growing and groaning thither:
   Nor doth my flower
   Want a spring-shower,
My sins and I joining together:

But while I grow in a straight line,
Still upwards bent, as if heav'n were mine own,
 Thy anger comes, and I decline:
What frost to that? what pole is not the zone,[1]
   Where all things burn,
   When thou dost turn,
And the least frown of thine is shown?

And now in age I bud again,
After so many deaths I live and write;
 I once more smell the dew and rain,
And relish versing: O my only light,
   It cannot be
   That I am he
On whom thy tempests fell all night.

These are thy wonders, Lord of love,
To make us see we are but flowers that glide:[2]
 Which when we once can find and prove,
Thou hast a garden for us, where to bide.
   Who would be more,
   Swelling through store,
Forfeit their Paradise by their pride.

---

[1] zone: hottest part of earth between tropics.
[2] glide: slip away.

2

Right

My crooked winding ways, wherein I live,
Wherein I die, not live: for life is straight,
Straight as a line ...
Give me simplicity, that I may live.

George Herbert, 'A Wreath'

Psalm 1

Blessed is the man that walketh not in the counsel of the
ungodly, nor standeth in the way of sinners, nor sitteth in
the seat of the scornful.
But his delight is in the law of the Lord; and in his law
doth he meditate day and night.
And he shall be like a tree planted by the rivers of water,
that bringeth forth his fruit in his season; his leaf also shall
not wither; and whatsoever he doeth shall prosper.
The ungodly are not so: but are like the chaff which the
wind driveth away.
Therefore the ungodly shall not stand in the judgment, nor
sinners in the congregation of the righteous.
For the Lord knoweth the way of the righteous: but the
way of the ungodly shall perish.

Truth

Balade de Bon Conseil
GEOFFREY CHAUCER

Flee from the press, and dwell with soothfastness,[1]
Suffice unto[2] thy good, though it be small;
For hoard hath hate, and climbing tickleness,[3]
Press hath envỳ, and weal blent overall;[4]
Savour no more than thee behovė shall;
Rule well thyself, that other folk canst rede;[5]
And Truth thee shall deliver, it is no dread.

Tempest thee nought all crooked to redress,
In trust of her that turneth as a ball:
Great restė stant in little busyness;
Be ware also to spurn against an awl;[6]
Strive not, as doth the crockė[7] with the wall.
Dauntė[8] thyself, that dauntest others' deed;
And Truth thee shall deliver, it is no dread.

That thee is sent, receive in buxomness,[9]
The wrestling for this world asketh a fall.
Here is no home, here n'is but wilderness:
Forth, pilgrim, forth! Forth, beast, out of thy stall!

[1] soothfastness: truthfulness.
[2] suffice unto: be satisfied with.
[3] tickleness: precariousness.
[4] weal blent overall: prosperity blinds one completely.
[5] rede: advise. 'Other folk' is the object of this verb.
[6] to spurn against an awl: to kick against the pricks.
[7] crocke: pot.
[8] Daunte: overcome.
[9] buxomness: submissiveness.

Know thy countrỳ, look up, thank God of all;
Hold the highway, and let thy ghost[1] thee lead;
And Truth thee shall deliver, it is no dread.

Envoy

Therefore, thou Vache,[2] leave thine old wretchedness
Unto the world; leave now to be thrall,[3]
Cry him mercỳ, that of his high goodnèss
Made thee of nought, and in especial
Draw unto him, and pray in general
For thee, and eek[4] for other, heavenly meed;[5]
And Truth thee shall deliver, it is no dread.

---

[1] ghost: spirit.
[2] Sir Philip Vache, to whom the poem is addressed.
[3] leave now to be thrall: cease now to be a slave.
[4] eek: also.
[5] meed: reward.

from *Christian Ethics*

THOMAS TRAHERNE

For man to act as if his soul did see
The very brightness of eternity;
For man to act as if his love did burn
Above the spheres, even while it's in its urn;
For man to act even in the wilderness
As if he did those sovereign joys possess
Which do at once confirm, stir up, inflame
And perfect angels – having not the same!
It doth increase the value of his deeds;
In this a man a Seraphim exceeds.

   To act on obligations yet unknown,
To act upon rewards as yet unshown,
To keep commands whose beauty's yet unseen,
To cherish and retain a zeal between
Sleeping and waking, shows a constant care;
And that a deeper love, a love so rare
That no eye-service may with it compare.

   The angels, who are faithful while they view
His glory, know not what themselves would do,
Were they in our estate! A dimmer light
Perhaps would make them err as well as we;
And in the coldness of a darker night
Forgetful and lukewarm themselves might be.
Our very rust shall cover us with gold,
Our dust shall sparkle while their eyes behold
The glory springing from a feeble state,
Where mere belief doth, if not conquer fate,
Surmount, and pass what it doth antedate.

Psalm 51

MILES COVERDALE

1. Have mercy upon me, O God, after thy great goodness: according to the multitude of thy mercies do away my offences.

2. Wash me thoroughly from my wickedness: and cleanse me from my sin.

3. For I acknowledge my faults: and my sin is ever before me.

4. Against thee only have I sinned, and done this evil in thy sight: that thou mightest be justified, and clear when thou art judged.

5. Behold, I was shapen in wickedness: and in sin hath my mother conceived me.

6. But lo, thou requirest truth in the inward parts: and shalt make me to understand wisdom secretly.

7. Thou shalt purge me with hyssop, and I shall be clean: thou shalt wash me, and I shall be whiter than snow.

8. Thou shalt make me hear of joy and gladness: that the bones which thou hast broken may rejoice.

9. Turn thy face from my sins: and put out all my misdeeds.

10. Make me a clean heart, O God: and renew a right spirit within me.

11. Cast me not away from thy presence: and take not thy holy Spirit from me.

12. O give me the comfort of thy help again: and stablish me with thy free Spirit.

13. Then shall I teach thy ways unto the wicked: and sinners shall be converted unto thee.

14. Deliver me from blood-guiltiness, O God, thou that art the God of my health: and my tongue shall sing of thy righteousness.

15 Thou shalt open my lips, O Lord: and my mouth shall shew thy praise.

16 For thou desirest no sacrifice, else would I give it thee: but thou delightest not in burnt-offerings.

17 The sacrifice of God is a troubled spirit: a broken and contrite heart, O God, shalt thou not despise.

18 O be favourable and gracious unto Sion: build thou the walls of Jerusalem.

19 Then shalt thou be pleased with the sacrifice of righteousness, with the burnt-offerings and oblations: then shall they offer young bullocks upon thine altar.

Psalm 139

MARY HERBERT, COUNTESS OF PEMBROKE

O Lord in me there lieth nought
  But to thy search revealèd lies:
    For when I sit
    Thou markest it;
  No less thou notest when I rise.
Yea, closest closet of my thought
  Hath open windows to thine eyes.

Thou walkest with me when I walk;
  When to my bed for rest I go,
    I find thee there,
    And ev'rywhere;
  Not youngest thought in me doth grow,
No, not one word I cast to talk,
  But yet unuttered thou dost know.

If forth I march, thou goest before,
  If back I turn, thou com'st behind;
    So forth nor back
    Thy guard I lack,
  Nay on me too thy hand I find.
Well I thy wisdom may adore,
  But never reach with earthy mind.

To shun thy notice, leave thine eye,
  O whither might I take my way?
    To starry sphere?
    Thy throne is there.

To dead men's undelightsome stay?
There is thy walk, and there to lie
    Unknown in vain I should assay.

O Sun, whom light nor flight can match,
    Suppose thy lightful, flightful wings
        Thou lend to me,
        And I could flee
    As far as thee the ev'ning brings,
Ev'n led to West he would me catch
    Nor should I lurk with western things.

Do thou thy best, O secret night,
    In sable veil to cover me,
        Thy sable veil
        Shall vainly fail;
    With day unmask'd my night shall be,
For night is day, and darkness light,
    O father of all lights, to thee.

Each inmost piece in me is thine:
    While yet I in my mother dwelt,
        All that me clad
        From thee I had.
    Thou in my fame hast strangely dealt;
Needs in my praise thy works must shine,
    So inly them my thoughts have felt.

Thou, how my back was beam-wise laid
    And raft'ring of my ribs, dost know;
        Know'st ev'ry point
        Of bone and joint,
    How to this whole these parts did grow,
In brave embroid'ry fair array'd
    Though wrought in shop both dark and low.

Nay, fashionless, ere form I took,
  Thy all-and-more beholding eye
    My shapeless shape
    Could not escape;
  All these, time-framed successively
Ere one had being, in the book
  Of thy foresight enroll'd did lie.

My God, how I these studies prize
  That do thy hidden workings show!
    Whose sum is such
    No sum so much,
  Nay, summ'd as sand, they sumless grow.
I lie to sleep, from sleep I rise,
  Yet still in thought with thee I go.

My God, if thou but one wouldst kill,
  Then straight would leave my further chase
    This cursèd brood
    Inur'd to blood
  Whose graceles taunts at thy disgrace
Have aimèd oft, and, hating still,
  Would with proud lies thy truth outface.

Hate not I them, who thee do hate?
  Thine, Lord, I will the censure be.
    Detest I not
    The cankered knot
  Whom I against thee banded see?
O Lord, thou know'st in highest rate
  I hate them all as foes to me.

Search me, my God, and prove my heart,
  Examine me, and try my thought;
    And mark in me

If aught there be
That hath with cause their anger wrought.
If not (as not) my life's each part,
Lord, safely guide from danger brought.

Confession

GEORGE HERBERT

O what a cunning guest
Is this same grief! within my heart I made
    Closets; and in them many a chest;
    And like a master in my trade,
In those chests, boxes; in each box, a till:[1]
Yet grief knows all, and enters when he will.

    No screw, no piercer can
Into a piece of timber work and wind,
    As God's afflictions into man,
    When he a torture hath design'd.
They are too subtle for the subtlest hearts;
And fall, like rheums,[2] upon the tendrest parts.

    We are the earth; and they,
Like moles within us, heave, and cast about:
    And till they foot[3] and clutch their prey,
    They never cool, much less give out,
No smith can make such locks, but they have keys:
Closets are halls to them; and hearts, high-ways.

    Only an open breast
Doth shut them out, so that they cannot enter;
    Or, if they enter, cannot rest,
    But quickly seek some new adventure.

[1] till: casket within larger box for safekeeping of valuables.
[2] rheums: rheumatic pains.
[3] foot: seize with talons.

Smooth open hearts no fastning have; but fiction
Doth give a hold and handle to affliction.

   Wherefore my faults and sins,
Lord, I acknowledge; take thy plagues away:
  For since confession pardon wins,
   I challenge here the brightest day,
The clearest diamond: let them do their best,
They shall be thick and cloudy to[1] my breast.

[1] to: compared to.

The Man of Life Upright

THOMAS CAMPION

The man of life upright,
   Whose guiltless heart is free
From all dishonest deeds
   And thought of vanity:

The man whose silent days
   In harmless joys are spent,
Whom hopes cannot delude
   Nor sorrow discontent:

That man needs neither towers
   Nor armour for defence,
Nor secret vaults to fly
   From thunder's violence.

He only can behold
   With unaffrighted eyes
The horrors of the deep
   And terrors of the skies.

Thus scorning all the cares
   That fate or fortune brings,
He makes the heaven his book,
   His wisdom heavenly things,

Good thoughts his only friends,
   His wealth a well-spent age,
The earth his sober inn
   And quiet pilgrimage.

The Character of a Happy Life

SIR HENRY WOTTON

How happy is he born or taught,
That serveth not another's will;
Whose armour is his honest thought,
And simple truth his highest skill;

Whose passions not his masters are;
Whose soul is still prepared for death,
Untied unto the world with care
Of princes' grace or vulgar breath;

Who envies none whom chance doth raise,
Or vice; who never understood
The deepest wounds are given by praise,
By rule of state, but not of good;

Who hath his life from rumours freed;
Whose conscience is his strong retreat;
Whose state can neither flatterers feed,
Nor ruin make accusers great;

Who God doth late and early pray,
More of his grace than goods to send,
And entertains the harmless day
With a well-chosen book or friend, –

This man is free from servile bands
Of hope to rise or fear to fall;
Lord of himself, though not of lands;
And having nothing, yet hath all.

Life Encompassed

DONALD DAVIE

How often I have said,
'This will never do,'
Of ways of feeling that now
I trust in, and pursue!

Do traverses tramped in the past,
My own, criss-crossed as I forge
Across from another quarter
Speak of a life encompassed?

Well, life is not research.
No one asks you to map the terrain,
Only to get across it
In new ways, time and again.

How many such, even now,
I dismiss out of hand
As not to my purpose, not
Unknown, just unexamined.

Ethics

C. K. WILLIAMS

The only time, I swear, I ever fell more than abstractly in
    love with someone else's wife,
I managed to maintain the clearest sense of innocence, even
    after the woman returned my love,
even after she'd left her husband and come down on the
    plane from Montreal to be with me,
I still felt I'd done nothing immoral, that whole disturbing
    category had somehow been effaced;
even after she'd arrived and we'd gone home and gone to
    bed, and even after, the next morning,
when she crossed my room undressed – I almost looked
    away; we were both as shy as adolescents –
and all that next day when we walked, made love again,
    then slept, clinging to each other,
even then, her sleeping hand softly on my chest, her gentle
    breath gently moving on my cheek,
even then, or not until then, not until the new day touched
    upon us, and I knew, knew absolutely,
that though we might love each other, something in her had
    to have the husband, too,
and though she'd tried, and would keep trying to overcome
    herself, I couldn't wait for her,
did that perfect guiltlessness, that sure conviction of my
    inviolable virtue, flee me,
to leave me with a blade of loathing for myself, a disgust
    with who I guessed by now I was,
but even then, when I took her to the airport and she started
    up that corridor the other way,

and we waved, just waved – anybody watching would have
thought that we were separating friends –
even then, one part of my identity kept claiming its integrity,
its non-involvement, even chastity,
which is what I castigate myself again for now, not the
husband or his pain, which he survived,
nor the wife's temptation, but the thrill of evil that I'd felt,
then kept myself from feeling.

Address to the Unco Guid,

Or the rigidly righteous

My son, these maxims make a rule,
And lump them ay thegither;[1]
The Rigid Righteous *is a fool,*
The Rigid Wise *anither:*
The cleanest corn that e'er was dight[2]
May hae some pyles o' caff[3] in;
So ne'er a fellow-creature slight
For random fits o' daffin.[4]

SOLOMON – *Ecclesiastes* 7:16
ROBERT BURNS

O ye wha are sae guid[5] yoursel,
  Sae pious and sae holy,
Ye've nought to do but mark and tell
  Your Neebours' fauts[6] and folly!
Whase life is like a weel-gaun[7] mill,
  Supply'd wi' store o' water,
The heapet happer's[8] ebbing still,
  An' still the clap plays clatter.

Hear me, ye venerable Core,[9]

[1] thegither: together.
[2] dight: sifted.
[3] caff: chaff.
[4] daffin: larking.
[5] guid: good.
[6] fauts: faults.
[7] weel-gaun: well-going.
[8] happer: hopper.
[9] Core: company.

As counsel for poor mortals,
That frequent pass douce[1] Wisdom's door
   For glaikit[2] Folly's portals;
I, for their thoughtless, careless sakes,
   Would here propone[3] defences,
Their donsie[4] tricks, their black mistakes,
   Their failings and mischances.

Ye see your state wi' theirs compar'd,
   And shudder at the niffer,[5]
But cast a moment's fair regard,
   What maks the mighty differ;
Discount what scant occasion gave,
   That purity ye pride in,
And (what's aft mair than a' the lave)[6]
   Your better art o' hiding.

Think, when your castigated pulse
   Gies now and then a wallop,
What ragings must his veins convulse,
   That still eternal gallop:
Wi' wind and tide fair i' your tail,
   Right on ye scud your sea-way;
But in the teeth o' baith to sail,
   It maks an unco leeway.

See Social-life and Glee sit down,
   All joyous and unthinking,
Till, quite transmugrify'd, they're grown
   Debauchery and Drinking:

[1] douce: sober.
[2] glaikit: giddy.
[3] propone: put forward.
[4] donsie: unlucky.
[5] niffer: exchange.
[6] lave: rest.

O would they stay to calculate
  Th' eternal consequences;
Or your more dreaded hell to state,
  Damnation of expences!

Ye high, exalted, virtuous Dames,
  Ty'd up in godly laces,
Before ye gie poor Frailty names,
  Suppose a change o' cases;
A dear-lov'd lad, convenience snug,
  A treacherous inclination –
But, let me whisper i' your lug,[1]
  Ye're aiblins[2] nae temptation.

Then gently scan your brother Man,
  Still gentler sister Woman;
Tho' they may gang a kennin[3] wrang,
  To step aside is human:
One point must still be greatly dark,
  The moving *Why* they do it;
And just as lamely can ye mark,
  How far perhaps they rue it.

Who made the heart, 'tis *He* alone
  Decidedly can try us,
He knows each chord its various tone,
  Each spring its various bias:
Then at the balance let's be mute,
  We never can adjust it;
What's *done* we partly may compute,
  But know not what's *resisted*.

---

[1] lug: ear.
[2] aiblins: maybe.
[3] kennin: little.

from *An Epistle Answering to One that Asked to be Sealed of the Tribe of Ben*

BEN JONSON

Men that are safe, and sure, in all they do,
   Care not what trials they are put unto;
They meet the fire, the test, as Martyrs would;
   And though Opinion stamp them not, are gold.
I could say more of such, but that I flee
   To speak my self out too ambitiously,
And showing so weak an act to vulgar eyes,
   Put conscience and my right, to compromise.
Let those that merely talk, and never think,
   That live in the wild anarchy of drink,
Subject to quarrel only; or else such
   As make it their proficiency, how much
They 'ave glutted in, and lecher'd out, that week,
   That never yet did friend, or friendship, seek
But for a Sealing: let these men protest.
   Or th' other on their borders, that will jest
On all souls that are absent; even the dead;
   Like flies, or worms, which man's corrupt parts fed:
That to speak well, think it above all sin,
   Of any company but that they are in,
Call every night to supper in these fits,
   And are received for the covey of Wits;
That censure all the town, and all th' affairs,
   And know whose ignorance is more than theirs;
Let these men have their ways, and take their times
   To vent their libels, and to issue rhymes,
I have no portion in them, nor their deal

Of news they get, to strew out their long meal;
I study other friendships, and more one,
    Than these can ever be; or else wish none ...
    Well, with mine own frail Pitcher, what to do
I have decreed: keep it from waves and press,
    Lest it be justled, crack'd, made nought, or less:
Live to that point I will, for which I am man,
    And dwell as in my Centre, as I can,
Still looking to, and ever loving heaven;
    With reverence using all the gifts thence given.
'Mongst which, if I have any friendships sent,
    Such as are square, well-tagg'd, and permanent,
Not built with canvas, paper, and false lights,
    As are the glorious scenes, at the great sights;
And that there be no fevery heats, nor colds,
    Oily expansions, or shrunk dirty folds,
But all so clear, and led by reason's flame
    As but to stumble in her sight were shame;
These will I honour, love, embrace, and serve:
    And free it from all question to preserve.
So short you read my character, and theirs
    I would call mine, to which not many stairs
Are asked to climb. First give me faith, who know
    My self a little. I will take you so,
As you have writ your self. Now stand, and then,
    Sir, you are Sealed of the Tribe of *Ben*.

The Shepherd Boy Sings in the Valley of Humiliation

JOHN BUNYAN

He that is down needs fear no fall,
  He that is low, no pride;
He that is humble ever shall
  Have God to be his guide.

I am content with what I have,
  Little be it or much:
And, Lord, contentment still I crave,
  Because Thou savest such.

Fullness to such a burden is
  That go on pilgrimage:
Here little, and hereafter bliss,
  Is best from age to age.

Lord, when the wise men came from far

SIDNEY GODOLPHIN

Lord, when the wise men came from far,
Led to thy cradle by a star,
Then did the shepherds too rejoice,
Instructed by thy angels' voice;
Blest were the wise men in their skill,
And shepherds in their harmless will.

Wise men in tracing nature's laws
Ascend unto the highest cause;
Shepherds with humble fearfulness
Walk safely, though their light be less;
Though wise men better know the way,
It seems no honest heart can stray.

There is no merit in the wise
But love (the shepherds' sacrifice).
Wise men, all ways of knowledge past,
To th' shepherds' wonder come at last;
To know, can only wonder breed,
And not to know, is wonder's seed.

A wise man at the altar bows
And offers up his studied vows
And is received; may not the tears
Which spring too from a shepherd's fears,
And sighs upon his frailty spent,
Though not distinct, be eloquent?

'Tis true, the object sanctifies
All passions which within us rise;
But since no creature comprehends
The cause of causes, end of ends,
He who himself vouchsafes to know
Best pleases his creator so.

When then our sorrows we apply
To our own wants and poverty,
When we look up in all distress
And our own misery confess,
Sending both thanks and prayers above,
Then though we do not know, we love.

Affliction (i)

GEORGE HERBERT

When first thou didst entice to thee my heart,
                    I thought the service brave.[1]
So many joys I writ down for my part,
                    Besides what I might have
Out of my stock of natural delights,
Augmented with thy gracious benefits.

I looked on thy furniture so fine,
                    And made it fine to me:
Thy glorious household-stuff did me entwine,
                    And 'tice me unto thee.
Such stars I counted mine: both heav'n and earth
Paid me my wages in a world of mirth.

What pleasures could I want, whose King I served?
                    Where joys my fellows were?
Thus argu'd into hopes, my thoughts reserved
                    No place for grief or fear.
Therefore my sudden soul caught at the place,
And made her youth and fierceness seek thy face.

At first thou gav'st me milk and sweetnesses;
                    I had my wish and way:
My days were straw'd with flow'rs and happiness;
                    There was no month but May.

[1] brave: fine, splendid.

But with my years sorrow did twist and grow,
And made a party unawares for woe.

My flesh began unto my soul in pain,
                    Sicknesses cleave my bones;
Consuming agues dwell in ev'ry vein,
                    And tune my breath to groans.
Sorrow was all my soul; I scarce believed,
Till grief did tell me roundly, that I lived.

When I got health, thou took'st away my life,
                    And more; for my friends[1] die:
My mirth and edge was lost; a blunted knife
                    Was of more use than I.
Thus thin and lean without a fence or friend,
I was blown through with ev'ry storm and wind.

Whereas my birth and spirit rather took
                    The way that takes the town;
Thou didst betray me to a lingring book,
                    And wrap me in a gown.
I was entangled in the world of strife,
Before I had the power to change my life.

Yet, for I threatned oft the siege to raise,
                    Not simpring all mine age,
Thou often didst with Academic praise
                    Melt and dissolve my rage.
I took thy sweetned pill, till I came where
I could not go away, nor persevere.

Yet lest perchance I should too happy be
                    In my unhappiness,

[1] Including Herbert's patrons at court: it is said that Herbert was an ambitious man.

Turning my purge to food, thou throwest me
                Into more sicknesses.
Thus doth thy power cross-bias[1] me, not making
Thine own gift good, yet me from my ways taking.

Now I am here, what thou wilt do with me
                None of my books will show:
I read, and sigh, and wish I were a tree;
                For sure I then should grow
To fruit or shade: at least some bird would trust
Her household to me, and I should be just.

Yet, though thou troublest me, I must be meek;
                In weakness must be stout.
Well, I will change the service, and go seek
                Some other master out.
Ah my dear God! though I am clean forgot,
Let me not love thee, if I love thee not.

[1] cross-bias: from bowls, deflecting from course.

To Heaven

BEN JONSON

Good and great God, can I not think of thee
 But it must, straight, my melancholy be?
Is it interpreted in me disease
 That, laden with my sins, I seek for ease?
O be thou witness, that the reins[1] dost know
 And hearts of all, if I be sad for show,
And judge me after, if I dare pretend
 To aught but grace, or aim at other end.
As thou art all, so be thou all to me,
 First, midst, and last, converted, one and three;
My faith, my hope, my love; and in this state
 My judge, my witness, and my advocate.
Where have I been this while exil'd from thee,
 And whither rap'd, now thou but stoop'st to me?
Dwell, dwell here still. O, being everywhere,
 How can I doubt to find thee ever, here?
I know my state, both full of shame and scorn,
 Conceiv'd in sin, and unto labour born,
Standing with fear, and must with horror fall,
 And destin'd unto judgement, after all.
I feel my griefs too, and there scarce is ground
 Upon my flesh t'inflict another wound.
Yet dare I not complain, or wish for death
 With holy PAUL, lest it be thought the breath
Of discontent; or that these prayers be
 For weariness of life, not love of thee.

---

[1] reins: literally, kidneys but here seat of the feelings.

Light Shining Out of Darkness

WILLIAM COWPER

God moves in a mysterious way,
  His wonders to perform;
He plants his footsteps in the sea,
  And rides upon the storm.

Deep in unfathomable mines
  Of never failing skill,
He treasures up his bright designs,
  And works his sovereign will.

Ye fearful saints fresh courage take,
  The clouds ye so much dread
Are big with mercy, and shall break
  In blessings on your head.

Judge not the Lord by feeble sense,
  But trust him for his grace;
Behind a frowning providence,
  He hides a smiling face.

His purposes will ripen fast,
  Unfolding ev'ry hour;
The bud may have a bitter taste,
  But sweet will be the flow'r.

Blind unbelief is sure to err,
  And scan his work in vain;
God is his own interpreter,
  And he will make it plain.

Part Five

END

What is the price of Experience? do men buy it
for a song
Or wisdom for a dance in the street? No it is
bought with the price
Of all that a man hath, his house his wife his
children.
Wisdom is sold in the desolate market where
none comes to buy
And in the withered field where the farmer
plows for bread in vain.

William Blake, *The Four Zoas* ('Night the
Second')

I

Time

These are the arks, the trophies I erect,
That fortify thy name against old age;
And these thy sacred virtues must protect
Against the dark, and Time's consuming rage.

Samuel Daniel, 'Let others sing of knights and
pallatines'

The Minute before Meeting

THOMAS HARDY

The grey gaunt days dividing us in twain
Seemed hopeless hills my strength must faint to climb,
But they are gone; and now I would detain
The few clock-beats that part us; rein back Time,

And live in close expectance never closed
In change for far expectance closed at last,
So harshly has expectance been imposed
On my long need while these slow blank months passed.

And knowing that what is now about to be
Will all *have been* in O, so short a space!
I read beyond it my despondency
When more dividing months shall take its place,
Thereby denying to this hour of grace
A full-up measure of felicity.

The Poplar-Field

WILLIAM COWPER

The poplars are felled, farewell to the shade
And the whispering sound of the cool colonnade,
The winds play no longer, and sing in the leaves,
Nor Ouse on his bosom their image receives.

Twelve years have elapsed since I last took a view
Of my favourite field and the bank where they grew,
And now in the grass behold they are laid,
And the tree is my seat that once lent me a shade.

The blackbird has fled to another retreat
Where the hazels afford him a screen from the heat,
And the scene where his melody charmed me before,
Resounds with his sweet-flowing ditty no more.

My fugitive years are all hasting away,
And I must ere long lie as lowly as they,
With a turf on my breast, and a stone at my head,
Ere another such grove shall arise in its stead.

'Tis a sight to engage me, if any thing can,
To muse on the perishing pleasures of man;
Though his life be a dream, his enjoyments, I see,
Have a being less durable even than he.

Love and Life

JOHN WILMOT, EARL OF ROCHESTER

All my past life is mine no more;
  The flying hours are gone,
Like transitory dreams given o'er
Whose images are kept in store
  By memory alone.

Whatever is to come is not:
  How can it then be mine?
The present moment's all my lot,
And that, as fast as it is got,
  Phyllis, is wholly thine.

Then talk not of inconstancy,
  False hearts, and broken vows;
If I, by miracle, can be
This livelong minute true to thee,
  'Tis all that heaven allows.

They say that Hope is happiness

LORD BYRON

They say that Hope is happiness;
   But genuine Love must prize the past,
And Memory wakes the thoughts that bless:
   They rose the first – they set the last;

And all that Memory loves the most
   Was once our only Hope to be,
And all that Hope adored and lost
   Hath melted into Memory.

Alas! it is delusion all;
   The future cheats us from afar,
Nor can we be what we recall,
   Nor dare we think on what we are.

Fragment: Home

PERCY BYSSHE SHELLEY

Dear home, thou scene of earliest hopes and joys,
The least of which wronged Memory ever makes
Bitterer than all thine unremembered tears.

Domestic Peace

ANNE BRONTË

Why should such gloomy silence reign,
   And why is all the house so drear,
When neither danger, sickness, pain,
   Nor death, nor want, has entered here?

We are as many as we were
   That other night, when all were gay
And full of hope, and free from care;
   Yet is there something gone away.

The moon without, as pure and calm,
   Is shining as that night she shone;
But now, to us, she brings no balm,
   For something from our hearts is gone.

Something whose absence leaves a void –
   A cheerless want in every heart;
Each feels the bliss of all destroyed,
   And mourns the change – but each apart.

The fire is burning in the grate
   As redly as it used to burn;
But still the hearth is desolate,
   Till mirth, and love, with *peace* return.

'Twas *peace* that flowed from heart to heart,
   With looks and smiles that spoke of heaven,

And gave us language to impart
   The blissful thoughts itself had given.

Domestic peace – best joy of earth!
   When shall we all thy value learn?
White angel, to our sorrowing hearth,
   Return, – oh, graciously return!

Surprised by Joy – Impatient as the Wind

WILLIAM WORDSWORTH

Surprised by joy – impatient as the Wind
I turned to share the transport – Oh! with whom
But Thee,[1] deep buried in the silent tomb,
That spot which no vicissitude can find?
Love, faithful love, recalled thee to my mind –
But how could I forget thee? Through what power,
Even for the least division of an hour,
Have I been so beguiled as to be blind
To my most grievous loss! – That thought's return
Was the worst pang that sorrow ever bore,
Save one, one only, when I stood forlorn,
Knowing my heart's best treasure was no more;
That neither present time, nor years unborn
Could to my sight that heavenly face restore.

[1] The poet's daughter, Catherine, died on 4 June 1812 at the age of three; this poem was written some time between 1813 and 1814.

Your Last Drive[1]

THOMAS HARDY

Here by the moorway you returned,
And saw the borough lights ahead
That lit your face – all undiscerned
To be in a week the face of the dead,
And you told of the charm of that haloed view
That never again would beam on you.

And on your left you passed the spot
Where eight days later you were to lie,
And be spoken of as one who was not;
Beholding it with a heedless eye
As alien from you, though under its tree
You soon would halt everlastingly.

I drove not with you.... Yet had I sat
At your side that eve I should not have seen
That the countenance I was glancing at
Had a last-time look in the flickering sheen,
Nor have read the writing upon your face,
'I go hence soon to my resting-place;

'You may miss me then. But I shall not know
How many times you visit me there,
Or what your thoughts are, or if you go
There never at all. And I shall not care.

---

[1] This poem, 'At Castle Boterel' and 'After a Journey' are part of
the sequence 'Poems of 1912–13', on the death of Hardy's wife,
Emma.

Should you censure me I shall take no heed,
And even your praises no more shall need.'

True: never you'll know. And you will not mind.
But shall I then slight you because of such?
Dear ghost, in the past did you ever find
The thought 'What profit,' move me much?
Yet abides the fact, indeed, the same, –
You are past love, praise, indifference, blame.

At Castle Boterel

THOMAS HARDY

As I drive to the junction of lane and highway,
  And the drizzle bedrenches the waggonette,
I look behind at the fading byway,
  And see on its slope, now glistening wet,
     Distinctly yet

Myself and a girlish form benighted
  In dry March weather. We climb the road
Beside a chaise. We had just alighted
  To ease the sturdy pony's load
     When he sighed and slowed.

What we did as we climbed, and what we talked of
  Matters not much, nor to what it led, –
Something that life will not be balked of
  Without rude reason till hope is dead,
     And feeling fled.

It filled but a minute. But was there ever
  A time of such quality, since or before,
In that hill's story? To one mind never,
  Though it has been climbed, foot-swift, foot-sore,
     By thousands more.

Primaeval rocks form the road's steep border,
  And much have they faced there, first and last,
Of the transitory in Earth's long order;

But what they record in colour and cast
    Is – that we two passed.

And to me, though Time's unflinching rigour,
    In mindless rote, has ruled from sight
The substance now, one phantom figure
    Remains on the slope, as when that night
        Saw us alight.

I look and see it there, shrinking, shrinking,
    I look back at it amid the rain
For the very last time; for my sand is sinking,
    And I shall traverse old love's domain
        Never again.

Joy Passing By

WILLIAM BARNES

When ice all melted to the sun,
And left the wavy streams to run,
We longed, as summer came, to roll
In river foam, o'er depth and shoal;
And if we lost our loose-bow'd swing,
We had a kite to pull our string;
      Or, if no ball
      Would rise or fall
With us, another joy was nigh
Before our joy all pass'd us by.

If leaves of trees, that wind stripp'd bare
At morning, fly on evening air,
We still look on for summer boughs
To shade again our sunburnt brows;
Where orchard-blooms' white scales may fall
May hang the apple's blushing ball;
      New hopes come on
      For old ones gone,
As day on day may shine on high,
Until our joys all pass us by.

My childhood yearn'd to reach the span
Of boyhood's life, and be a man;
And then I look'd, in manhood's pride,
For manhood's sweetest choice, a bride;
And then to lovely children, come
To make my home a dearer home.

But now my mind
Can look behind
For joy, and wonder, with a sigh,
When all my joys have pass'd me by!

Was it when once I miss'd a call
To rise, and thenceforth seem'd to fall;
Or when my wife to my hands left
Her few bright keys, a doleful heft;[1]
Or when before the door I stood
To watch a child away for good;
Or where some crowd
In mirth was loud;
Or where I saw a mourner sigh;
Where did my joy all pass me by?

[1] heft: weight.

The Widow to her Hour Glass

ROBERT BLOOMFIELD

Come, friend, I'll turn thee up again:
Companion of the lonely hour!
Spring thirty times hath fed with rain
And cloth'd with leaves my humble bower,
  Since thou hast stood
  In frame of wood,
Or chest or window by my side:
At every birth still thou wert near,
Still spoke thine admonitions clear,
  And, when mine husband died.

I've often watch'd thy streaming sand,
And seen the growing mountain rise,
And often found Life's hopes to stand
On props as weak in Wisdom's eyes:
  Its conic crown
  Still sliding down,
Again heap'd up, then down again;
The sand above more hollow grew,
Like days and years still filt'ring through,
  And mingling joy and pain.

While thus I spin, and sometimes sing,
(For now and then my heart will glow)
Thou measur'st Time's expanding wing:
By thee the noontide hour I know:
  Though silent thou,
  Still shalt thou flow,

And jog along thy destin'd way:
But when I glean the sultry fields,
When earth her yellow harvest yields,
　　Thou gett'st a holiday.

Steady as truth, on either end
Thy daily task performing well,
Thou'rt meditation's constant friend,
And strik'st the heart without a bell:
　　Come, lovely May!
　　Thy lengthen'd day
Shall gild once more my native plain;
Curl inward here, sweet woodbine flow'r;
'Companion of the lonely hour,
　　I'll turn thee up again.'

The Aged Lover Renounceth Love

THOMAS, LORD VAUX

I loathe that I did love,
  In youth that I thought sweet,
As time requires for my behove,
  Methinks they are not meet.

My lusts they do me leave,
  My fancies all be fled,
And tract of time begins to weave
  Grey hairs upon my head.

For age with stealing steps
  Hath clawed me with his crutch,
And lusty life away she leaps
  As there had been none such.

My Muse doth not delight
  Me as she did before;
My hand and pen are not in plight,
  As they have been of yore.

For reason me denies
  This youthly idle rhyme;
And day by day to me she cries,
  'Leave off these toys in time.'

The wrinkles in my brow,
  The furrows in my face,

Say, limping age will lodge him now
  Where youth must give him place.

The harbinger of death,
  To me I see him ride,
The cough, the cold, the gasping breath
  Doth bid me to provide

A pickaxe and a spade,
  And eke a shrouding sheet,
A horse of clay for to be made
  For such a guest most meet.

Methinks I hear the clark
  That knolls the careful knell,
And bids me leave my woeful wark,
  Ere nature me compel.

My keepers knit the knot
  That youth did laugh to scorn,
Of me that clean shall be forgot
  As I had not been born.

Thus must I youth give up,
  Whose badge I long did wear;
To them I yield the wanton cup
  That better may it bear.

Lo, here the barëd skull,
  By whose bald sign I know
That stooping age away shall pull
  Which youthful years did sow.

For beauty with her band
  These crooked cares hath wrought,

And shippëd me into the land
   From whence I first was brought.

And ye that bide behind,
   Have ye none other trust:
As ye of clay were cast by kind,
   So shall ye waste to dust.

I Look Into My Glass

THOMAS HARDY

I look into my glass,
And view my wasting skin,
And say, 'Would God it came to pass
My heart had shrunk as thin!'

For then, I, undistrest
By hearts grown cold to me,
Could lonely wait my endless rest
With equanimity.

But Time, to make me grieve,
Part steals, lets part abide;
And shakes this fragile frame at eve
With throbbings of noontide.

The Forerunners

GEORGE HERBERT

The harbingers[1] are come. See, see their mark;
White is their colour, and behold my head.
But must they have my brain? must they dispark
Those sparkling notions, which therein were bred?
      Must dullness turn me to a clod?
Yet have they left me, *Thou art still my God.*[2]

Good men ye be, to leave me my best room,
Ev'n all my heart, and what is lodged there:
I pass not,[3] I, what of the rest become,
So *Thou art still my God* be out of fear.
      He will be pleased with that ditty;
And if I please him, I write fine and witty.

Farewell sweet phrases, lovely metaphors.
But will ye leave me thus? when ye before
Of stews and brothels only knew the doors,
Then did I wash you with my tears, and more
      Brought you to Church well drest and clad:
My God must have my best, ev'n all I had.

Lovely enchanting language, sugar-cane,
Honey of roses, whither wilt thou fly?
Hath some fond lover 'tic'd thee to thy bane?

---

[1] harbingers: forerunners sent ahead of a royal progress to requisition lodgings by chalking doors.
[2] See Psalms 31:14.
[3] pass not: care not.

And wilt thou leave the Church, and love a sty?
        Fie, thou wilt soil thy broider'd coat,
And hurt thy self, and him that sings the note.

Let foolish lovers, if they will love dung,
With canvas, not with arras clothe their shame:
Let folly speak in her own native tongue.
True beauty dwells on high: ours is a flame
        But borrow'd thence to light us thither.
Beauty and beauteous words should go together.

Yet if you go, I pass not; take your way:
For *Thou art still my God* is all that ye
Perhaps with more embellishment can say.
Go birds of spring: let winter have his fee,
        Let a bleak paleness chalk the door,
So all within be livelier than before.

The Forgiven Past

LAURA RIDING

That once which pained to think of,
Like a promise to oneself not kept
Nor keepable, now is grown mild.
The thistle-patch of memory
Claims our confiding touch;
The naked spurs do not draw blood,
Yielding to stoic pressure
With awkward flexibility.

We are glad it happened so
Which long seemed traitorous to hope,
False to the destined Otherwise;
Since by those failures-of-the-time
We learned the skill of failure, time –
Waiting to hold the seal of truth
With a less eager hand,
Sparing the authentic signature
For the most prudent sanctions,
Lest the wax and ink of faith be used
Before to hope's reverses
Succeed the just realities,
And we be spent of welcome
Save for a withered smile.

The transformation of old grief
Into a present grace of mind
Among the early shadows which
The present light inhabit,

As the portentous universe
Now upon earth descends
Timidly, in nostalgic bands
Of elemental trials and errors:
This is how truth is groved,
With wayside nights where sleeping
We wake to tell what once seemed cruel
As dream-dim – in the dream
As plain and sure as then,
In telling no less dark than doubtful.

This is how pleasure relives history,
Like accusation that at last
Settling unrancorous on lies
Gives kinder names to them –
When truth is so familiar
That the false no more than strange is,
Nor wondrous evil strange
But of a beggar's right to tenderness
Whom once in robes of certainty
We stood upon illusion's stage
And then, to expiate our self-deceit,
Sent forth in honesty's ill rags.

Psalm 90

THE BIBLE, AUTHORIZED VERSION

Lord, thou hast been our dwelling place in all generations.
Before the mountains were brought forth, or ever thou
   hadst formed the earth and the world, even from
   everlasting to everlasting, thou art God.
Thou turnest man to destruction; and sayest, Return, ye
   children of men.
For a thousand years in thy sight are but as yesterday
   when it is past, and as a watch in the night.
Thou carriest them away as with a flood; they are *as* a
   sleep: in the morning they are like grass which groweth up.
In the morning it flourisheth, and groweth up; in the
   evening it is cut down, and withereth.
For we are consumed by thine anger, and by thy wrath are
   we troubled.
Thou hast set our iniquities before thee, our secret sins in
   the light of thy countenance.
For all our days are passed away in thy wrath: we spend
   our years as a tale that is told.
The days of our years are threescore years and ten; and if
   by reason of strength they be fourscore years, yet is their
   strength labour and sorrow; for it is soon cut off, and we
   fly away.
Who knoweth the power of thine anger? even according
   to thy fear, so is thy wrath.
So teach us to number our days, that we may apply our
   hearts unto wisdom.
Return, O Lord, how long? and let it repent thee
   concerning thy servants.

O satisfy us early with thy mercy; that we may rejoice
and be glad all our days.

Make us glad according to the days wherein thou hast
afflicted us, and the years wherein we have seen evil.

Let thy work appear unto thy servants, and thy glory
unto their children.

And let the beauty of the Lord our God be upon us: and
establish thou the work of our hands upon us; yea, the
work of our hands establish thou it.

Wait a little!

ANONYMOUS (FOURTEENTH CENTURY)

Loverd, thou clepedest[1] me,
And I nought ne answered thee
But[2] wordės slow and sleepy:
'Tholė[3] yet!! Thole a litel!'
But 'yet' and 'yet' was endėless
And 'thole a litel' a long way is.

[1] clepedest: called.
[2] But: except
[3] Tholė: wait.

2

Death

Man that is born of a woman hath but a short time to live, and is full of misery. He cometh up, and is cut down, like a flower; he fleeth as it were a shadow, and never continueth in one stay. In the midst of life we are in death ...

Book of Common Prayer

In Time of Pestilence

THOMAS NASHE

Adieu, farewell earth's bliss,
This world uncertain is;
Fond are life's lustful joys,
Death proves them all but toys,
None from his darts can fly.
I am sick, I must die.
            Lord, have mercy on us!

Rich men, trust not in wealth,
Gold cannot buy you health;
Physic himself must fade,
All things to end are made.
The plague full swift goes by.
I am sick, I must die.
            Lord, have mercy on us!

Beauty is but a flower
Which wrinkles will devour;
Brightness falls from the air,
Queens have died young and fair,
Dust hath closed Helen's eye.
I am sick, I must die.
            Lord, have mercy on us!

Strength stoops unto the grave,
Worms feed on Hector brave,
Swords may not fight with fate,
Earth still holds ope her gate.

Come! come! the bells do cry.
I am sick, I must die.
    Lord, have mercy on us!

Wit with his wantonness
Tasteth death's bitterness;
Hell's executioner
Hath no ears for to hear
What vain art can reply.
I am sick, I must die.
    Lord, have mercy on us!

Haste, therefore, each degree,
To welcome destiny.
Heaven is our heritage,
Earth but a player's stage;
Mount we unto the sky
I am sick, I must die.
    Lord, have mercy on us!

In Hospital

Vigil

WILLIAM ERNEST HENLEY

Lived on one's back,
In the long hours of repose,
Life is a practical nightmare –
Hideous asleep or awake.

Shoulders and loins
Ache – – – !
Ache, and the mattress,
Run into boulders and hummocks,
Glows like a kiln, while the bedclothes –
Tumbling, importunate, daft –
Ramble and roll, and the gas,
Screwed to its lowermost,
An inevitable atom of light,
Haunts, and a stertorous sleeper
Snores me to hate and despair.

All the old time
Surges malignant before me;
Old voices, old kisses, old songs
Blossom derisive about me;
While the new days
Pass me in endless procession:
A pageant of shadows
Silently, leeringly wending
On ... and still on ... still on!

Far in the stillness a cat
Languishes loudly. A cinder
Falls, and the shadows
Lurch to the leap of the flame. The next man to me
Turns with a moan; and the snorer,
The drug like a rope at his throat,
Gasps, gurgles, snorts himself free, as the night-nurse,
Noiseless and strange,
Her bull's eye half-lanterned in apron
(Whispering me, 'Are ye no sleepin' yet?'),
Passes, list-slippered and peering,
Round ... and is gone.

Sleep comes at last –
Sleep full of dreams and misgivings –
Broken with brutal and sordid
Voices and sounds that impose on me,
Ere I can wake to it,
The unnatural, intolerable day.

What the Doctor Said

RAYMOND CARVER

He said it doesn't look good
he said it looks bad in fact real bad
he said I counted thirty-two of them on one lung before
I quit counting them
I said I'm glad I wouldn't want to know
about any more being there than that
he said are you a religious man do you kneel down
in forest groves and let yourself ask for help
when you come to a waterfall
mist blowing against your face and arms
do you stop and ask for understanding at those moments
I said not yet but I intend to start today
he said I'm real sorry he said
I wish I had some other kind of news to give you
I said Amen and he said something else
I didn't catch and not knowing what else to do
and not wanting him to have to repeat it
and me to have to fully digest it
I just looked at him
for a minute and he looked back it was then
I jumped up and shook hands with this man who'd just
    given me
something no one else on earth had ever given me
I may even have thanked him habit being so strong

The Dying Animals

GAVIN EWART

The animals that look at us like children
in innocence, in perfect innocence!
The innocence that looks at us! Like children
the animals, the simple animals,
have no idea why legs no longer work.

The food that is refused, the love of sleeping –
in innocence, in childhood innocence
there is a parallel of love. Of sleeping
they're never tired, the dying animals;
sick children too, whose play to them is work.

The animals are little children dying,
brash tigers, household pets – all innocence,
the flames that lit their eyes are also dying,
the animals, the simple animals,
die easily; but hard for us, like work!

On the Death of Mr Robert Levet

A Practiser in Physic

SAMUEL JOHNSON

Condemned to Hope's delusive mine,
   As on we toil from day to day,
By sudden blasts, or slow decline,
   Our social comforts drop away.

Well tried through many a varying year,
   See Levet to the grave descend;
Officious, innocent, sincere,
   Of every friendless name the friend.

Yet still he fills affection's eye,
   Obscurely wise, and coarsely kind;
Nor, lettered arrogance, deny
   Thy praise to merit unrefined.

When fainting nature called for aid,
   And hovering death prepared the blow,
His vigorous remedy displayed
   The power of art without the show.

In misery's darkest caverns known,
   His useful care was ever nigh,
Where hopeless anguish poured his groan,
   And lonely want retired to die.

No summons mocked by chill delay,
   No petty gain disdained by pride,

The modest wants of every day
    The toil of every day supplied.

His virtues walked their narrow round,
    Nor made a pause, nor left a void;
And sure the Eternal Master found
    The single talent well employed.

The busy day, the peaceful night,
    Unfelt, uncounted, glided by;
His frame was firm, his powers were bright,
    Though now his eightieth year was nigh.

Then with no fiery throbbing pain,
    No cold gradations of decay,
Death broke at once the vital chain,
    And forc'd his soul the nearest way.[1]

[1] First printed version of poem from *The Gentleman's Magazine*
August 1783; most editions now print 'freed' for 'forc'd' – but
Johnson also feared death.

She dwelt among the untrodden ways

WILLIAM WORDSWORTH

She dwelt among the untrodden ways
   Beside the springs of Dove,
A Maid whom there were none to praise
   And very few to love:

A violet by a mossy stone
   Half hidden from the eye!
— Fair as a star, when only one
   Is shining in the sky.

She lived unknown, and few could know
   When Lucy ceased to be;
But she is in her grave, and, oh,
   The difference to me!

Silence, and Stealth of Days

HENRY VAUGHAN

Silence, and stealth of days! 'tis now
        Since thou art gone,
Twelve hundred hours, and not a brow
        But clouds hang on.
As he that in some cave's thick damp
        Locked from the light,
Fixeth a solitary lamp,
        To brave the night
And walking from his sun, when past
        That glimmering ray
Cuts through the heavy mists in haste
        Back to his day,
So o'er fled minutes I retreat
        Unto that hour
Which showed thee last, but did defeat
        Thy light, and power,
I search, and rack my soul to see
        Those beams again,
But nothing but the snuff to me
        Appeareth plain;
That dark, and dead sleeps in its known,
        And common urn,
But those fled to their Maker's throne,
        There shine, and burn;
O could I track them! but souls must
        Track one the other,
And now the spirit, not the dust
        Must be thy brother.

Yet I have one *pearl* by whose light
All things I see,
And in the heart of earth, and night
Find Heaven, and thee.

On the Death of Emily Jane Brontë

CHARLOTTE BRONTË

My darling, thou wilt never know
The grinding agony of woe
   That we have borne for thee.
Thus may we consolation tear
E'en from the depth of our despair
   And wasting misery.

The nightly anguish thou art spared
When all the crushing truth is bared
   To the awakening mind,
When the galled heart is pierced with grief,
Till wildly it implores relief,
   But small relief can find.

Nor know'st thou what it is to lie
Looking forth with streaming eye
   On life's lone wilderness.
'Weary, weary, dark and drear,
How shall I the journey bear,
   The burden and distress?'

Then since thou art spared such pain
We will not wish thee here again;
   He that lives must mourn.
God help us through our misery
And give us rest and joy with thee
   When we reach our bourne!

They are all Gone into the World of Light!

HENRY VAUGHAN

They are all gone into the world of light!
    And I alone sit ling'ring here;
Their very memory is fair and bright,
    And my sad thoughts doth clear.

It glows and glitters in my cloudy breast
    Like stars upon some gloomy grove,
Or those faint beams in which this hill is dressed,
    After the sun's remove.

I see them walking in an air of glory,
    Whose light doth trample on my days:
My days, which are at best but dull and hoary,
    Mere glimmering and decays.

O holy hope! and high humility,
    High as the Heavens above!
These are your walks, and you have showed them me
    To kindle my cold love,

Dear, beauteous death! the jewel of the just,
    Shining nowhere, but in the dark;
What mysteries do lie beyond thy dust;
    Could man outlook that mark!

He that hath found some fledged bird's nest, may know
    At first sight, if the bird be flown;

But what fair well, or grove he sings in now,
     That is to him unknown.

And yet, as Angels in some brighter dreams
     Call to the soul, when man doth sleep:
So some strange thoughts transcend our wonted themes,
     And into glory peep.

If a star were confined into a tomb
     Her captive flames must needs burn there;
But when the hand that locked her up, gives room,
     She'll shine through all the sphere.

O Father of eternal life, and all
     Created glories under thee!
Resume thy spirit from this world of thrall
     Into true liberty.

Either disperse these mists, which blot and fill
     My perspective (still) as they pass,
Or else remove me hence unto that hill,
     Where I shall need no glass.

The Passionate Man's Pilgrimage

supposed to be written by one at the point of death[1]
attributed to SIR WALTER RALEGH

Give me my Scallop shell of quiet,
My staff of Faith to walk upon,
My Scrip of Joy, Immortal diet,
My bottle of salvation:
My Gown of Glory, hope's true gage,
And thus I'll take my pilgrimage.

Blood must be my body's balmer,
No other balm will there be given
Whilst my soul like a white Palmer
Travels to the land of heaven,
Over the silver mountains,
Where spring the Nectar fountains:
And there I'll kiss
The Bowl of bliss,
And drink my eternal fill
On every milken hill.
My soul will be a dry before,
But after, it will ne'er thirst more.

And by the happy blissful way
More peaceful Pilgrims I shall see,
That have shook off their gowns of clay,
And go apparel'd fresh like me.
I'll bring them first

---

[1] Ralegh was under sentence of death from 17 November to 6 December, 1603.

To slake their thirst
And then to taste those Nectar suckets[1]
At the clear wells
Where sweetness dwells,
Drawn up by Saints in Christal buckets.

And when our bottles and all we,
Are filled with immortality:
Then the holy paths we'll travel
Strewed with Rubies thick as gravel,
Ceilings of Diamonds, Sapphire floors,
High walls of Coral and Pearl Bowers.

From thence to heaven's Bribeless hall
Where no corrupted voices brawl,
No Conscience molten into gold,
Nor forg'd accusers bought and sold,
No cause defer'd nor vain spent Journey,
For there Christ is the King's Attorney:
Who pleads for all without degrees,
And he hath Angels, but no fees.

When the grand twelve million Jury
Of our sins with sinful fury,
Gainst our souls' black verdicts give,
Christ pleads his death, and then we live,
Be thou my speaker taintless pleader,
Unblotted Lawyer, true proceeder,
Thou movest salvation even for alms:
Not with a bribed Lawyer's palms.

And this is my eternal plea,
To him that made Heaven, Earth and Sea,

[1] suckets: sweetmeats, usually fruit candied in syrup.

Seeing my flesh must die so soon,
And want a head to dine next noon,
Just at the stroke when my veins start and spread
Set on my soul an everlasting head.
Then am I ready like a palmer fit,
To tread those blest paths which before I writ.

Seneca's Troades, *Act II, Chorus*

JOHN WILMOT, EARL OF ROCHESTER

After death nothing is, and nothing, death:
The utmost limit of a gasp of breath.
Let the ambitious zealot lay aside
His hopes of heaven, whose faith is but his pride;
    Let slavish souls lay by their fear,
    Nor be concerned which way nor where
    After this life they shall be hurled.
Dead, we become the lumber of the world,
And to that mass of matter shall be swept
Where things destroyed with things unborn are kept.
    Devouring time swallows us whole;
Impartial death confounds body and soul.
    For Hell and the foul fiend that rules
    God's everlasting fiery jails
    (Devised by rogues, dreaded by fools),
With his grim, grisly dog that keeps the door,
    Are senseless stories, idle tales,
        Dreams, whimseys, and no more.

Cobwebs

CHRISTINA ROSSETTI

It is a land with neither night nor day,
  Nor heat nor cold, nor any wind nor rain,
  Nor hills nor valleys: but one even plain
Stretches through long unbroken miles away,
While through the sluggish air a twilight grey
  Broodeth: no moons or seasons wax and wane,
  No ebb and flow are there along the main,
No bud-time, no leaf-falling, there for aye: –
No ripple on the sea, no shifting sand,
  No beat of wings to stir the stagnant space:
No pulse of life through all the loveless land
And loveless sea; no trace of days before,
  No guarded home, no toil-won resting-place,
No future hope, no fear for evermore.

Upon the Image of Death
attributed to ROBERT SOUTHWELL

Before my face the picture hangs,
  That daily should put me in mind
Of those cold qualms and bitter pangs,
  That shortly I am like to find:
    But yet, alas, full little I
    Do think hereon, that I must die.

I often look upon a face
  Most ugly, grisly, bare and thin;
I often view the hollow place,
  Where eyes and nose had sometimes been;
    I see the bones across that lie,
    Yet little think that I must die.

I read the label underneath,
  That telleth me whereto I must;
I see the sentence eke[1] that saith
  'Remember, man, that thou art dust!'
    But yet, alas, but seldom I
    Do think indeed that I must die.

Continually at my bed's head
  A hearse doth hang, which doth me tell,
That I ere morning may be dead,
  Though now I feel myself full well:

---

[1] eke: also.

But yet, alas, for all this, I
Have little mind that I must die.

The gown which I do use to wear,
  The knife wherewith I cut my meat,
And eke that old and ancient chair
  Which is my only usual seat;
    All these do tell me I must die,
    And yet my life amend not I.

My ancestors are turned to clay,
  And many of my mates are gone,
My youngers daily drop away,
  And can I think to 'scape alone?
    No, no, I know that I must die,
    And yet my life amend not I.

Not Solomon, for all his wit,
  Nor Samson, though he were so strong,
No king nor person ever yet
  Could 'scape, but death laid him along:
    Wherefore I know that I must die,
    And yet my life amend not I.

Though all the East did quake to hear
  Of Alexander's dreadful name,
And all the West likewise did fear
  To hear of Julius Caesar's fame,
    Yet both by death in dust now lie.
    Who then can 'scape, but he must die?

If none can 'scape death's dreadful dart,
  If rich and poor his beck obey,
If strong, if wise, if all do smart,

Then I to 'scape shall have no way.
Oh! grant me grace, O God, that I
My life may mend, sith I must die.

Written the Night before he was Beheaded

CHIDIOCK TICHBOURNE

My prime of youth is but a frost of cares,
  My feast of joy is but a dish of pain,
My crop of corn is but a field of tares,
  And all my good is but vain hope of gain;
My life is fled, and yet I saw no sun;
And now I live, and now my life is done.

My tale was heard, and yet it was not told;
  My fruit is fallen, and yet my leaves are green;
My youth is spent, and yet I am not old;
  I saw the world, and yet I was not seen;
My thread is cut, and yet it is not spun;
And now I live, and now my life is done.

I sought my death, and found it in the womb,
  I lookt for life and saw it was a shade;
I trod the earth and knew it was my tomb,
  And now I die, and now I was but made;
My glass is full, and now my glass is run,
And now I live, and now my life is done.

To *Fanny Brawne*

JOHN KEATS

This living hand, now warm and capable
Of earnest grasping, would, if it were cold
And in the icy silence of the tomb,
So haunt thy days and chill thy dreaming nights
That thou wouldst wish thine own heart dry of blood
So in my veins red life might stream again,
And thou be conscience-calmed – see here it is –
I hold it towards you.

Hymn to God my God, in my Sickness

JOHN DONNE

Since I am coming to that holy room,
  Where, with my choir of saints for evermore,
I shall be made thy music; as I come
  I tune the instrument here at the door,
  And what I must do then, think here before.

Whilst my physicians by their love are grown
  Cosmographers, and I their map, who lie
Flat on this bed, that by them may be shown
  That this is my south-west discovery[1]
  Per fretum febris,[2] by these straits to die,

I joy, that in these straits, I see my west;
  For, though their currents yield return to none,
What shall my west hurt me? As west and east
  In all flat maps (and I am one) are one,
  So death doth touch the resurrection.

Is the Pacific Sea my home? Or are
  The eastern riches? Is Jerusalem?
Anyan,[3] and Magellan, and Gibraltar,
  All straits, and none but straits, are ways to them,
  Whether where Japhet dwelt, or Cham, or Shem.[4]

---

[1] my south-west discovery: passage to the New World.
[2] per fretum febris: by the strait, and heat, of fever.
[3] Anyan: Annam, the strait dividing America from Asia.
[4] The sons of Noah who, dividing the world between them, held Europe, Africa and Asia respectively.

We think that Paradise and Calvary,
    Christ's Cross, and Adam's tree, stood in one place;
Look Lord, and find both Adams met in me;
    As the first Adam's sweat surrounds my face,
    May the last Adam's blood my soul embrace.

So, in his purple[1] wrapped receive me Lord,
    By these his thorns give me his other crown;
And as to others' souls I preached thy word,
    Be this my text, my sermon to mine own,
    Therefore that he may raise the Lord throws down.

[1] purple: Christ's blood, His imperial robe.

Leaves A-Vallen

WILLIAM BARNES

There the ash-tree leaves do vall
　　In the wind a-blowen cwolder,
An' my childern, tall or small,
　　Since last Fall be woone year wolder;
Woone year wolder, woone year dearer,
　　Till when they do leäve my he'th,[1]
I shall be noo mwore a hearer
　　O' their vaïces or their me'th.[2]

There dead ash leaves be a-toss'd
　　In the wind, a-blowen stronger,
An' our life-time, since we lost
　　Souls we lov'd, is woone year longer;
Woone year longer, woone year wider,
　　Vrom[3] the friends that death ha' took,
As the hours do teäke the rider
　　Vrom the hand that last he shook.

No. If he do ride at night
　　Vrom the zide the zun went under,
Woone hour vrom his western light
　　Needen meäke woone hour asunder;
Woone hour onward, woone hour nigher
　　To the hopevul eastern skies,
Where his mornen rim o' vier
　　Soon ageän shall meet his eyes.

[1] he'th: hearth.
[2] me'th: mirth.
[3] Vrom: from

Leaves be now a-scatter'd round
    In the wind, a-blowen bleaker,
An' if we do walk the ground,
    Wi' our life-strangth woone year weaker;
Woone year weaker, woone year nigher
    To the pleäce where we shall vind
Woone that's deathless vor the dier,
    Voremost[1] they that dropp'd behind.

---

[1] Voremost: Foremost.

On his Dead Wife

JOHN MILTON

Methought I saw my late espousèd saint
  Brought to me like Alcestis from the grave,
  Whom Jove's great son[1] to her glad husband[2] gave,
  Rescued from death by force, though pale and faint.
Mine, as whom washed from spot of childbed taint
  Purification in the old Law did save,
  And such as yet once more I trust to have
  Full sight of her in heaven without restraint,
Came vested all in white, pure as her mind.
  Her face was veiled, yet to my fancied sight
  Love, sweetness, goodness, in her person shined
So clear as in no face with more delight.
  But O as to embrace me she inclined,
  I waked, she fled, and day brought back my night.

[1] son: Hercules.
[2] husband: Admetus.

from *Lycidas*[1]

JOHN MILTON

Ye valleys low, where the mild whispers use
Of shades and wanton winds and gushing brooks,
On whose fresh lap the swart star sparely looks,
Throw hither all your quaint enamelled eyes,
That on the green turf suck the honied showers,
And purple all the ground with vernal flowers.
Bring the rathe[2] primrose that forsaken dies,
The tufted crow-toe, and pale jessamine,
The white pink, and the pansy freaked with jet,
The glowing violet,
The musk rose, and the well-attired woodbine,
With cowslips wan that hang the pensive head,
And every flower that sad embroidery wears.
Bid amaranthus all his beauty shed,
And daffadillies fill their cups with tears,
To strew the laureate hearse where Lycid lies.
For so to interpose a little ease,
Let our frail thoughts dally with false surmise;[3]
Ay me! whilst thee the shores and sounding seas
Wash far away, where'er thy bones are hurled,
Whether beyond the stormy Hebrides,
Where thou perhaps under the whelming tide
Visit'st the bottom of the monstrous world;
Or whether thou, to our moist vows denied,

[1] The poet's friend, Edward King, here named Lycidas, drowned at sea in 1637.
[2] rathe: early.
[3] King's body was never in fact recovered.

Sleep'st by the fable of Bellerus old,
Where the great Vision of the guarded mount[1]
Looks toward Namancos and Bayona's hold.[2]
Look homeward, Angel,[3] now, and melt with ruth:
And, O ye dolphins, waft the hapless youth.

Weep no more, woeful shepherds, weep no more,
For Lycidas, your sorrow, is not dead,
Sunk though he be beneath the watery floor;
So sinks the day-star[4] in the ocean bed,
And yet anon repairs his drooping head,
And tricks his beams, and with new-spangled ore
Flames in the forehead of the morning sky:
So Lycidas sunk low, but mounted high,
Through the dead might of him[5] that walked the waves,
Where, other groves and other streams along,
With nectar pure his oozy locks he laves,[6]
And hears the unexpressive nuptial song,
In the blest kingdoms meek of joy and love.
There entertain him all the saints above,
In solemn troops and sweet societies,
That sing, and singing in their glory move,
And wipe the tears for ever from his eyes.

[1] mount: St Michael's Mount.
[2] i.e. Spain.
[3] St Michael.
[4] day-star: sun.
[5] Christ.
[6] laves: washes.

His Litany, to the Holy Spirit

ROBERT HERRICK

In the hour of my distress,
When temptations me oppress,
And when I my sins confess,
   Sweet Spirit comfort me!

When I lie within my bed,
Sick in heart, and sick in head,
And with doubts discomforted,
   Sweet Spirit comfort me!

When the house doth sigh and weep,
And the world is drown'd in sleep,
Yet mine eyes the watch do keep;
   Sweet Spirit comfort me!

When the artless Doctor sees
No one hope, but of his Fees,
And his skill runs on the lees;
   Sweet Spirit comfort me!

When his Potion and his Pill,
Has, or none, or little skill,
Meet for nothing, but to kill;
   Sweet Spirit comfort me!

When the passing-bell doth toll,
And the Furies in a shoal

Come to fright a parting soul;
   Sweet Spirit comfort me!

When the tapers now burn blue,
And the comforters are few,
And that number more than true;
   Sweet Spirit comfort me!

When the Priest his last hath pray'd,
And I nod to what is said,
'Cause my speech is now decay'd;
   Sweet Spirit comfort me!

When (God knows) I'm tossed about,
Either with despair, or doubt;
Yet before the glass be out,
   Sweet Spirit comfort me!

When the Tempter me pursu'th
With the sins of all my youth,
And half damns me with untruth;
   Sweet Spirit comfort me!

When the fames and hellish cries
Fright mine ears, and fright mine eyes,
And all terrors me surprise;
   Sweet Spirit comfort me!

When the Judgment is reveal'd,
And that open'd which was seal'd,
When to Thee I have appeal'd;
   Sweet Spirit comfort me!

from *In Memoriam*

ALFRED, LORD TENNYSON

L

Be near me when my light is low,
    When the blood creeps, and the nerves prick
    And tinge; and the heart is sick,
And all the wheels of Being slow.

Be near me when the sensuous frame
    Is rack'd with pangs that conquer trust;
    And Time, a maniac scattering dust,
And Life, a Fury slinging flame.

Be near me when my faith is dry,
    And men the flies of latter spring,
    That lay their eggs, and sting and sing
And weave their petty cells and die.

Be near me when I fade away,
    To point the term of human strife,
    And on the low dark verge of life
The twilight of eternal day.

Lead, Kindly Light, amid the encircling gloom

JOHN HENRY NEWMAN

Lead, Kindly Light, amid the encircling gloom,
    Lead Thou me on!
The night is dark, and I am far from home –
    Lead Thou me on!
Keep Thou my feet; I do not ask to see
The distant scene, – one step enough for me.

I was not ever thus, nor pray'd that Thou
    Shouldst lead me on.
I loved to choose and see my path; but now
    Lead Thou me on!
I loved the garish day, and, spite of fears,
Pride ruled my will: remember not past years.

So long Thy power hath blest me, sure it still
    Will lead me on,
O'er moor and fen, o'er crag and torrent, till
    The night is gone;
And with the morn those angel faces smile
Which I have loved long since, and lost awhile.

A Hymn to God the Father

JOHN DONNE

Wilt thou forgive that sin where I begun,
    Which was my sin, though it were done before?
Wilt thou forgive that sin, through which I run,
    And do run still: though still I do deplore?
      When thou hast done, thou hast not done,[1]
        For, I have more.

Wilt thou forgive that sin which I have won
    Others to sin? and, made my sin their door?
Wilt thou forgive that sin which I did shun
    A year, or two: but wallowed in, a score?
      When thou hast done, thou hast not done,
        For I have more.

I have a sin of fear, that when I have spun
    My last thread, I shall perish on the shore;
But swear by thy self, that at my death thy son
    Shall shine as he shines now, and heretofore;
      And, having done that, thou hast done,
        I fear no more.

[1] done: punning on the poet's own name.

Fear no more the heat o' the sun

WILLIAM SHAKESPEARE

Fear no more the heat o' the sun,
   Nor the furious winter's rages;
Thou thy worldly task hast done,
   Home art gone, and ta'en thy wages:
Golden lads and girls all must,
As chimney-sweepers, come to dust.

Fear no more the frown o' the great;
   Thou art past the tyrant's stroke:
Care no more to clothe and eat;
   To thee the reed is as the oak:
The sceptre, learning, physic, must
All follow this, and come to dust.

Fear no more the lightning-flash,
   Nor the all-dreaded thunder-stone;
Fear not slander, censure rash;
   Thou hast finished joy and moan:
All lovers young, all lovers must
Consign to thee, and come to dust.

No exorcizer harm thee!
Nor no witchcraft charm thee!
Ghost unlaid forbear thee!
Nothing ill come near thee!
Quiet consummation have;
And renownëd be thy grave!

INDEX OF TITLES

INDEX OF FIRST LINES

INDEX OF AUTHORS

ACKNOWLEDGEMENTS

The editor and publishers wish to thank the following for permission to use copyright material:

Anvil Press Poetry Ltd for Carol Ann Duffy, 'Prayer' from *Mean Time*, 1993;

Bloodaxe Books and Farrar, Straus & Giroux, Inc. for C. K. Williams, 'Ethics' from *A Dream of Mind*, 1992. Copyright © 1992 by C. K. Williams;

Marion Boyars Publishers Ltd with University of California Press for Robert Creeley, 'The Rain' from *Poems 1950–1965 (For Love)* and *Collected Poems of Robert Creeley, 1945–1975*. Copyright © 1983 The Regents of the University of California;

Carcanet Press for Hugh MacDiarmid, 'At My Father's Grave' from *Complete Poems*; Donald Davie, 'Life Ecompassed' from *Collected Poems*; C. H. Sisson, 'The Temple', 'Evasion' and 'Narcissus' from *Collected Poems*; Les Murray, 'Poetry and Religion' and 'An Absolutely Ordinary Rainbow' from *Collected Poems*; with Farrar, Straus & Giroux, Inc. for Les Murray, 'The Last Hellos', 'The Say-but-the-word Centurion Attempts a Summary' from *Subhuman Redneck Poems and Collected Poems*. Copyright © 1997 by Les Murray; with Georges Borchardt, Inc. on behalf of the author for John Ashbery, 'Blue Sonata' from *Houseboat Days*, Viking Penguin, 1977. Copyright © 1975, 1976, 1977 by John Ashbery; and with New Directions Publishing Corporation for William Carlos Williams, 'To Daphne and

---

[1] In conformity with the late author's wish, her Board of Literary Management asks us to record that, in 1941, Laura (Riding) Jackson renounced, on grounds of linguistic principle, the writing of poetry: she had come to hold that 'poetry obstructs general attainment to something better in our linguistic way-of-life than we have'.